ASHEN TOMORROW

T.K. Blackwood

Chromatic Aberration

Dedicated to the men and women who stand in harm's way in the name of freedom.

And if you think you're safe then you're a little too late 'cause we've come to kill you in the Summer of Hate

CHEMLAB

When two tribes go to war, a point is all that you can score. We've got two tribes, we got the bomb! We got the bomb!

FRANKIE GOES TO HOLLYWOOD

1

August 1993

The summer sun rose, cold and gray, over the dark waters where the Barents Sea met the Norwegian Sea. Interlopers cruised these inhospitable, icy waters at the crown of the world. The combined naval power of NATO flexed its unmatched might. Destroyers, cruisers, aircraft carriers, and all their sundry support craft ran from horizon to horizon. They left broad, white wakes in their passing as they cruised east—into the realm of the enemy.

Admiral Ernest Alderman, the undisputed master of these waves, could not shake the sensation that they were sailing into the mouth of hell itself. Dante had got it right, he thought. It wasn't fire and brimstone. Deepest hell was deathly cold.

Despite the chilly, despondent solitude of the Arctic circle, the bridge of USS *Bastogne* was alive with activity, as busy as every other ship in the fleet. This was a combat deployment after all.

To the south, just over the horizon, the rocky fjords of Norway's northern-most coastline beckoned silently. Hammerfest—a uniquely Scandinavian name for a city, Alderman thought—was the northernmost city on the planet earth. with more than 6,000 souls calling that place home. That was, assuming the city's Soviet occupiers hadn't decimated them as they had so many other places in a vain attempt to cow the locals into submission through brutality.

"There they go," a nearby officer said, squinting through a pair of binoculars.

Alderman came to stand beside him and raised his own binoculars. He peered out at the distant shapes of a flock of boats peeling away from a cluster of slate-gray warships.

"Royal Marines," Alderman said.

"Yes, sir."

The landing ships were joined a moment later by a squadron of helicopters. After they vanished beyond the horizon some minutes later, two pairs of British harrier jets cruised after them. The Brits had largely missed the Soviet deathride in the Norwegian Sea, but were more than making up for that fact with their hell-driven liberation of Norway.

When the Soviets had invaded Sweden, they'd left most of Norway's coastline indefensible. That nation was so narrow as to be nearly one dimensional at places, and so they had concentrated all their defenses closer to the Soviet border and along the coast. When motor-rifle regiments began bypassing them, all resistance crumpled in a rush. NATO lines collapsed back to a handful of tightly-held pockets on the coast. Now the reverse was happening. With the seas firmly in Western control, NATO was free to land forces up and down the length of the country, cutting off desperately fleeing Soviet formations.

What started as a daring, bold surprise attack had quickly become a trap for the Warsaw Pact. It was a mistake Alderman was intent to make them keep paying for.

"Godspeed to them," Alderman said, lowering his binoculars.

"Not much left now," the captain beside him said.

"No," Alderman agreed. It was a sense they all shared, a feeling of things coming to a head. The end within sight.

"With the Finns rebelling, the whole Russian supply line is basically cut. All those guys are trapped in Sweden," the captain continued. "How much you want to bet that, instead of ferrying in more marines, we're going to be mostly ferrying POWs back to the camps in Scotland?"

"We'll be shipping guns to the Finns too before too long," Alderman said. "Soviets underestimated them twice in one century. I'm not sure they'll recover from it this time."

"Hope not," the captain said. He fell silent as he and Alderman watched a pair of F-18 Hornets wheeled into position on

Bastogne's deck and made ready to launch.

"After that—after Norway and Sweden—think we're going into Finland?" The captain sounded equal parts eager and afraid.

"If the Finns invite us," Alderman said, watching as the Hornets hooked into Bastogne's catapult system. "Don't see why they wouldn't."

"And then... Russia?"

It was a question Alderman had considered, though he didn't want to.

"Escalation" was a dirty word before the war and it was no less so now. For as terrible as this war was—all the fighting and dying—they all knew it could get worse. Much worse.

For now, each side was content to treat this as a contest of arms, not an existential struggle. That could always change, and change quickly.

Not only that, but even if the Soviets obliged the West to try, it would be logistically difficult—maybe impossible.

"Last time American troops trod Russian soil in anger was Vladivostok in 1919," Alderman said.

It was a non-answer. Truthfully, he didn't know what would happen next. History generally didn't look kindly on nations which invaded Russia. It seldom turned out well for the invader. But without invasion how could there be anything like victory? Would the Soviets give up like good sports? Or would they take things to the fiery, bitter end?

Alderman supposed he would find out either way.

The Hornets took off in sequence, flung from the deck by the catapult, engines roaring. A pair of F-14 Tomcats were close behind them.

On the horizon, USS *Shiloh* launched its own aircraft. Jet fighters climbed away in pairs, joining together into attack groups in the skies above, a sliver of the striking power at Alderman's fingertips.

Sensing that the captain still wanted an answer, Alderman spoke again. "I don't know if we'll go into Russia, but at least we're taking the war to them. They're going to have to face reality sooner than later."

The Tomcats took off and more planes took their place, an unending dance of men and machines. He knew their destination—Arkangelsk. He'd rather it was the naval base at Polyarny, but that place was swarming with air defenses—layer after layer of surface to air missiles backed by squadrons of interceptors. A tough nut to crack. For now they would stick to softer targets, just something to remind the Soviets that they weren't untouchable. Too long they'd waged war on others with impunity. Convinced, it seemed, of the childish delusion that they could bomb everyone and no one could bomb them. Alderman was happy to disabuse them of that notion. War would bare its grim visage on Soviet soil now.

The attack squadrons formed up overhead, wheeling into formation.

"Sir," *Bastogne*'s CAG said, looking over to Alderman. "All squadron leaders report ready."

Alderman nodded. "God speed. Send them in."

***

Lancer 103 was one of a half dozen F-14 Tomcats providing air cover for the strike package cruising into range of Soviet radar coverage on their Barents Sea coast. Combat action was, for Captain David "Rabbit" Barlow, old hat by now. He'd seen the elephant as it were, but it was still terrifying all the same.

"Sixty seconds out," Robert "Gomez" Adams said from the Tomcat's backseat. As the fighter's Radar Intercept Officer he handled the aircraft's sophisticated instruments and weapons while Rabbit mostly handled the actual flying. "After that, assume they have us."

Ground-based radar was sure to pick them up by that point. Knowing that the enemy was moments away from spotting them did nothing to still Rabbit's fluttering heart. He took a deep breath of dry, oxygen-rich air through his mask and let it out slowly. He tried to keep his grip on the sticks loose, casual, but found himself tensing up from time to time. For some stupid reason, Rabbit had thought that once they kicked the Soviet's ass in the Norwegian Sea their jobs would be done. That's it, check and mate, game over, good job, everybody.

They'd sail into Scappa Flow or wherever as goddam heroes. Tickertape parades, kisses from pretty women, champagne for days.

Delusional. The war wasn't over yet.

Not over, but altered. The Soviets had gambled big in October of '92. And lost big. The vast bulk of their surface navy had been sunk. Sent to the bottom or up in flames. If he closed his eyes he could still picture flocks of orange life rafts cluttering the dark, pitching surface of the sea. He could feel the vibration of his Tomcat's vulcan cannon, see planes going down in spiraling smoke trails.

What was left of the enemy's once-proud navy was damaged, worn out, and broke down. Their submarine fleet—terror of the North Atlantic in the early days of the war—was exhausted, all but destroyed. The days of the Soviet Union as a naval power were gone, hopefully forever. But that only meant that their mission to counter Soviet sea power had been superseded by a new, greater emphasis on supporting the land war.

"Nails," Gomez said, voice high with tension. "They're painting us."

Rabbit resisted the urge to radio in, honoring the communications blackout they observed. Instead he looked left and right at the other Tomcats of the attack force. Somewhere below and ahead of them were the Hornets which carried the laser-guided bombs intended for Arkangelsk, welcoming them officially to the war.

"Ground radar?" Rabbit asked.

"Looks that way," Gomez replied tightly. He fiddled with his console for a moment. "Wait a minute..."

Something about his tone curdled Rabbit's blood. "What?"

"Uhh... shit. Nails. Four O'clock."

Off to their right. That couldn't be land-based radar.

"Gotta be a patrol," Rabbit said. He pulled back on the stick slightly, gaining a little altitude before pulling to the side, banking to face this new threat. "Let's go radar active."

Gomez flipped on the Tomcat's nosecone-mounted radar and painted the enemy. "Tally! Two bogeys, dead ahead. Angels nine, closing fast."

A joust.

Rabbit swore and toggled on his radio. "Lancer 100, this is 103. Bogeys four O'clock. Moving to engage."

"Affirm 103. Good hunting."

"Ducky, you see them?" Rabbit looked to his left and saw Lancer 108 hovering a few hundred yards off his wing.

"Dead to rights, Rabbit. You do the honors."

It was time to kill. "Gomez?"

"Phoenix. Do it."

"Lancer 103, fox three." Rabbit fired.

The Tomcat bounced with weapons release. The Phoenix itself was as heavy as it was big. It fell quickly away before its booster activated and the large deadly missile screamed off toward the enemy.

"They're going cold," Rabbit said, watching on radar as both contacts turned away from the Tomcats, drawing them away from the other planes of their formation and robbing the Phoenix of its lethal velocity.

"Stay on them," Ducky said.

A minute later the Phoenix splashed, missing wide. So long as the Russians were running it would be hard to catch them.

Rabbit let them have another fox three. He wasn't keen to get into a dogfight with the weight of those missiles holding him back. It was hard enough to turn in the Tomcat without them.

Below them, the white-gray ocean gave way to a dull green countryside. Rabbit was too focused on chasing his quarry to realize he was now—for the first time in his life—flying over Soviet territory.

"They're fast," Rabbit growled, watching the enemy making distance on him. "Gotta be Foxbats."

"SAM! SAM!" Gomez blurted breathlessly. "SAM, nine O'clock!"

Rabbit didn't think, he reacted.

"103 defending!" He broke right, turning away from the enemy surface to air missile and dove. Gravity's possessive grip on him lessened. He seemed to float in his restraints as they inverted and plunged down toward Russia.

Rabbit banged his fist against the countermeasures release button and a spray of flares and chaff puffed out behind them. He breathed hard, feeling blood shifting around in his body with sickening ease.

"Ooooh shit!" Gomez said. He rattled around in the backseat, swiveling his head and craning his neck, trying to track the enemy missile visually. "It's—shit! Missed! Missed us!"

Rabbit levelled out but caught sight of another missile climbing into the air from their right before he could relax. "Defending again!"

He cranked away from it and dove. "Ducky!" He could manage no more, grunting and grinding his teeth as he fought G-forces. More countermeasures sprayed from 103. The Russian pilots had led them straight into an ambush. Clever bastards.

"They're coming back for us," Ducky said, sounding more calm than Rabbit felt. "108, fox one!"

As the world spun outside 103's cockpit, Rabbit saw the contrail of a Soviet SAM missile flash by them and he gasped. Two SAMs dodged in a row. That was some kind of luck. When he levelled out again he was surprised to see treetops and telephone poles. They were low. Dangerously low. Low enough that climbing back to altitude wasn't an option. It would rob them off too much speed, making them sitting ducks for the Soviet interceptors closing on them.

"Splash!" Ducky said as he struck one of the Soviet planes from the sky.

Rabbit worked his foot pedals and ruddered the Tomcat around in a broad turn, bringing its nose on line with the remaining enemy aircraft. Pulling back on the stick he sighted it.

"I got tone!" Gomez said.

"103, fox one!" Rabbit fired and the Sparrow streaked away, passing over desolate taiga before catching the distant Foxbat in the wing with a puff of smoke. "Splash!"

The MiG tumbled from the sky, spiraling down to the ground. Even though the distance was extreme, Rabbit saw the ejector sea fire and a parachute deploy a few moments before the plane crashed into the woods.

He pulled back on the stick, gaining more altitude to rejoin Ducky as they turned back for the coast. Ahead of them he saw a pair of fireballs on the horizon, the Hornets working their targets in Arkhangelsk.

"Lancers, all targets serviced," Lancer 100 said. "Break for the coast and make for Point Delta."

"103 affirm," Rabbit said as they peeled away.

"Look at that," Gomez said, pressing his helmet against the Tomcat's cockpit glass as he peered down on the blown bridge over the Dvinia River. "Absolutely wrecked."

Rabbit didn't know how much difference a blown bridge would really make, but maybe it would make the Soviets think they were preparing another amphibious landing or something. "That's peanuts, man," Rabbit said. "Wait till we clear out some of these SAMs and run a flight of B-52s straight up their ass." He could still feel adrenaline coursing through him. His hands trembled on the controls.

"Think Ivan will think we're going nuclear?" Gomez asked.

Rabbit hadn't thought of it. Now that he had, he wished he hadn't. The nuclear specter that haunted everyone seemed to have been dispelled as weeks became months and no one opened Pandora's box. It was sobering to remember that could change at any moment. "If they were going to pop off they would have done it by now," Rabbit said with what he hoped sounded like confidence.

Gomez said nothing. He wasn't convinced. For that matter, neither was Rabbit. They turned back toward *Shiloh*, home, and safety.

2

As the bombs fell on the bridge and the air defenses around Arkangelsk, the prison laborers or the Cellulose-Paper Complex hurried to shelter wherever they could find it. It wasn't that they were ordered to do so; rather the guards themselves abandoned their posts to find hiding places. With no guards to beat them into obedient lines, the prisoners let animal survival instincts guide their actions.

Andrei Gradenko hurried out of the paper plant as part of a stream of panicked prisoners and guards. He couldn't imagine that a paper mill would make a suitable military target, but he saw no reason to chance it. Bursting from the dank, musky interior, he sucked in a breath of relatively clean air as he hurried across the open yard. Mud squelched and sucked at his loose boots, giving him an awkward, broad gait.

A gust of hot air buffeted him and he fell to the ground, knees sinking into the muck. He thought it was from a bomb blast until he saw the American F-18 scream by, barely higher than the roof of the paper plant. A wash of noise left him deafened, staring up at the enemy aircraft in shock and horror.

Arkangelsk was hardly as remote as somewhere like Omsk or Novosiborisk, but it was very far from the front lines.

Or it had been.

The Hornet banked up, climbing away as it unleashed ordinance. The bombs made a graceful parabolic arc. Gradenko watched them sailing across the sky, crossing over the Dvinia River to strike the bridge there directly.

He propped himself up on his elbows and saw the flash of the explosions a moment before the thunderclap boom reached him.

Like magic, the entire bridge buckled, slumped, and caved in, dropping into the river.

More bombs fell north of the city, exploding among what he could only imagine were more militarily significant targets, radar installations or anti-aircraft batteries, maybe.

Some of the guards got back to their feet, gawking blankly at the smoke starting to drift up. A dozen voices swore at once.

"Get the prisoners together! Collect them!" A sergeant shouted, kicking a prone guard in the ribs. "Get up, comrade!"

For a moment Gradenko realized that there were nearly a hundred prisoners here and only three or four guards. With the chaos and confusion there was no more perfect attempt to escape. He could throw himself on the prone guard and wrestle his rifle away from him. The others could fall on the guards, beat them, take their weapons, and break free of this place. Together they would smash the gates, disarm the guards, and drive on to freedom and safety.

Instead Gradenko only laid there and watched as the guards got their bearings, organized themselves, and started shouting commands at the prisoners again.

No one else did anything either. With no one seeming to know what to do, the prisoners were herded into groups and left to sit on the muddy ground while the guards talked among themselves and—presumably—with the commandant of the base.

After close to an hour they received orders.

"Up! Everyone up!" They were herded like cattle toward the gates of the base.

"They are going to kill us," Dragomirov wheezed, limping along beside Gradenko. He wasn't sure when the former spymaster had found him. Somehow he was still as sneaky in sickness as he had been in health.

Gradenko looped an arm under Dragomirov's shoulder and helped him to walk. He could feel Dragomirov shiver though he was sweating, hot to the touch. No doubt he was slowly dying from infection, not long for this world.

Truthfully, Gradenko wouldn't mind being shot. He welcomed a quick death at this point. A bullet would be a mercy compared to a lifetime in this terrible place or a slow, miserable decline like Dragomirov. Instead of a shallow grave and firing line, he saw a battered tuck full of shovels arriving at the base gate. Not death, but more work.

The gates were opened, the prisoners issued shovels and buckets and marched in a disordered column into the heart of the city, toward the destruction of the bridge.

Dragomirov winced, failed to stifle a groan, and staggered slightly.

Before either he or Gradenko could fall, another man—this one in Swedish military fatigues—swooped in to quickly steady him.

"Thank you," Gradenko said, speaking English.

The man, Johan, nodded ascent but said nothing else.

Within minutes the prisoners—a mixture of criminals, political dissidents, and Western POWs—reached the destroyed bridge where they were driven to work with the shovels and buckets, scooping up bits of broken concrete and carrying it to a dump truck which arrived shortly after.

Dragomirov could hardly walk, let alone work. He carried a bucket of concrete chips a few meters before collapsing.

Gradenko swore under his breath and stepped away from the work line to his friend. "Comrade, please get up." He gave a surreptitious glance at a nearby guard.

"Can't," Dragomirov moaned, holding his guts tightly. "Can't."

"They will kill you," Gradenko hissed.

Dragomirov just shook his head, jaw clenched in pain.

Before despair could overtake him, Johan appeared again. "Here. Quick." He took one of Dragomirov's arms, Gradenko the other. Together they dragged the sick man to the dump truck and laid him down beneath it, nestled in the shadow of the huge wheel. "We will move him when the truck is full," Johan said.

Gradenko nodded. He wanted to feel relief, but he only felt horror. Sorrow.

The monotony of work burned these feelings from his mind before long. Clearing this rubble with shovels was like trying to dig to China with a spoon, but it proceeded steadily through weight of numbers alone.

Once the truck was full and the sun was dipping low, Johan and Gradnko collected the unconscious Dragomirov from beneath the vehicle before he might be crushed.

For a moment Gradenko thought Dragomirov was finally dead until he touched his wrist and he groaned.

"Come on, comrade."

The prisoners walked back to the camp under the watchful eyes of the guards. It wasn't as if they could go far. The whole city was locked down tight by a battalion of old reservists who watched the coast anxiously. Sick, malnourished men in prison jumpsuits would be spotted right away. Spotted and liquidated.

Gradenko parted ways with Johan, returning to the prisoner barracks where he laid down Dragomirov again.

The former KGB man didn't stir. He breathed shallowly and lay still. His eyes were closed, his forehead slick with sweat.

Gradnko watched him desperately, wishing he could do more. When he was satisfied that Dragomirov wouldn't rise again, he left the barracks and went for the POW's side of the camp.

Normally the Soviets and Western prisoners didn't interact. They had no reason to and more than that, no ability to. A language barrier was a difficult enough obstacle among friends, it was insurmountable between enemies. Gradenko was different.

"Hello," he said, using English as he approached a group of enemy soldiers in dirty uniforms.

"Gradenko," Johan said with a tone approaching joviality. "How is your friend?"

"Not well," Gradenko said, frowning as he stood among the soldiers, sailors, and airmen. "I hope maybe I can get him medicine from the guards." Gradenko wasn't sure how exactly he would manage that yet. He had nothing to trade, certainly nothing to offer that the guards couldn't take from him if they truly wanted to.

"He's fucked," the voice was American, harsh, cold. "I've seen that look. Gangrene. Pretty sure." The man shrugged, looking pathetically small and thin beneath his bulky woodland camo jacket. "He'll be dead soon."

Gradenko knew it was true which was why he didn't argue, though he wanted to. He hung his head a little and an uncomfortable silence settled over the group.

"Gradenko, chess?" another soldier asked with a hopeful smile, trying to lighten the mood.

"Yes, of course." Gradenko had discovered his skill at chess was a commodity in high demand among the POWs with few other avenues for entertainment.

They took seats on upturned plastic buckets with an improvised board set up between them. The pieces were mostly nuts, bolts, a few coins, and any other trash which could be scrounged up. It took a bit of imagination and memory to see them as pawns, knights, bishops, kings, and queens.

His opponent, a Danish lieutenant, set the board eagerly, keen for a rematch. He fared no better this time than he did the last.

In Gradenko's childhood, chess had been a national pastime in the Soviet Union, an obsession. It was taught in school, read about in newspapers, and watched on television. International games were headline news. If the Soviet Union's greatest minds—greatest chess masters—could defeat their Western opponents, then there was nothing they couldn't do. Men like Kasparov, Taimanov, and Zagorovsky were heroes and idols for a generation of young people. And so Gradenko had become proficient at the game.

"Damn," the Dane said as Gradenko checkmated him.

Gradenko had dragged the game out as long as he felt he could without insulting his intelligence.

"Next time," the Dane said, rising from his seat to be replaced by the American who reset the pieces.

"Next time," Gradenko agreed with a bland smile. It helped, he thought, that at some level he was still an enemy to these men. They wanted to beat him badly enough to keep playing him even though they kept losing. There was something admirable about their determination. He wondered what would happen if he started losing.

Johan took a seat next to Gradenko as he watched the game. "Instead of medicine, you should find us cigarettes, *tovarisch*." His ironic use of the word "comrade" never failed to amuse Gradenko.

"If I could get cigarettes, why should I give them to you?" Gradenko asked with a hint of jest.

"Not a gift," Johan replied, eyes on the game. "A prize pool."

It was harder than against the Dane, but Gradenko checkmated the American.

"I still think you're getting help on a radio earpiece," the American teased as he stood up, beaten, this time replaced by Johan. It was near dark now so they played in the meager light of dusk. This would be the last game of the day.

"Why is it that you care so much for your friend?" Johan asked as he advanced a rook. "If what you say is true, and he is the KGB Chairman, then he should be no friend of yours."

"I owe him," Gradeno said. Sometimes he wondered if telling Johan and the other POWs his identity was a mistake. He'd expected fury or scheming. Any kind of response, really. Instead they just seemed amused to share a prison camp with the one-time General Secretary of the Communist Party. "He saved my son and he tried to save me from this place." Gradenko matched Johan's move with a sweep of his bishop.

"Ah, that is noble. Noble?" Johan checked the word and the American nodded, confirming it.

English was the only language they had in common and few of them had anything like mastery over it—including the American.

The game went on, pieces traded in an ever escalating struggle until the board was sparsely populated.

"There were many I thought I could trust," Gradenko said. "Dragomirov was the only one who proved loyal to the end."

"That's fucking ironic," the American said.

"I suppose now you see error," Johan said. "Error to trust. Error to make these choices." There was a coldness to his eyes. No doubt he was thinking of the decision made to drag Sweden into this war, a decision which had catastrophic consequences for him. Gradnko didn't know if Johan knew or even suspected how direct a role Gradenko himself had played in that decision. He hoped he never found out. "Yes," he said. "Many times I made many mistakes, but I am one man. What can I do?"

"Spoken like a true Russian," Johan said, eliciting derisive laughter from the others.

It rankled Gradenko. It was easy to preach about swimming against the current, much harder when you saw just how strong that current was. He said nothing and took Johan's bishop.

"I think," Gradenko said finally. "We make better friends than enemies." He looked at Johan and saw him grinning confidently. When he looked down and studied the board, he saw why. He realized, with rising consternation, that he'd been goaded into taking that bishop and had totally opened his defense. He was mated in two moves.

Johan said nothing. He didn't need to, he knew.

After hesitating with his hand over the piece, Gradenko tipped his king.

Johan met Gradnko's gaze and gave him a tight smile, offering a hand.

Gradenko shook. "Yes. We are together now. Together against the Russian bastards," he said.

The others laughed.

"We must survive together," Johan answered, eyes tightening.

"Yes," Gradenko said. It was the only way to get through this.

3

Crocodile Tears's gas turbine engine screamed as the M1 Abrams main battle tank clattered forward over open German countryside. What might have once been a pretty view was marred by a smoldering wheeled APC in the middle of the field, surrounded by the charred bodies of dead Soviet riflemen. A grave for a dozen men.

Captain Don Vance opened the hatch of his tank and risked lifting his head out for a better look. He rested one hand on the grips of the .50 caliber gun mounted here. Not so long ago he'd been forced to use an identical weapon in defense of his tank. He could still sometimes feel the dull tug in his thigh, tracing the path of the metal splinter cast through his leg. It was a sobering reminder of his own mortality.

Beyond the destroyed BTR was an abandoned civilian pickup truck which had been hastily painted olive green. Its driver's side door was peppered with shrapnel impacts and it sat on flat tires.

"Shit, is that a Toyota?" Vance's gunner Waxman asked, standing in his own open hatch beside Vance.

"I think so," Vance said.

Crocodile Tears crossed the ground near the pickup and Vance satisfied himself that it really was empty. The bed was full of discarded weapons and equipment. He saw one of the unusual, wok-like helmets that the East Germans used. It lay discarded on the ground nearby with no evidence of its owner anywhere.

"Hard to believe," Waxman said as they saw more abandoned gear and an overturned BTR further ahead. It looked like these had been hit by artillery or airstrikes. It was all the same to Vance, it was one less thing to have to worry about.

"Cutthroat Six, this is Three Six. Contact front." The voice of one of Vance's platoon leaders carried clearly over his headphones.

"Six affirms. Tanks?"

"Not sure. Bounced off our armor but there's something ahead in that group of trees. Maybe an old T-55 or something." The lieutenant read off a grid reference and Vance ducked down into his tank to check it. "We pulled back," the lieutenant continued, sounding a little shaken from his brush with death.

"Six copies," Vance said. "That's just ahead of us. We'll flush it out. Cutthroat Five, copy?"

"Five Copies," TJ buzzed back. "Lead on."

Vance didn't have to look back to know that TJ's tank—*Candyass*—was close behind him.

"Let's nail the bastard," Vance said, directing his driver—Kinney—as they accelerated and pulled left, circling around a muddy bottom to cross the field. Vance slammed his hatch closed and pressed his forehead to the padded sights, peering ahead as he searched for targets. In a minute he saw the cluster of trees that Three Six had described. Vance didn't see anything but he wasn't going to take chances. "Gunner, sabot, trees ahead."

Patterson, the tank's teenage loader, pressed the floor pedal to open the ammunition rack and drew out a shell before sliding it home and closing the breach. "Up!"

Waxman opened his mouth and fired. "Shot!"

Crocodile Tears recoiled and the shell passed through where whatever was hiding in the trees would be. There was no flash, no explosion. Nothing. Vance had time to wonder if it had moved when he caught movement. Infantry.

"Gunner, HEAT!"

Maybe it was an ATGM team. Didn't explain the shell that Three Six had taken, but it wouldn't matter in a moment.

"Up!"

"Shot!"

Crocodile Tears spoke again, this time the shell was packed with high explosives, not an armor-piercing penetrator. It burst in the trees with a devastating bang, shredding foliage and felling a pine.

TJ's tank cruised past them, circling left and peppered the woods with machine gun fire, suppressing whatever might still be alive.

A couple more pines toppled over, their trunks splintered. Another caught fire and burned, but nothing moved.

Vance counted heartbeats. "Alright, let's advance."

They drove up, moving closer. When they were within a hundred yards, Vance saw their target finally, but felt only shock. He could barely believe it.

"That's an anti-tank gun," he said.

The antique weapon would have looked more at home in the Second World War or in a museum. It was a towed anti-tank cannon, crew served, left here to ambush pursuing forces. Vance didn't realize he'd broadcast over the radio until TJ replied.

"A what?"

"An AT gun," Vance repeated. "Looks like maybe a..." it took him a moment to dredge the designation from the dusty depths of his memory. "A T-12."

"T-12 is what... a hundred millimeters?" TJ asked. "That can't breach our front armor."

"Yeah," Vance said. "I think they figured that out the hard way."

The gun was surrounded with an improvised screen of brush and undergrowth which smoldered. Around it were three dead men—no. Two dead men. One dying.

Vance cruised slowly by and he watched the enemy soldier rolling slowly side to side in the pine straw like a dreamer trying to wake from a nightmare. It would be over for him soon enough.

Beyond the open ground, Vance's company found a road and followed it on. A couple destroyed and abandoned Soviet trucks marked their line of retreat. NATO was unstoppable, smashing the enemy from the air and rolling them on the ground. The

Warsaw Pact was collapsing faster than the Western forces could pursue them.

Some Apache gunships passed by low overhead, hunting for enemy resistance. Vance would be surprised if they found any. They were maybe thirty miles from the Czechoslovakian border, still inside West Germany, recapturing territory that had initially been lost in the opening days of the war. Within a few minutes they reached the town of Himmelkron.

The town itself was remarkably intact, though nothing moved. The streets were deserted. Windows were shuttered and curtains drawn. It felt dead. Vance hoped the locals were just hiding. A medieval abbey of lichen-blotched gray stone loomed over the town from a gently sloped hill.

Vance's infantry cleared the streets swiftly, moving by squads between the buildings. Only once the infantry gave the all clear did Vance bring his tanks up.

Vance signalled Kinney to slow as they approached a crossroads in the town where a trio of M113 APCs covered in foliage were parked.

Vance opened his hatch. "Any trouble?" he called down to Kelly, the infantry's captain.

Kelly moved closer, shouting over the idle roar of Vance's tank. "Nah! Reds all vamoosed. Locals are in their basements, seems like. A couple of them said the Russians fell back north." He pointed in that direction.

Vance followed his gesture. "Cool. We'll go after them. Tell them the German army is behind us. They're continuing on to Czechoslovakia. I think we're going for Berlin."

Kelly gave Vance a thumbs up and Vance set Kinney driving again.

Outside of town Vance heard the freight train howl of artillery passing overhead, going west to east. Friendly. Maybe the Germans were softening up the enemy near the Czech border.

Ahead, the road was jammed up with American tanks. Vance pulled in behind them. Before he had a chance to radio for feedback, he saw an M113 command APC coming back this way, its top bristling with antennas. It slowed to a halt and Major Esposito emerged from the hatch.

"Captain!" Esposito called to Vance, looking flush with excitement. "This is it! This is the big fucking drive!"

"Breakthrough?" Vance said the golden word, almost not daring to hope. Breakthrough, a *real* breakthrough would mean the end.

Esposito nodded eagerly. "Brits tore a hole in the line ahead, said we're clear to go. Berlin or bust! Follow on behind Rodriguez. Put the hammer down and lock the throttle. We're through!"

Vance could scarcely believe it. It didn't feel real. It might not be. He couldn't shake that nagging voice in his head. This wasn't the first time they'd reportedly cracked the enemy line, though with how exhausted they were, Vance had to believe the end was here.

"You with me?" Esposito asked.

"With you, sir!" Vance replied.

"Go!" Esposito said, gesturing toward Berlin with a chopping gesture. "Havoc! Go get em!"

4

It was gray and drizzling when Jan Adamcik and the other Czechoslovakians assembled for morning roll call. Standing in an orderly line they waited silently to call "here" when their name was read.

Adamcik tried to ignore the steady dampening of his shoulders as the rain grew only more intense.

"Sergeant Adamcik, Jan." The voice was accented, German, like all the guards of this camp. It was also without malice.

"Here," Adamcik said.

The Germans didn't really seem to know what to do with the Czechoslovakians. In many ways they were just as much victims of the Soviets as anyone else. In other ways...

Adamcik thought of the dead men and women in the park in Nuremberg, the chatter of machine guns. How much death and destruction had he and his people seen visited on the West Germans? How much had they participated in? How much could they have prevented?

Finally the count finished. All present and accounted for. "Dismissed."

The men broke ranks, trudging through the mud back for their pre-fabricated metal barracks or to mill about aimlessly in the open. The world—as much as they could access anyway —was hemmed in by towering barbed wire fences and coils of razor wire. The perimeter fence was dotted with guard towers and humorless reservists on patrol. This war was very personal to the people of Germany, more than to many others in NATO. For them it was both a "brother war" against their lost cousins in the East, and a war of survival. Their homes and yards were the battlefield, their children the collateral damage.

Adamcik walked the length of the perimeter fence, keeping a safe distance away as he made for the shoddy barn that acted as their mess hall.

They were treated well which almost seemed to make things worse. He would have understood beatings, deprivation, hardship, torture. Instead he'd received food, warm clothes, toiletries, even a pack of playing cards from the Red Cross. He received better treatment in enemy captivity than he often did in service to the Czechoslovakian People's Army.

Enemy. He was having to rethink that word. The Soviets had never been comrades, not really, but the West hadn't either. It left him and the others in a strange no-man's land. Now he could not help but think they had all been fighting for the wrong side this whole time. It was sobering to think of all the blood and sweat shed in service of uncaring slave drivers.

"Hey, Adamcik." Janco, his old gunner, jogged to catch up with him. He offered Adamcik a cigarette, another kindness from their captors.

Adamcik declined with a raised hand. "What is it?"

Janco shrugged, walking alongside his old commander in the rain, their boots squelching. "They say the Americans reached the border." Adamcik didn't have to ask which border he meant. "But they have not crossed yet."

Adamcik didn't know how to feel about that. Western invasion—or liberation—would end Soviet occupation of his country. He would celebrate that. But it would also bring war home. He'd seen first hand what it had done to Germany. He'd been the one to bring it. "Soon then," he said.

Janco grunted ascent.

They continued their walk. Adamcik saw many familiar faces. Gaspar, the mechanic-turned-driver playing a game of cards with Ambroz, his old lieutenant. He saw Captain Zetov, Sergeant Coufal, and many others idly passing the time. Adamcik had no illusions that there would be any Czechoslovakian People's Army left to return to when this war ended. One way or another that was finished.

"What are you thinking?" Janco asked.

"I am wondering if we made the right choice," Adamcik said. "To surrender ourselves."

Before Janco could ask him to elaborate, a pair of German soldiers approached. "Sergeant Adamick, come," one said in stiff Czech, gesturing to him to follow.

Adamcik and Janco exchanged a look before Adamcik followed mutely behind them. He was taken out of the main enclosure and into a nearby featureless building. After being quickly patted down he was taken into a small room with a metal table and two chairs, one taken by a man in woodland camouflage—an American uniform.

As Adamcik sat, he was surprised to see not the American flag on the man's sleeve, but instead the red, white, and blue of the Czechoslovakian flag. Adamcik eyed this stranger warily, but the man in the American uniform just smiled blandly back.

"Sergeant Adamcik," he said. "I am Captain Vesely." His Czech was flawless, native.

Adamcik regarded him for another moment in silence. "I can tell you nothing more than what I told the others," Adamcik said finally. "I served with the First Tank Regiment of the Czechoslovakian People's Army. My company was abandoned by our regiment in the retreat. We collectively made the choice to surrender ourselves and our equipment. We had no desire to fight on anymore. We wanted nothing but defeat of the Soviets and liberation of our people." Adamcik rattled these details off in quick succession, hardly pausing. He'd said it all before.

Vesely, surprisingly, said nothing, and only grinned back. When Adamcik too fell silent, the captain surprised him by asking: "have you enjoyed your time here?"

"Enjoyed?" Adamcik repeated the strange question. "No."

"Why not?" Vesely asked. "You are safe, clothed, fed."

Adamcik sensed this was no normal interrogation. He was being led to a conclusion, what that was he couldn't see yet. "Yes," he agreed, "but that is not enough."

"You want freedom?"

Adamcik nodded stiffly. "Of course. But it is also hard to sit and watch, and do nothing."

Vesely nodded as if he understood. Maybe he did. "There are many of our nation who feel the same."

Adamcik could not help but feel suspicious at his use of the phrase 'our nation' while Vesely wore the uniform of NATO.

"Many feel that we have been fighting the wrong enemy," Vesely finished.

Adamcik said nothing.

"Do you?" Vesely asked.

"I... I do not know. I do not love the Russians," Adamcik started, stopped, and then continued. "In fact, I hate them. I hate them for what they did to us. What they made us into. We were like slaves to them. But..."

"But?"

"But I do not always believe that the enemy of my enemy is my friend. How can I trust the Germans or the Americans any more than I trust the Russians?"

"How can that be true?" Vesely asked, "when you gave your whole company's tanks over to them?"

Again Adamcik said nothing.

"Surely you believe they are here for good." Vesely waited for Adamcik to respond. When he did not he continued on undaunted. "I deserted the army and fled the country ten years ago," Vesely said. "I crossed the border into Germany and then immigrated to the United States in 1983."

Adamcik remained silent.

"Does this bother you?" Vesely asked.

"No," Adamcik replied truthfully after thinking it over.

"Do you know what I am doing here?"

Adamcik could think of no reason and so shook his head.

"I have come to recruit men for a military unit. Men with experience and training. I have been tasked by the Czechoslovak provisional government to create an armored company. Tanks and infantry."

"Provisional government?" Adamcik asked suspiciously.

Vesely nodded. "Yes. One which will replace the communist puppet apparatus in Prague and hold free elections when this war is over."

It was too good to be true, too much to imagine. Adamcik could scarcely believe it. He forced himself to consider this for a few moments before finally speaking. "You want me to enlist?"

"I want you to command a platoon," Vesely said.

Adamcik gaped at him. "Platoon? No. I am only a sergeant..."

"And I was once only a lieutenant," Vesely said with that infinitely calm smile. "I have heard of your surrender. I have spoken with others who know you. The men of your company respect you. They elected you to lead them. If you join now, then I am sure many of them will too."

It was a prospect Adamcik hadn't considered. It was not just his life on the line but those of all his men as well, all the men who trusted him and looked to him. He'd failed such men before. He thought of Charvat, his old driver, and Macek, the would be mutineer, both killed by firing squad. Killed as he stood and watched.

"I... do not know." After another moment he added, "we do not know Western tanks. We have not been trained on them."

"We have enough captured T-72s and BMPs to outfit a motor rifle division," Vesely said without missing a beat. "A company will be no trouble."

"Who will we fight for?" Adamcik said finally. "The Americans?"

Vesely tapped the patch on his sleeve. "We fight for our own country. We are not slaves, Adamcik, but free men."

It was a prospect as enticing as it was terrifying. Free men were responsible for their own actions. He thought again of those poor lost souls at Nuremburg. What could he have done to save them? But the past was the past. It could not be changed. The future... that was still open to be written. For as much as he wished he was, Adamcik was no coward. He was a man of action. He stood and offered a hand to Vesely.

Vesely stood, grinning wider, and shook it. "Welcome to the Legion."

5

Rastayev was hardly chief among General Pyotr Strelnikov's lieutenants. In fact, he paled when placed alongside men like Sidorov and Lukin, who Strelnikov could not help but think of as his left and right hands. But Rastayev—who had been a mere colonel at the start of the war—had been made general by Strelnikov on one major virtue: he was trustworthy.

It was hollow comfort. Things had slipped so badly that now Strelnikov himself was forced to value loyalty over skill. Once he stabilized things he promised himself he would clean the upper echelons of the Soviet military and set it on the path to greatness. Once everything was ordered again. Once they'd won the war.

Passing through Warsaw, Strelnikov looked from the Lada's window at the endless column of military vehicles which lined the road. The men gathered here represented everything which could be collected by the way of reinforcements. Everything which was left. Battle hardened veterans mingled with grizzled reservists and raw conscripts. There were far too few of the former and far too many of the latter for Strelnikov's taste. More troublingly, the equipment he saw on display was ancient and poorly maintained. He saw only older model tanks and APCs and a motley mix of uniforms. His foot soldiers wore no body armor and often wore camouflage from thirty years ago.

It was even worse than that. In addition to the ubiquitous Ural trucks which carried the army's supplies the final few kilometers from the rail head to the frontlines, was a menagerie of civilian vehicles. Busses, dump trucks, cargo vans, cars, and work vehicles. These vehicles—looted from the Germans and

Poles—would work as a stop gap measure, but the logistical strain of trying to maintain such a varied fleet only compounded the problems they faced.

Strelnikov's stomach churned unhappily and he scowled out the window. His brow furrowed in consternation. It seemed to him that the war machine was in danger of coming apart, rattling itself to pieces.

One thing that Strelnikov did not see on the streets of this Polish city was civilians. The entire city was locked down, patrolled closely by Soviet soldiers. All those who could had fled. All those who could not made do. Their fear of the Soviets kept them complacent for now. That equation might reverse if their fear of the enemy overcame their fear of their overlords. Steps would have to be taken to ensure that did not happen.

Strelnikov made a mental note of that just before his motorcade reached the entrance of the hotel which served as headquarters for the army front here.

A phalanx of officers in parade dress stood waiting for them. At last he saw something uniform about the army.

Strelnikov climbed from the car and snugged his peaked cap in place before returning the salute of the honor guards. He walked the row of officers, noting their ascending rank until at last he came to a familiar—if unwelcome face.

"General Turgenev," Strelnikov said with a wan smile. "How long has it been? Last we spoke I believe you had transferred me back to Moscow under General Tarasov's orders."

Turgenev shifted uncomfortably but maintained Strelnikov's gaze. Though unimaginative and thick-headed, at least he could not be said to be a coward. He saluted Strelnikov stiffly. "I believe that you are correct."

There was no love lost between them. In fact, Turgenev might well prove to be one of the first men Strelnikov purged from the army when the opportunity presented itself. Unlike Rastayev, who hung by his side like a dog, Turgenev was far from loyal. But Strelnikov knew the old goat wouldn't act without orders. It was his weakness. He was a slave to his orders. Strelnikov had little use for unimaginative sycophants like Turgenev, but he trusted him at least to carry out orders. Right now that was all he needed.

"I hope to get a briefing about the situation before I issue any orders," Strelnikov said before gesturing into the hotel, an unspoken command for Turgenev to lead the way. He did so.

Within a few minutes the general staff of the front settled into an expansive conference room whose windows overlooked Warsaw.

"I want open and honest speech," Strelnikov said, removing his cap and setting it down on the lacquered surface of the table as he sat. "Dressing up problems with fancy words will only compound problems. Be forthcoming and we can face them together." He looked to Turgenev. "Speak."

The general was silent for a moment as he gathered his thoughts. "To speak openly and honestly," he said at last, "the situation is grim." When Strelnikov didn't blow up, he continued, standing at the foot of the table. "NATO forces are advancing on all fronts. The enemy is entering into the German Democratic Republic. Berlin itself is now under threat." As he spoke he seemed to become more animated, more agitated. "They are at the gates of Budapest. Yugoslavia is lost, Bulgaria all but undone." Turgenev flashed a sharp look at a nearby staff officer who bustled over, laying a map of Eastern Europe on the table so that Turgenev might better outline the problem. "Panic has spread through the army. East German units are deserting en masse. Czechoslovak units are rebelling, Polish forces are threatening mutiny. Poland..." Trugenev paused to shake his head sadly. "It is a whole separate issue."

"Tell me," Strelnikov said.

"Where to begin?" Turgenev spread his hands helplessly. "Protests. Riots. A general strike. The Polish People's Army is—at this point—politically unreliable. I have pulled them back and now hold them under our direct supervision. All heavy weapons and equipment I have ordered sent back to depots or issued as replacements to other units."

Effectively Turgenev disarmed them. It was a start, but insufficient.

"Gather what remaining Polish forces there are and send them out of the country," Strelnikov said. "If they remain here they will only melt away and join the dissenters."

"We cannot rely on them to hold the line," Turgenev insisted.

"Send them to Hungary," Strelnikov said. "A counterattack at Budapest. They may at least soak up Western bullets."

Silence reigned as the order was transcribed.

"For those Poles in open rebellion, there will be reprisals." Strelnikov continued. He glanced out the window at the city beyond. Maybe it was fate that the city he'd come to fame for subduing in '89 would now be the heart of his grand counterattack. "I expect strikers to be made example of and all public displays met with bayonets." He turned back to Turgenev and the others. "Do not worry about civilian casualties. In a war such as this, there are no civilians."

Turgenev waited for this order to be taken down before continuing, seemingly unimpressed with Strelnikov's bold words. "At present the front is collapsing. As our allies break their trust with us, it creates fresh holes in our line. All I can do is withdraw and shrink our lines to avoid a total collapse." Finally, Turgenev presented the situation in a single sentence. "We are in danger of losing everything."

Strelnikov nodded as if he had been told the weather forecast. He could not alter reality by force of will alone. However bleak, however unpleasant the situation, it was what it was. All that remained was what to do next. "Suggestions?" He looked around at the officers.

At first none spoke.

"We might reconsider our policy on special weapon deployment," Rastayev said, voice subdued.

"Special weapons" was a neat euphemism for the Soviet Union's considerable stockpile of biological, chemical, and nuclear weapons.

"Out of the question," Strelnikov barked angrily. "Do you

not think that NATO has their own special weapons to match ours? Have you seen the state of our NBC defense troops? Decontamination gear, chemical suits, gas masks? Do you think our men still carry these things?"

Rastayev shrank from Strelnikov's fury, averting his eyes.

"To open the gates of Armageddon here is to invite defeat in a shorter time and on a greater scale. No." Strelnikov shook his head. "We will win as we have in the past." Seeing as there were no subsequent suggestions, he saw free to issue his orders. Strelnikov snapped his fingers and another aide appeared with another map. He unrolled it over Turgenev's. This one was marked with units and movements.

"Operation Floodland," Strelnkov said. "I have drawn the preliminaries up on the train ride here, but now we will sort out the specifics. "It hinges on a bolstered defense of the Danube River to the south. I have sent Comrade General Dmitriyev to Leningrad to take command of the front against Finland and Comrade General Sidorov to take command in Prague." He indicated the army fronts on the map as he spoke. He wished with all his heart for generals of greater caliber, men like Tarasov, Mamedov, Gurrov—men lost to this bloody struggle never to return. But if wishes were horses then beggars would ride.

"With our flanks secured," Strelnikov continued, "I will lead a counterattack toward Berlin to blunt the enemy advance. This force will use Comrade General Rastayev's division, General Turgenev's army front, and whatever else can be spared."

Turgenev raised an eyebrow. "A counterattack?"

"Just so."

"Do you see the risk in gambling everything on such a thrust?' Turgenev asked before belatedly adding, "Comrade General."

Strelnikov could not help but laugh. It was cold and mirthless. "It is a gamble, yes. But if we do not gamble, comrade, then we cannot win. If we allow things to proceed as they have been then surely we will lose." No one objected or corrected him, but Strelnikov saw the horror and worry on their faces. "So many good men have been lost," he continued. "We will ensure that it is not in vain."

Turgenev took all this in before speaking. "For our flanks to be secure then we must consider Romania. The Bulgarian People's Army is in open mutiny now," he said. "The country is lost."

Strelnikov looked at the map with distaste. "If Bulgaria is lost... so be it. But the Danube must be held at all costs."

6

The broad avenues of Sofia were packed edge to edge and end to end with a never ending flow of traffic, both foot and vehicular. Because of the dense press, cars and trucks—even military ones—all moved about the same speed as the pedestrians on foot. The air was full of the smell of exhaust and the murmur of idling engines and a thousand conversations.

"Look at them all, Jean," Pete Owens said, astounded as he looked over the crowd from his vantage point on the back of a Bulgarian BMP.

"Less talking, more shooting." Jean Carson, Associated Press, couldn't count how many times she'd had to remind her cameraman of that in the past few days. As the communist system faltered and failed across Eastern Europe, they encountered more and more scenes which would have been unimaginable just a few years ago.

She had to excuse his amateurish shock, since this was all so unprecedented. After decades of restriction and repression, the iron curtain was coming down with a reverberating crash of metal. All that remained now was to see how the pieces fell.

Both sides of the street were flanked by looming, blocky, symmetrical buildings in a style which Jean would have called "Federal" but might more accurately have been "Tsarist." Either way, it wouldn't have looked out of place in Washington D. C.

The windows of these government buildings were open, full of the pale faces of curious and stunned onlookers as people filtered through the capitol. They inched closer to the Communist Party Headquarters building which sat dead ahead at the crook of a Y-shaped intersection. The colonnaded facade of the building was crowned with a cupola and, atop that, a towering flagpole currently flying the tricolor of the Bulgarian People's Republic.

The same flag flew from the aerial of the BMP Jean and Pete rode atop. Unlike the flag on the headquarters building though, the flag on the BMP had its coat of arms crudely cut out of the top left corner, leaving a gaping hole—the flag of the anti-communist forces. That flag was echoed around them hundreds of times. People in the crowd carried it. I hung from windows and fluttered on rooftops. The voice of the people was unmistakable. The wind of change was here.

Pete swept the scene with the unfeeling lens of his camera, recording it all for re-broadcast in the Western world. It would be, Jean imagined, a sorely needed moral boost to see the evil empire crumbling at last. Freedom had come to Bulgaria as it no doubt would to Germany, Czechoslovakia, Poland, Romania, and Hungary. Someday.

"Incredible," Jean breathed. All the bleeding and dying almost seemed worth it.

The Bulgarian soldiers they rode with seemed just as elated. They raised their rifles in salute and called out to the crowd who cheered them. Horns honked, people laughed, cried, sang, and stood in mute shock.

They drove slowly past a small open space in the crowd where Jean saw more mutinying Bulgarian soldiers. These had their officers held at gunpoint, their hands bound behind their back where they kneeled on the sidewalk, surrounded by a jeering crowd. More ominously was a handful of dead men in Soviet uniforms around them, advisors and commissars. The leash holders.

"Pete, here. Here!" Jean called. To her Bulgarian companions she added "*Blagodarya*!" Thanks, or so she had been told. It was the only Bulgarian she spoke.

They waved farewell as she jumped and landed awkwardly from the armored vehicle. Pete came down a moment later beside her, grunting and cradling the camera. Jean forged ahead, leading Pete carefully.

"American," she said. "Associated Press." The words were like a spell, the crowd made way for her, perhaps compelled by the novelty of seeing a pushy American woman more than any particular respect for the news media.

Without an interpreter, any meaningful interaction was really impossible. They'd left Cristo, their Greek interpreter, back with the Greek army outside Sofia for now. It had been decided —at levels far over Jean's head—that the optics of self-liberation would look better and so the Greeks had held back, allowing their now Bulgarian allies to enter the city. It was the same story with European Turkey to the east. Turkish army units re-crossed the Maritsa River and were driving for the Black Sea, aiming to cut Istanbul off from the rest of the Soviet empire.

Pete filmed the scene of the Bulgarian officers taken captive and the cheering crowd.

A sergeant with a thick, drooping mustache approached them. "American?"

"Yes," Jean said, resisting the urge to follow up with: 'how could you tell?'

"Good!" He said, beaming, pleased with his English and with seeing them here. "American friends."

"Yes, friends," Jean repeated.

He beamed at the camera when Pete focused on him, His comrades in arms collected behind him to mug for the camera, posing with their assault rifles.

"What have these men done?" Jean asked, straining the sergeant's tenuous grasp of English.

"Damn communists," he said after a moment of thought. "Damn Russians. Eh.... enemy!"

"The enemy?"

"Enemy of me. Enemy of you," he said. "Russian bastards."

Jean filled in the gaps for him. These were the oppressors. The ones who'd sold his country into poverty and slavery. The ones who'd marched them into the sights of Greek guns to die in droves.

Before they could stammer through any more awkward conversation, a tremor ran through the crowd, a thousand voices stilling at once.

At first, Jean's stomach tensed, her blood chilled. A panic would mean a stampede, a crush. She'd only just started to look for shelter when she saw that the crowd wasn't afraid, they were awed. Fingers pointed, voices raised. There was movement on the cupola of the communist party building.

Jean went to nudge Pete's arm but he was already filming, camera shouldered, adjusting the zoom to capture the movement.

A lone figure crept from an open window and clambered carefully along the rooftop before scaling a ladder toward the flag. After some struggle, Jean saw the flag flutter away, cut loose.

The man produced a new flag from a bag at his side and affixed it to the pole. When he released it, the wind caught it and unfurled it, exposing the flashing hole where the coat of arms had been removed.

The crowd erupted as one, the sound deafening, almost overpowering. The elated cry of freedom.

Jean was floored and could only gawk at Pete. Spectacle over, he gawked back. "It's a total rebellion," he said, stunned.

Jean corrected him. "It's a revolution."

7

For all Esposito's talk of "putting the hammer down and locking the throttle" the advance north from Himmelkron was anything but breakneck by peacetime standards. A two hour drive by car took closer to two days for the men and machines of Cutthroat Company. It wasn't the enemy which slowed them down, or rather, it wasn't enemy *action* which slowed them. Instead they were delayed by the volume of surrenders and the roads clogged with refugees and abandoned vehicles.

They crossed the inner-German border without fanfare. A long, parallel row of chainlink fences topped with coils of razorwire marked it, along with multilingual signs warning of dire consequences should the border be violated intentionally or otherwise.

Vance's Abrams tanks tore through the fence like tissue paper, engines roaring as they crumpled the wire beneath their tracks.

He'd expected a fight, or at least greatly reinforced barricades and anti-tank obstacles. Instead the engineers trailing behind them had little to do but start sweeping the border for mines and marking clear paths.

"Looks like they're too busy running to fight," TJ said over the radio.

Vance rubbed bleary eyes. He'd slept hardly a wink since they'd started the advance. Crawling through fields, villages, and alongside choked highways both night and day took its toll.

"Don't count on that to hold out," Vance said. "Leipzig is ahead."

Everyone knew that the Soviets would fight for it even if the Germans didn't.

The road told a different story. Just as before, it was lined with the debris of a dissolving army. Weapons, uniforms, helmets, tanks, trucks, APCs, all lay forgotten.

"Cutthroat Six, One Six. I see a white flag ahead. Looks like civilians, sir."

Vance tapped his mic on. "Civilians?"

"Affirmative. About a dozen of them in the main highway. They're blocking the way but..."

Vance really hated when strange things happened. He almost longed for a platoon of T-62s to blow sky high. Anything other than whatever the hell this was.

"Copy," Vance said. "Hold position and wait one. I'll be there."

Sure enough when he found his first platoon further up the road their tanks were pulled off the main highway guns trained —almost comically—on a small gaggle of men in suits and plain clothes standing under a white sheet tied to a long pole a couple hundred yards away.

Vance had Kinney halt and took a look at the Germans through his gunsights. They shifted anxiously, but stood firm, watching him watch them. He sighed. "One Six, shoot anything that shoots at me. Copy?"

"Copy, Six. Good luck."

Vance toggled to TJ's frequency. "TJ, hold back." He didn't add: 'just in case they kill me.'

"Be careful."

Vance switched over to his intercom. "Driver advance slow. Take us up to those civilians."

Crocodile Tears crept forward with a rattle of treads, moving down the center of a two lane road. Open, rolling countryside unfolded to either side of them and they passed a guide sign marking the city ahead as Leipzig.

When he got within ten yards of the civilians they took a few fearful steps back but otherwise remained firm. He slowed to a halt and stood up, leaning out of the turret. "English?' he called down hopefully.

"You are American?" a white-haired man in a plain suit called back by way of response.

"Yeah," Vance said. "Captain Vance."

He saw relief on the faces of the men here. He wondered who it was they were dreading to encounter. Maybe the French.

"We are here on behalf of the city of Leipzig and its people," the white-haired man said with surprisingly good English. "We are here to surrender the city to you."

Vance had accepted a lot of surrenders by this point, including a whole Czechoslovakian combat team, but an entire city was new to him. "I'm just a captain," he said. "I don't know that I can accept your surrender." When he saw their faces fall to horror and dismay he quickly added. "But I'll find out. No one will fire on or harm you. Are there any forces in the city?"

"Forces?" the German repeated uncertainly.

"Soldiers. Tanks. Army."

"No," he said quickly. A little too quickly. "No soldiers. That is over. They have left their guns and their posts. Just boys. frightened boys."

"Frightened boys can still be soldiers." Vance spoke from experience.

"They have given that up," the man insisted. "We will cause no trouble and no blood will be spilled unless you are the ones to spill it."

Vance shook his head. "Let me talk to my superior. Wait here." He disappeared back into the tank and flipped on the battalion command radio. "Hammermill Six, Cutthroat Six Actual, I'm being offered the surrender of the city of Leipzig."

"Say again, Cutthroat?"

Vance repeated the message and a moment later Esposito himself came on the radio. "What's the play?" he asked.

"I think they're sincere. Looks like the village elders or some shit. They're telling me the only soldiers in the city are deserters. They want to surrender the whole city without a fight."

There was a long delay. Esposito coordinating with regiment command, Vance imagined. When he came back he spoke with authority. "We can consider it an open city. There will be no fighting if we're allowed to pass through and enter it as we see fit to. Only condition is that they need to turn over the deserters as POWs."

"If they don't go for that?" Vance asked.

"Do they have any guns?" Esposito asked.

"No, sir."

"Then they don't have any choice, do they?"

A hard truth, but immutable. "No, sir. I'll let them know." He stood up again and met the eyes of the anxious delegates of Leipzig. "I can accept your surrender on two conditions. First, that we can pass freely into and through your city and second, that all the soldiers in your city must turn themselves over as prisoners of war."

"We have no power to compel them to surrender," the white-haired man said, equal parts defiant and afraid.

"We have the power to do that,"Vance assured him. "I just need your word you won't interfere. They are soldiers of war and will be treated fairly."

"My word," the German repeated, seeming to understand the concept. "You will have it if I have yours that they will be treated well."

Vance could not help but put an edge in his voice. "They will be treated better than your people treated ours. This is the only deal I can offer you. Take it or leave it."

There was no real choice at all.

After assuring him they would comply with the American demands, the German delegates stepped aside and let Vance's tanks continue on toward the city.

TJ brought his tank alongside Vance's, lifting one headphone to shout over to him. "Better than blasting militia out of basements and highrises, huh?"

Vance nodded. "Next stop, Berlin."

"What are the odds they also give that one up without a fight?" TJ asked.

Vance didn't want to speculate. "Go in expecting to burn it down," he said. "I don't think we'll be rushing in to shake their hands when we get there."

"Hey, at least this one was a cakewalk," TJ said, pulling his headphones back down.

"Yeah," Vance did likewise and Kinney put the tank in gear. But he didn't think this luck would hold much longer.

8

It seemed strange to Petty Officer John Rayburn that there was a time—not so long ago when he'd looked forward to ending the long period of uneasy boredom and ceaseless training he and the Marines of his company had endured in Northern Italy. Now, with his feet sore, his uniform caked with dirt, eyes heavy with fatigue, he only dreamed about a time when he could leave this hellish place behind.

Gravel crunched between Rayburn's boots and the road as he walked, trailing at the rear of the platoon as they moved slowly ahead.

They walked to either side of the road to Budapest flanked by dense stands of trees and brush that mostly hid the flat, open countryside around them from view. He was directly behind Wierzbowski who lugged a heavy M240 machine gun at the ready, head swiveling, neck craned as he struggled to make out targets ahead.

Rayburn carried the same rifle that many of the Marines around him did, although—as a Navy corpsman—his primary responsibility wasn't fighting, it was medical triage. In that sense, his first aid kit was more important to him than the weapon in his hands.

Turning his head to the right, Rayburn caught glimpses of an open field which ran nearly to the horizon. Towering smokestacks of some industrial facility that broke that flat plane far off. Not his problem.

"What a shithole," Wierzbowski muttered, frowning at the empty space. "Bomb this shit to the stone age, man. Who cares?"

No one objected. Rayburn was too tired to do much other than grunt in response.

"At least they could let us drive there," Keyes said from the other side of the road, glancing back over his shoulder at the Amphibious Assault Vehicle, *Decimator*.

"*Decimator* ain't bullet proof," Sergeant Washington replied. "You gonna look like Swiss-fucking-cheese if we let your ass ride into Budapest."

Ahead of them all, Lieutenant Eichmann consulted closely with the platoon radioman, talking in hushed voices.

"Right," the lieutenant said finally, turning back to the platoon and raising his voice. "Recon reports contact ahead. Enemy infantry dug in. We're advancing to contact. Weapons free. Anything that moves is hostile."

"Fuckin-A," Wierzbowski said, adjusting his grip on his machine gun.

The Marines increased their pace, walking fast, subconsciously bowing their heads and hunching their backs to keep low as they moved steadily nearer to the reported enemy position. Sunlight warmed the pavement, sending trickles of sweat down Rayburn's back that he tried to ignore. He felt like a bundle of nerves. The fact that the birds had fallen silent did nothing to help with that.

Machine gun fire lashed the treeline around them and sent the Marines to ground with startled shouts.

Rayburn threw himself flat on the asphalt and belly crawled into the undergrowth to the right. Bullets cracked and zipped by, what felt like only inches overhead.

"Enemy front! Contact contact!"

Wierzbowski crawled forward until he found a gap in the foliage facing out across an open field toward the enemy. There was no sign of any people at all, just an ugly brown scar which marked the parapet of a crude trench cut along the edge of an open farm. It was target enough.

Wierzbowski unfolded his weapon's bipod, shouldered it, and began belting suppressive fire across the enemy works.

Rayburn came as close to Wierzbowski as he dared, unable

to shake the knowledge that machine gunners made inviting targets. He added his own meager fire to Wierzbowski's, peppering the trench aimlessly with the Marines.

The enemy wasn't budging.

"Soviets!" Keyes said, rolling onto his back to reload. "Gotta be."

Rayburn agreed. Anyone else would have bolted at first contact. Only the Soviets had any fight left in them. "Probably a Guards unit!" Rayburn called back, yelling over his ringing ears. That was pure conjecture, but it felt better to go toe to toe with the Soviet elite instead of run of the mill conscripts.

Within a few minutes, *Decimator* herself waded into the fight. Though she was far from bulletproof, she packed a wallop. The forty millimeter grenade launcher in her turret began to burp rhythmically. The small explosive rounds peppered the enemy trenches, bursting around and above them. As the AmTrac tore into the enemy, Soviet return fire began to slacken off.

"Washington! Pivot right!" Lieutenant Eichmann called, waving his hand that way. "Get along this road and flush them!"

Sergeant Washington shouted confirmation and then slunk back from the treeline, calling to Keyes, Rayburn, Weirsbowski, and the rest of his squad. They withdrew to the relative safety of the treeline on the opposite side of the road and picked their way forward. They moved at a low crouch, edging closer to the enemy trenches.

Rayburn hardly felt his fatigue now that he was in the grip of battle. Even fear seemed alien to him. All he worried about was being ready to fight, ready to act. He had a job to do.

Bullets stitched the trees around them, singing through the foliage. Some struck trunks and branches, showering the Marines with bits of bark.

Keyes swore under his breath as everyone ducked.

"Move!" Washington shouted, pausing to wave his men on. "Get up!"

Finally they reached a section of the road nearly perpendicular to the Soviet trench. Rayburn saw that the enemy earthworks curled in toward a sprawling suburb half-visible ahead, running parallel to the road. It was about a hundred yards away over open ground, but he didn't see any movement.

Washington had his squad lay flat and wait. In another minute, mortar fire whistled in, exploding along the Soviet lines. It did no apparent damage, but at least put the fear of God into them. Hopefully. When it slackened off, the Marines went forward.

"Let's go!"

Wierzbowski fired from the hip, short stuttering bursts as they jogged through the open farmland toward the trench. Rayburn wasn't sure it did any good, but no one fired back at them.

Once they were within twenty or so yards, they went to ground again.

"Rayman, grenade!" Washington said.

They both pulled pins nearly simultaneously.

Rayburn released the spoon and watched the safety handle fall away. He felt a thrill as he counted to three, holding the live explosive and then hurled it overhand toward the trench. A perfect shot. It banked off the parapet and landed inside.

Before it could explode he saw an enemy figure rise up, clambering out of the trench to escape it, making a run for it.

He couldn't outrun Keyes' gun.

The Soviet fell flat on his face, riddled with bullets, and slid back into the trench a moment before the grenade exploded.

"Go!" Washington bolted to his feet, leading Rayburn and Keyes into the trench. They slid down the dirt parapet and landed in the muddy bottom.

One Soviet was dead, another lay on the ground, groaning, but otherwise motionless. His back was peppered with splinters from a grenade and he bled profusely.

Washington fired his weapon twice into him to make him dead before they moved on.

Rayburn adjusted his medical bag and stepped over the dead men, following Washington through the trench. It zigzagged through the rich Hungarian earth. They cleared each bend with grenades and blind bursts of gunfire while Wierzbowski and the others provided overwatch.

"Infantry in the open!" Wierzbowski shouted before cutting down some withdrawing Soviet soldiers.

Rayburn's heart thundered in his ears while they cleared the rest of the trench. It was smaller than he had supposed initially, maybe designed for a platoon of enemy infantry but held by less than that. Soon, all the Marines piled into the trench, working their way to the rear of the network. They moved closer to the village it screened, no doubt another enemy strongpoint.

Rayburn peeked his head through a gap in the parapet and, to his surprise, saw a figure waving a white towel, standing at the edge of the village.

"Sergeant," Rayburn said, pointing.

"I see him," Washington said before raising his voice. "Come on!" He beckoned with a hand. "We won't shoot you!"

After some hesitation, the enemy soldier moved forward and was suddenly joined by a dozen others, men in khaki uniforms with their hands held high.

"Hungarians?" Wierzbowski asked.

"Maybe." Rayburn wasn't sure. He just knew they weren't Soviets.

The foreign soldiers had made it halfway to the trench when long ripping bursts of machine gun fire cut them down in the open.

"Cease fire! Cease fire!" Rayburn shouted in horror. He could only watch helplessly as the surviving enemy soldiers panicked, some fleeing back toward the village, others fleeing toward the Americans.

"Who's firing!?" Washington shouted, "Cease fire, god dammit!"

It was only then that they realized the fire came not from the Americans, but from the enemy lines, shooting the surrendering men in the back.

Wierzbowski swore angrily, sighted his weapon on the source

of the fire and returned fire vengefully. It was too late.

Within a minute *Decimator* chuffed out a storm of grenades, demolishing the offending house and reducing it to kindling, but the damage was done. When at last everything fell silent, all the soldiers who had hoped to surrender were dead in the field. Murdered.

The Marines watched with impotent fury and horror until finally they were clear to advance again. Climbing from the trench they moved forward on foot in a long, shaky line.

Rayburn jogged ahead of the others, breathing hard, hoping he might find someone to save, but knowing that he wouldn't. When he reached the dead men he stood over them and could do nothing but stare.

Wierzbowski reached him next, scowling down at the bodies before kneeling and rolling one over. His khaki uniform was stained a bloody shade of red, his face a rictus mask of pain. His steel helmet was marked with a white eagle bearing a shield.

"They're fucking Polish, man," Weirzbowski said in dismay. "What the fuck."

"Shit," Rayburn said. "Russians didn't let them surrender."

Wierzbowski stood back up, baring his teeth toward the enemy. "We'll see what happens next time a Russian wants to call it even." His tone left no doubt to his meaning.

Rayburn was too shocked to do more than watch Wierzbowski stalk forward, following the others of the unit on, continuing toward the enemy, hunting for targets to pay the price of what had happened.

9

The monotony of the gulag wasn't pleasant, but it was safe, or at least familiar. Change to that schedule was never welcome, and so when instead of being sent into the paper plant the prisoners were gathered in ranks in the yard, Gradenko felt only apprehension. He noted that none of the POWs were here, only the Soviet convicts who stood in neat rows, moved into compliance by the threat of violence from the sneering guards.

"Stand up straight and pay attention!" a guard snapped, kicking a prisoner in the calf. Gradenko made himself as tall as he could even as Dragomirov slumped against him, only semi-lucid, muttering under his breath.

"Be quiet," Gradenko hissed.

Mercifully Dragomirov obeyed, swaying slightly on his feet.

The prisoners were dirty, scrawny, unshaven, and sickly looking. Their jumpsuits had begun life a navy blue color but now matched the muddy brown of the ground.

Opposite them were a handful of soldiers—true soldiers—not the sniveling guards of this place. They wore the accoutrements of battle, steel pot helmets and military fatigues. At their center was an aging, overweight officer in a peaked cap. A colonel. He looked over the prisoners like a man surveying the pitiful remains of a buffet. For a little while, no one spoke. Finally, the colonel raised his voice. "Men," he said. "I am Colonel Ivanov of the 286th Motor Rifles."

He spoke as if he represented the Tsar's personal guard. The unit name meant nothing to even Gradenko who ought to know more about the organization of the army than anyone else here.

"I have come with an offer for you. An offer of life."

The colonel drew in a deep breath before continuing. "The Motherland calls on its sons to defend her. The enemy must be thrown back and to do that we must have men. My regiment has openings for riflemen. Foot soldiers." He looked over the prisoners, looking for anything like recognition.

Gradenko pointedly did not meet his gaze, staring at the mud at the colonel's boots.

"For all men who join me and sign a term of service to fight, you will be granted amnesty by order of General Strelnikov. You will be issued with boots, a rifle, a uniform, and food."

That last prospect made Gradenko's stomach rumble weakly. Even army rations sounded like a feast compared to the gruel he subsisted on here.

"And, most importantly, you will be granted freedom," the colonel finished. "We will take all men who can see and walk." A low bar, but it excluded at least Dragomirov. "Who will join me?"

No one moved.

"Come on." The colonel persisted, undaunted. "Who will volunteer? Who will redeem themselves?"

His soldiers walked the line of prisoners, looking each of them in the face as if searching for something. Gradenko let his eyes roll off them.

At last a timid hand went up. The prisoner who raised it was quickly pulled from the line by the soldiers.

"Who else?"

In this way, a trickle of men signed their lives to the army.

Gradenko knew what fate awaited those desperate enough to agree. The men who volunteered here could expect to be marched into minefields and sent to charge enemy trenches or defend hopeless positions. However terrible it was here, an old man like him had better odds in a gulag than on a battlefield in a penal battalion. It was a lottery of survival, only worse than that. A lottery was guaranteed to have a winner.

Gradenko waited in tense silence as the army picked the men it could. He felt a sudden shock when he saw the last of them to step forward was Radomir, once the Soviet minister of petroleum, now cannon fodder.

Radomir and Gradenko caught each other's eye. Each expression filled with pity and remorse. Gradenko recognized a few others who joined as KGB, Dragomirov's men, their decision compelled either by desperation or misplaced patriotism.

Finally, when the colonel saw no more would come, he took his reluctant recruits and marched them out of the camp and toward waiting trucks. Gradenko expected they would ultimately join a dingy column of reservists and march into the enemy guns in Sweden, Turkey, or Germany.

"The rest of you, move! To work!" The guards drove the remaining prisoners toward the plant.

Gradenko caught Dragomirov's arm and helped him stumble along. Dragomirov's eyes were glassy, unfocused. He spent a lot of time muttering or whispering, conversing with the unseen. Gradenko was not a superstitious man, but he could not help but imagine that Dragomirov was talking with the dead.

"They are going to Finland," Johan said, falling into step beside Gradenko as the POWs joined the remaining Soviet prisoners.

"Finland?"

Johan nodded. "There has been an uprising, I am told. Worse, the army units in Leningrad are mutinying, refusing to fight."

Gradenko had no difficulty believing that. Things were bad indeed for Strelnikov to rally prisoners to the army. The choice wasn't without precedent in Russian history, but it was a desperate one.

"I hope you will forgive me if I say my hopes are with the Finns," Johan said, only a hint of jest in his tone.

Gradenko truthfully wasn't sure who he wanted to win at this stage. The war was a travesty, there was no denying that, but that did not mean he craved the defeat of his nation. "I hope that it will accelerate the end of this war," he said finally.

Johan looked at Dragomirov, frowning sympathetically. "How is he?" He did not even bother to address the man directly anymore.

Gradenko could only shake his head.

"I will help you to take him back," Johan said.

Together they carried Dragomirov across the yard and into the prisoner barracks. Some of the gulag's actual criminals watched them from where they sat on their bunks. Their eyes were mirthless, hungry.

"Here," Gradenko eased Dragomirov down onto his cot, wincing as he gasped.

"Reports," Dragomirov said, eyes flying wide. It was the first clear word he'd said all day. "The reports will reflect this..." his eyes dimmed, glancing around, jaw working noiselessly.

"I am sure they will, comrade," Gradenko said.

"What did he say?" John asked.

"He is reliving his life," Gradenko explained, touching Dragomirov's forehead. He was burning hot.

The KGB man's eyes fluttered closed and he breathed, hard and slow, as if from exertion. Gradenko thought that each pause between his breaths might be his last.

Johan stood beside Gradenko, saying nothing. There was nothing which could be said. The truth was obvious and unavoidable.

Dragomirov was a dead man.

10

Adamcik's lieutenant rank felt foreign to him, almost heavy. It was a burden he'd never wanted, or even felt qualified to bear. "Damn Vesely," he muttered to himself as he walked along the quartet of parked tanks which made up his platoon. *His* platoon. The idea was as foreign as his rank, or as the number of tanks. The Czechoslovakian army he'd been inducted into followed the structure of the Soviet system; a platoon was three tanks, not four. Much like the American-cut of his new uniform, it would be something to get used to.

"Good morning, Lieutenant," Sergeant Coufal said, standing between his driver and gunner and beaming at Adamcik, relishing in his superior's new rank and discomfort.

"Morning," Adamcik replied gruffly. His eyes went from the men to the tank. It was a T-72 dotted with explosive reactive armor blocks, no different than the tank he'd surrendered. Almost. Coufal's tank, like all the tanks in the Legion, was painted in the green, brown, and black blotches of American woodland camo. When coupled with the distinctive three-pointed white stars marked on the roof of the turret and flanks of the tank for identification, it was almost wholly different.

"All ready then?" Adamcik asked.

"Ready, Comrade Lieutenant," Coufal said, slipping into old habits easily. "Ready to go home."

Adamcik smiled at the thought. Home, the reason they were doing all of this. It was tantalizingly close by, just a few hours drive away, waiting for them to enter.

"Me too," Adamcik said before continuing his inspection. The tanks of his platoon were parked on a broad concrete expanse, the depot of some German division which was away at the front now. It was their temporary home as they finished "refresher training." The name was a joke. It was little more than a crash course. Of course, it was still nearly as long as their original, truncated military training had been.

The morning air was still cool, not yet warmed by the summer sun, but already unpleasantly humid. The calling of birds competed with the muttering of engines.

Adamcik gave greetings to each of his crews in turn before reaching his tank, another T-72 in American woodland, this one with a Czechoslovakian flag flying from its radio aerial.

Adamcik studied it for a moment until Janco poked his head up from the gunner's hatch. "You like it?"

"It will make us a very inviting target," Adamcik said. "I thought you might want *Zlato* to survive the war intact."

Janco clicked his tongue. "No, no. Not *Zlato*. She was lost to us when you surrendered her. *Milacku*." Darling.

"*Milacku*?" Adamcik repeated dubiously. "Janco, you really have been too long away from women."

His gunner grinned back enigmatically. "Which is why I am excited to go home."

Home. That constant refrain. It had become an almost religious calling among the men.

"You won't stay a sergeant long with such idle day dreaming."

Janco showed his new rank proudly but did not argue with Adamcik. "I just want to know when we leave. Soon, yes?"

"Soon," Adamcik repeated. "We wait only on the captain's word."

Janco grumbled, smile vanishing. "I signed up so we might fight," he says. "At least in the prison I did not have to work."

"And we *will* fight," Adamcik said, hoping that was true. He too was frustrated with the days of inactivity and bureaucratic reorganization. "Soon."

"I hope this is true," Janco said before returning to work.

Leaving him behind, Adamcik continued down the line of vehicles, this time passing by a platoon of BMPs done up as the tanks were. Among the infantry loitering around the armored beasts he saw Zetov, once Captain Zetov, now Private Zetov. He gave Adamcik a knowing look though he did not smile. When Adamcik nodded at him he returned the gesture. Adamcik hoped he would find penance in this service.

Beyond the BMPs he found who he was looking for. A tank on a hydraulic lift was being looked over by a team of technicians including Adamcik's one-time driver Gaspar.

"The whole suspension is shot," Lieutenant Ambroz said, voice sour. "I won't go home missing a tank. Sort it out in short order. Quick."

"Yes, Lieutenant," Gaspar said unhappily, glancing at Adamcik.

Ambroz followed his glance, looking over his shoulder to see Adamcik. A tense silence followed. Adamcik had once been his subordinate, but now was his equal in rank. Adamcik was certainly his superior in the estimation of the men of the company who had followed him into captivity. Ambroz knew how to command, but it was Adamcik who had led.

Adamcik broke the silence. "Ambroz," he said politely. "Tank trouble?"

"For now," Ambroz replied, his hard expression softening somewhat. "For now," he said again, glancing sternly at the mechanics. "We left all our qualified technicians with the Soviets." He meant it as a joke, but it fell flat. There was always that reminder, that sticking point of his loyalty. The men here knew Ambroz had served the regime unapologetically and more enthusiastically than any of them had done. Whatever his reasons for doing that, however pragmatic, it hadn't been forgotten.

"I am certain it will be set in order," Adamcik said placatingly. "Have you seen Captain Vesely?"

Ambroz shook his head, looking no happier. Vesely, an outsider, had eclipsed his importance and rank almost as much as Adamcik had. "No. He is waiting for the most dramatic moment I suspect."

Vesely's penchant for flair was unusual among the normally dour and plain men of the 1st Tank Regiment, but that only made him stand out more.

A breathless soldier dashed up to the garage entrance, leaning on the open doorway and he blurted. "It's time. The captain is ready!"

Adamcik and Ambroz exchanged a glance.

"He wants everyone. Get your men!" And then the messenger was off to spread the word.

Needing no further encouragement, Adamcik and Ambroz gathered their platoons and joined the press of Czechoslovakians gathering at the foot of a T-72 which served as a stage for Vesely.

Vesely beamed down at all of them, looking over each of them as they jostled close, eager to hear the command they all knew was coming. "Men," he began. "It's time."

A cheer went up. Adamcik, and even Ambroz, raised their voices and their arms.

"We are going home!" Vesely continued as the other shouted praise. "The vanguard of an army to liberate all Czechoslovakia. In short minutes now we will be transporting our vehicles to the front where we will deploy, advance, and drive the enemy out!"

There was more cheering. Adamcik was swept up in the moment with the rest of them. Scarce months ago he'd seen lifting the Soviet bootheel from his home as impossible. He'd seen no choice but to meekly go along with their orders under fear of death. Now? Now, the weak had become strong.

Vesely's smile faded. "I am very proud of every man here. Every single one of you. You have never shied from a fight but now may fight for what you believe. But I know that this is not as it should be. Those we face on the battlefield may be our countrymen."

The elation faded to mourning.

"We may kill those who still profess loyalty to the abortion of a state squatting in Prague and Bratislava like a demon spawn," Vesely went on, undaunted. "But we do whatever we must." He clasped a hand over his heart. "I have sworn my life to see Czechoslovakia free, no matter the cost! But I will hold no one else to my pledge. I offer you this last choice: if you feel you cannot raise your hand in anger against a brother, then you may leave the unit and return to be a prisoner of war, your honor intact." No one spoke or moved. Vesely looked them over sternly, his eyes passing across Adamcik and sending a shiver up his spine. "Once we cross the line—once we are home—to refuse your duty will be considered desertion and dealt with accordingly. Think carefully where your loyalties lie."

Adamcik resisted the urge to glance at Ambroz to measure his expression. He was sure many others felt the same way.

After a few more tense moments Vesely nodded again. "Very good. See to your tanks and we will depart!"

11

After a headlong charge in pursuit of the enemy, a breakdown was almost a welcome relief. Vance leaned on an ash tree nearby, sipping from his canteen and taking bites from a hot mixture of pork, rice, and barbecue sauce. As far as MRE menu items went, it wasn't bad. Or maybe he was just very hungry. As he wolfed the last of his meal down he wiped his mouth, took a drink from his canteen, and tossed his trash into a ditch by the road.

Crocodile Tears was in a bad way, an entire replacement engine block had just finished being hoisted in by a winch mounted to a recovery vehicle. In some cases it was just faster to replace the whole thing than to try to sort the exact cause of a failure. The new block was painstakingly installed under the diligent attention of a handful of mechanics.

Vance turned away, walking along the dusty East German road. It looked for the most part like the West German roads he had seen, maybe worse for wear. The country here was flatter, less hilly, but otherwise little different.

Of more interest was the lone BRDM—an East German armored car—abandoned on the roadside. Its hatches were all flung open and it was surrounded by a pile of uniforms. The men inside had melted away, slipping from the army before it became a death sentence for them.

Also here was Vance's crew, rifling through the car and its contents.

"AK?" Kinney asked, holding the carbine out to Waxman.

"Man, they won't let me take that back. I want one of those weird-ass bucket helmets these dudes wear." Waxman kicked around the discarded uniforms, frowning at the padded leather tanker helmets in evidence.

Patterson sat on the edge of the BRDM and grinned proudly, turning a knife over in his hands, studying the blade of his trophy.

Kinney, having dropped the AK, whistled. "Check it out!" He stooped over and slid a belt from the loops of a discarded pair of trousers. "Belt buckle. Hammer and sickle."

Vance peered at it. "That's a compass, not a hammer and sickle."

"What?" Kinney asked, dismayed, frowning at it. "Bogus."

"I'll take it," Waxman said, holding out his hand."

"Forget it. I'm still keeping it."

"Where you think these guys went?" Patterson asked, sheathing his captured knife and hopping off the armored car.

"Home," Vance said, turning his head to look in the direction of the nearest village.

"Lucky bastards," Kinney muttered.

"They've got to be close to done, right?" Waxman asked, directing his question to Vance. Vance eyed the abandoned junk. "Ivan's got deep pockets."

"Yeah, but not bottomless," Waxman countered. They were both thinking the same thing. Surely, at some point, the enemy would break down completely.

Behind them, the engine swap was just about complete when TJ's tank, *Candyass*, threw open its hatch. "Vance!" He called. "You on?"

In response, Vance jogged back to his tank, scaled the side, and slipped through the hatch, plugging in his headset.

"I am now," he said.

"Get on battalion net," TJ said.

Vance complied. "Cutthroat Six to Hammermill, say again Hammermill."

"Brawler has encountered enemy armor coming in from the east near Wunsiedel. Move your company up to ambush position and cover the withdrawal." Hammermill fed detailed information to Vance who scribbled notes on his laminated map square with a grease pen.

"Copy, Cutthroat moving. Tell Jones we're getting in blocking positions at Krohenhammer."

"Good hunting, Cutthroat."

Vance raised his head from his hatch and called out to the mechanics. "You guys done?"

"Just finished, sir!"

Vance flashed a thumbs up, his heart beating hard as his crew clambered back in, taking their places and readying the tank for battle.

"Six to platoon leads," Vance said. "We're rolling. Brawler needs backup. We're taking position west of Krohenhammer and setting up blocking positions. Find good cover and concealment, check targets, and be ready to fight enemy armor."

The tanks of Cutthroat roared out, moving from reserve into position behind Brawler Company.

After a few minutes of driving, Vance spotted a gap in a hedgerow running perpendicular to the road.

"Driver left. Take us into that gap."

Crocodile Tears peeled off, taking position while the rest of the company moved closer, guns trained on the road. Shortly after assuming position, Brawler Company's tanks and APCs filtered back past them, racing for safety, fewer in number than they had been.

Vance grimaced as a pockmarked M113 cruised by in a hurry. He hoped the troops in the back weren't equally shot full of holes.

Second Platoon's leader saw the enemy first. "Contact front, enemy armor." His warning was followed by the cacophonous boom of cannons as the Abrams tore into the enemy.

Fireballs blossomed skyward as ammunition cooked off. Billowing puffs of black smoke rolled out, marring the azure sky.

Vance watched carefully through his periscopes and reported back to Esposito. "Contact with enemy. Brawler's past us. We are heavily engaged. If Brawler can regroup and move back we'd really appreciate it!"

"Copy Cutthroat Six, we'll send what we can. Hammermill out."

Vance saw one of his tanks fire smoke grenades and reverse a moment before a shell deflected off its turret armor with a kinetic flash. Another struck it in the front, penetrating the belly armor. The tank continued rolling backwards, the driver likely dead, but now with smoke boiling out of its open hatches. A single crewman scrambled free of the fiery turret and leaped away even as the tank kept backing up until it vanished from view.

"Gunner left," Vance said.

"I see em!" Waxman pivoted *Crocodile Tears*' turret to cover this gap a moment before the first enemy made themselves known, a T-80, top shelf stuff for the Soviets.

Waxman didn't wait to call the target before he fired. "Shot!"

The T-80 vanished in a burst of smoke and fire. Hit. Killed.

The enemy answered this indignity with a spray of autocannon fire from an unseen BMP further ahead. Tracer fire pulsed from the smoke, searching for the Americans, shells crashing across fields and trees.

"Driver reverse!" Vance called.

Kinney pulled them back, slinking away from the probing autocannon fire.

Vance caught a clear glimpse of the T-80 they'd hit. It was smoldering badly. The driver struggled free of his hatch, his uniform smoking. He landed on the ground and thrashed around in agony. Vance imagined he was screaming if he still could—if his lungs weren't already scorched. He seemed to roll around for an eternity as Vance willed him to hurry up and die. He lost sight of them as they backed into cover in a thick stand of trees.

Minutes later, Brawler returned to the fight, sweeping in on the right to strike the Soviets. Anyone who stuck their nose out got it shot away immediately. It was a fight in which the first to shoot nearly always won, and the first to be seen nearly always died. Bit by bit the firepower stalemate was broken by aggressive maneuvering.

American infantry probed close enough to pour gunfire into the thinly-armored BMPs and drive them back. Shoulder-launched anti-tank missiles ruptured two of these vehicles and left them and their crews burning.

As the coup du grace, a helicopter gunship thundered in low, picking off a pair of tanks with TOW missiles before the whole attack ran out of steam and pulled back.

"Hammermill, this is Cutthroat, enemy is withdrawing, permission to reconsolidate? I want to pull back a klick or two." Vance hated to follow a victory with a retreat, but the ground they were bleeding over was meaningless, not worth the blood they would spill to hold it if the enemy came back, especially not if the Soviets followed the attack with a shower of shells, as was their custom.

After a pause Esposito came back. "Hammermill confirms, Cutthroat. Draw back and consolidate with Brawler."

He pulled back just in time. Like clockwork, a heavy artillery barrage plowed and churned the earth minutes later. Soviet shells clawed the ground where the American line had been. Had they remained, those craters would have become graves for his men. Vance watched trees toppling in the bombardment from a few kilometers away. It looked to him like the Soviets had finally found their backbone, or at least more soldiers. So much for breakthrough.

12

There was little for Strelnikov to see of General Rastayev's grand counterattack except for a steady stream of vehicles moving forward. Tanks, trucks, and APCs filled the road as they advanced past Rastayev's headquarters and Strelnikov's judging gaze. East Germany's open fields and farmland made for nearly ideal viewing conditions for watching these massive attacks go forward, but even so, it was only a keyhole view of the overall attack.

Much of what could be spared in terms of new equipment had been allocated to these men and even then, it seemed to be held together with shoestring and hope. Aluminum and steel seldom quit, but flesh, blood, and bone were exhausted. They fought on with weapons pulled from half-forgotten warehouses and depots. Strelnikov only hoped it was enough.

Beside him, a radio sitting on a folding table set up beneath an awning warbled and buzzed as battalion commanders gave orders and updates. One constant refrain was the ceaseless demand for fire support.

The air overhead, absent any Soviet aircraft, was full of the howl of outgoing shells. If there was one thing the Soviets did not lack, and probably never would, it was artillery. Anywhere the Americans resisted, anywhere they broke through, was met with heavy fusillades of shells. Spots of particularly fierce fighting began to look like an image of 1917 as open fields became cratered, dead moonscapes.

"Schonefeld has been taken by the 209th," Rastayev said to Strelnikov, fidgeting uneasily.

Strelnikov moved away wordlessly, sorely missing Mishkin's

skillful staff work. He eyed the map which had been set up here and nodded to himself. "Good." Still, he could not help but reflect that at the beginning of this conflict success had been measured in cities and countries, now it was measured in villages.

"Comrade," Rastayev said, moving to stand beside Strelnikov. "Even if we drive them back another ten kilometers I do not think we will do more than slow their attack." He kept his voice low, well aware of the infectious nature of defeatism.

Strelnikov gave his subordinate a cold, unsympathetic look. It wasn't because of his pessimism, in fact, Strelnikov agreed with his assessment. No, it was because Rastayev so utterly failed to grasp the purpose of what they were doing here. "Irrelevant," Strelnikov said finally. "Destruction of the enemy is not our purpose today." His contempt curdled to open disgust. "Do you really believe the surest method to destroy our enemy is to attack them head on?"

"N-no, comrade," Rastayaev muttered.

Strelnikov shook his head. The ranks of his leadership were as destitute as his stockpiles. "We guide them. Steer them. Yes?" He gestured with his hands. "By punishing the enemy for attempting to move to the south or north, we steer them toward a central attack."

"Central?"

"Berlin," Strelnikov said, now too weary to show displeasure. "We drive them to Berlin. The NATO forces there fought to the last at the start of hostilities. They demonstrated clearly how difficult it is to extract a determined defender from an urban area." Strelnikov had seen only the barest glimpse of West Berlin's ruin, but it was enough to convince him again of the futility of urban warfare.

"I do not think NATO can be compelled to enter Berlin..." Rastayev replied hesitantly.

"No, but he can be driven to the suburbs," Strelnikov said. "The highway interchanges around the city are necessary if they hope to advance on the Oder river and beyond. He has no choice and so we will make it painful for him. Mines have been sown, killing fields marked out, entrenchments constructed. We funnel them further and further into the ground of our choosing."

Rastayev seemed to understand the tactics, but the broader strategy was lost on him.

More artillery fire sailed far overhead, shrieking through the air to crash down on the distant enemy, steel tearing flesh.

"If we can bleed them in Berlin, Prague, and Budapest," Strelnikov explained, "then we may have a chance." Satisfied at least that Rastayev might continue the attack on his own, Strelnikov saluted him, though it was only perfunctory.

Rastayev returned it quickly, his dull eyes flickering with apprehension. "We will press them, Comrade General, and hold them, but what to do when we can do no more?"

Strelnikov didn't answer right away. He looked to his left and watched a platoon of BTR's draped in camo netting cruise by. What was the life expectancy for one of those eight-wheeled armored vehicles on the battlefield? What of its crew? Days? Hours? Minutes? It all boiled down to math. For all Strelnikov's belief in the power of morale and aggression, he could not stand in the way of numbers. If he ran out of BTRs and men to crew them before the enemy ran out of missiles and bombs then it was over for him. It was a reality he would rather not dwell on. Certainly not when he believed he'd found a way to cheat that reality.

"Americans are fickle," he said finally. "For them a dead platoon is a disaster. They have started wars over less." He tore his eyes from the BTR and looked back to Rastayev. "They will see bodies on the news and wonder what it is all for. They are fighting only because their politicians demand it. This war has no bearing on them. Once their people demand peace we will fracture their defense and victory will be ours."

"But with their Conscription Act, surely the Americans are prepared to fight. Surely they understand what is at stake." Rastayev said, forgetting his place. At least, Strelnikov thought, he showed initiative.

"It plays right into our hands. More dead boys."

Rastayev only looked more troubled. "If they fight for nothing, what is it that we fight for?"

The consequence of a liberated officer corps was an officer corps which started to think for itself. A double edged sword. Strelnikov was finding that he had a renewed appreciation for the tightly-held obedience the government had established among its officers before. Sometimes he would rather not be faced with uncomfortable questions.

"We fight for our homes," Strelnikov said automatically. "We fight for the Motherland. For our families. For victory." He gave a final look around, saluted Rastayev one last time, and left before he was forced to answer more uncomfortable questions. He had no time to remain idle, his work, it seemed, was never done.

13

Dragomirov, once the chairman of the State Security Comittee —the KGB—lay dead on a ratty cot in a gulag in Arkhangelsk with the air smelling like sweat and flatulence. His face was slack, eyes half-lidded, jaw agape. At least he wasn't suffering any longer.

Gradenko stood over his body and stared down at it, cold and empty. He felt that he should feel sadness or relief, instead he only felt as though he were seeing a portent of the future. Dragomirov's life had been spent in the service of the Soviet Union, or more accurately in the pursuit of power. Now he was dead, unmourned. Forgotten. His fate was to be Gradenko's.

"Only the dead escape this place," Gradenko muttered to himself as he slowly drew a thin blanket over Dragomirov's face. He'd died here alone while Gradenko slaved in the plant. Had he been lucid in his final moments? Called out for someone? Gradenko would never know. He only hoped it came quickly.

Shadows fell on Gradenko, cast by the bare light bulb hanging from the central beam in the shoddily-made barracks.

"Move aside," a gruff voice said.

Gradenko looked back and saw the men he was afraid to see. Their faces were as implacable as the frontal armor of a main battle tank, eyes colder than infrared spotlights. These were the true criminals of this place.

"Move?" Gradenko repeated dumbly, his mind refusing to understand.

Even silhouetted by the lightbulb, Gradenko saw the leader of these men grin. "Whatever he had is ours now."

They intended to search Dragomirov.

"And you," he added.

"W-we have nothing," Gradenko blurted, partly true. They had nothing worth stealing.

One of the criminals spat on Gradenko's boots. "Liar. We know who you are. Who he was. Men like you do not come empty-handed."

It was ludicrous to think that either he or Dragomirov had anything which the guards would not have taken. He could not be sure if their belief in hidden treasure was genuine or simply artifice to spark an altercation with a man now truly alone. A false flag.

Gradenko backed up until his legs struck the edge of Dragomirov's cot, his mind racing. If he resisted, they would kill him. If he submitted, then he would be their slave, another poor wretch who subsisted only on whatever they did not steal from him. Dragomirov would have never allowed that. Never.

Gradenko didn't have any choice. "There is... a watch."

"A watch?" one of the convicts asked.

"A Rolex," Gradenko repeated. "He kept it hidden."

"Get it," another said sharply.

Gradenko turned back around, giving one sorrowful glance at Dragomirov's empty face, and then slid his hands into his friend's coat pocket. It took only a moment to find Dragomirov's most precious possession.

"Here it is," Gradenko said, drawing, turning, and plunging the glass shiv into a criminal's stomach. Gradenko felt the slightest resistance as the blade pierced his shirt and then his belly.

The thug made a sound between a gasp and a grunt and grabbed Gradenko's wrist—too late.

"Son of a whore!" One of them cried, shoving Gradenko back automatically.

He kept a death grip on the shiv as he toppled back, landing hard on the earthen floor of the barracks. The other men in this place scrambled away automatically. Some cried in fright, others shouted warnings or encouragement.

Gradenko fought back to his feet as the two un-stabbed

criminals closed on him, their own shivs shining in the light. Here he would die, but it would be better to die a man than live as a slave.

He raised his knife, steeling himself for pain and blood when suddenly a harsh voice cut the chaos.

"Do not move!"

Like a nuclear icebreaker plowing the Arctic, a guard shoved his way through the prisoners, brandishing a club. Another followed behind him clutching an automatic rifle.

"What is this!?" one of the guards demanded, staring at the scene in horror.

Gradenko's glass blade dripped blood and the man he stabbed slumped against a bed, clutching his gut. "He stabbed me!" the prisoner said, voice edged with panic.

The guard pushed him aside and moved on Gradenko. It was only when he entered the light cast by the bulb that Gradenko saw the guard was worried. Worried for him.

"What is this? Give that to me!" the guard pried the shiv from Gradenko's hands.

"Does he have blood on him?" the other guard asked anxiously.

The first looked him over and shook his head. "No. He is clean."

"He stabbed me!" the criminal repeated.

"Shut up or *I* will stab you," the guard barked over his shoulder, not taking his eyes off Gradenko. "Come. Get up."

Gradenko did so numbly, utterly confused.

"You have a visitor."

So far as Gradenko knew, no one here had ever had a visitor or even been allowed to have a visitor. He was escorted quickly out of the dank barracks, away from the wounded, bewildered prisoner and across the muddy yard. They took him to a concrete guard post which was ringed by a mixture of prison guards and soldiers with rifles. It was only when he was taken inside and he saw his visitor that he understood why everything had happened as it did.

"Citizen Andrei Gradenko, Comrade General!" the guard said, pulling Gradenko into the light and into sight of General

Mishkin.

Mishkin stood at the far end of the spartan room, hands clasped behind his back. Between them was a simple wooden table and two chairs. The shock on Mishkin's face was unmistakable. He spent a long time staring as if trying to reassure himself that this was, in fact, the former general secretary.

Gradenko had never considered it until now, but he was nearly unrecognizable. He sported a thick, graying beard. His hair was shaggy and streaked white. His paunch was long gone and he now had a gaunt look to him with deep set eyes and prominent cheekbones.

Finally, Mishkin collected himself, nodded once, twice, then waved at the guards. "Leave us."

The guards traded nervous looks with each other. Had they made a mistake by neglecting to keep good care of Gradenko? Rather than voice their concerns they slipped out and closed the door behind them.

"Comrade, please," Mishkin said, gesturing to a chair. He put a polite smile on his face, but could not hide the worry in his eyes.

Gradenko eyed the chair warily before sitting.

Mishkin sat opposite him, fidgeting with his peaked cap in his hands. He seemed to have difficulty deciding whether to meet Gradenko's gaze or avoid it.

A minute of painful silence passed. Ordinarily it would be taken up with pleasantries. How are you? How are your children? Are you eating well? None of these questions were appropriate. Finally Mishkin opted for the direct approach.

"The war continues," he said finally, voice soft. "We've lost Ezerum and the enemy is nearing Berlin. The Finns are rebelling and the Bulgarians have mutinied." He took a shallow breath, the floodgates open now. "And... I've just learned this morning that the Iraqi government has separately initiated peace talks with the West. They found they bit off more than they could swallow."

Gradenko would not shed a single tear for the Iraqis, they should never have been relied on in the first place.

"At this rate the enemy will be driving into the Armenian SSR and approaching Tbilisi within a month," Mishkin said. "Maybe less." He sighed.

Gradenko said nothing though Mishkin gave him ample opportunity to do so as he fell into silence again.

Finally Mishkin forged ahead. "General Strelnikov... he refuses to negotiate. He cannot see the reality of the situation. He would choose death over dishonor. I beleive..." Mishkin paused, swallowed, glanced at the door. "I believe that he has lost his mind."

None of this was new information to Gradenko. "And why does this concern me?" he asked finally. He leaned back in the chair, back aching. "Chairman Dragomirov died today. Did you know that? Did they tell you?"

Mishkin's eyes widened and then he looked away. "No," he said.

"He has," Gradenko said again. "He is dead and I will join him soon if there is any mercy in this world. You come to me to tell me the war is a mistake, that it is going badly. This is what I told your General Strelnikov before he threw me in this place to die, to be forgotten." Gradenko's hate flowed free now, no longer restrained by a mixture of fear and self-discipline. No, he had nothing left to fear. "My wife," he said, breathing in sharply as a spike of pain lanced through his heart. "My wife was shot and killed as we tried to escape." He shook his head, feeling tears wanting to come, but not letting them. "I should have left before this ever started. She might still be alive."

"Comrade, I... I understand you have suffered, that you have suffered terribly and unjustly. But..." Mishkin said, steeling his nerves to look Gradenko in the eye again. "The Soviet Union needs you."

Gradenko said nothing. He folded his arms over his chest and leaned back in his chair, nonplussed. A weak appeal to patriotism would not sway him.

"The enemy air attack on Arkhangelsk earlier this month caused a great deal of... consternation among high command,"

Mishkin explained.

"You mean among Strelnikov's people," Gradenko said.

Mishkin ignored him. "There was a concern that this attack was intended to be nuclear. The enemy has not dared to attack our soil directly yet, not since the attack which started this war. If it had been nuclear... I do not need to tell you what would have happened next."

Gradenko imagined everything evaporating in rolling mushroom clouds, a blanket of sterilizing radioactive ash encircling the world. "No."

"Everyone is nervous, Mishkin said, looking suddenly downcast. "Everyone is afraid. Everyone but General Strelnikov..." He seemed to collect his resolve. "The war must end," Mishkin said, leaving no doubt of his conviction. He met Gradenko's cold eyes again. "And you must help me."

Gradenko laughed at him. His voice was hoarse, rough, unused to making such sounds. "Help you? How? What can I do from here?" he said.

"Maybe you could do more from... somewhere else," Mishkin said, shifting slightly in his seat.

This was almost more shocking even than Dragomirov's death, than plunging a knife into a man's body. Mishkin covered Gradenko's surprised silence with more words.

"If you could be taken from this place and sent abroad—to the West—then you could negotiate a peace."

"I have no authority to negotiate peace," Gradenko said, feeling as though he was explaining this to a child. "The West would not cooperate with me, and even if they did, Strelnikov would not respect any treaty I made." He paused for a moment. "If you want peace, don't send me to London or Paris. Send me to Moscow." Gradenko leaned over the table, resting his arms on the rough surface. "Let me find peace there."

Mishkin looked troubled. "Comrade, you are asking too much."

"If you cannot grant me that much then how can I be expected to do anything?" Gradenko said. "If there is to be peace it can only be obtained through diligent work and danger." He thought of his son's attempt to contact the West. "Sacrifice must be made. It will not be easy."

Mishkin mulled it over, warring with himself. What Gradenko was asking went against his every instinct, every fiber of who he was. All his life, Mishkin had been first a loyal soldier and second a servant of the Soviet Union. The question he was forced to ask himself now was: how did he choose to honor these oaths?

He did not answer quickly, allowing a minute of silence to lapse but, when he did finally speak, it was with finality. "I will get you from this place," he said, the words without doubt. "I will find a way to free you and then you will help me."

Second chances. "If you will get me free," Gradenko said, "then I will give my life to the cause of peace." After all, he had nothing else to live for.

14

An Italian armored platoon cruised past the Marines who stood on the shoulder of the road, pressing on into the heavy sounds of battle ahead. Rayburn lifted his helmet and wiped sweat from his brow, only reluctantly settling that weight back on his head.

"Hot," Keyes said from behind him, tugging futilely at the collar of his uniform to try to create some airflow.

"A lot hotter for the commies," Wierzbowski said. The M240 rested across his shoulders and he had his arms draped over it casually. "Hear that?"

Rayburn cocked his head and listened to the thundering boom of guns, artillery. "Sounds like a bad day."

Wierzbowski grinned and laughed. "Hell yeah, dude. It's the summer of hate!"

The last of the Italians passed by and Eichmann waved the Marines back onto the road to follow along in their wake. Decimator and the other AmTracks of the company roared, treads squeaking as they pulled back onto the pavement.

"Let's roll," Washington said.

Rayburn adjusted his slung rifle and followed the others. "I didn't know Europe was so goddam hot."

The company continued on, edging closer to their target: Budapest. It was invisible over the horizon but marked by columns of smoke. They were just starting to hit the suburbs of the city and—with some luck—that was the most they would ever have to see.

After the Italians had passed, another column took their place, this one going the opposite direction.

Wierzbowski whistled low. "Poor bastards."

The road was filled by civilians, mostly on foot, but some crawling along in Ladas and old work trucks. They carried their few worldly possessions on their back, men, women, children, the young and the old marching together.

The artillery fire grew only more intense as they drew nearer. Now they could hear the sharp crack and whistle of shells falling and bursting with more clarity.

Rayburn saw wounded among the civilians, some shambling along with crudely bandaged wounds, others born on stretchers or laid out in the bed of trucks, whimpering and groaning. Their course soon carried them to the banks of the broad Danube river.

Rayburn looked to his right and saw the far bank, enemy held. It was gray, crowded, and industrial. It was also riddled with shell holes, a consequence of intermittent NATO shelling.

Now they also heard the rattle of machine gun fire as the Italians clashed with the enemy around the city. It sounded fierce enough that Rayburn was glad not to be part of it.

"Off the road," Eichmann said, moving his way back down the column and waving at his platoon. "Shift left!"

Without argument or hesitation, Rayburn and the Marines scrambled away, moving off the road and sliding down into a gully which ran along behind endless blocks of Soviet-style apartment buildings.

"ATGMs on the far bank," Washington said, explaining the sudden movement.

Rayburn noted that the civilians kept moving along the road unhindered by fear of enemy fire. He supposed they had nothing worth attacking with anti-tank missiles.

A child's cries carried over the general mutter of the evacuating populace. It was a pitiful sound, one which broke through even Wierzbowski's casual bravado. He grimaced and looked up, seeing a woman stumbling along the road in a panic, clutching a child no older than five, covered in blood and crying.

Before Rayburn could move, he saw Rivers, another corpsman in the unit, jog up the slope to the road, already opening his medical bag.

"Thank God for Doc," Keyes said, relaxing slightly as Rivers reached the woman.

"Everyone take five!" Eichmann said as the AmTracs settled into cover. "Drain bladders and hydrate." Once the message was relayed, he pressed down the column, headed toward the company HQ.

Rayburn stood and watched Doc triage the wounded child. The injury looked superficial, a heavy bleeding head wound. The mother's relief as Rivers wrapped the child's head in gauze was enormous. Pent up tears of joy rolled down her cheeks and she covered her mouth, sobbing in relief as her baby was given a new lease on life

Rayburn wished all triage turned out so happily. He turned away and sat down in the shadow cast by *Decimator* alongside Wierzbowski and Keyes. Wierzbowski lit a cigarette and blew smoke, looking toward the nearby apartment block. "Bet they got some good vodka in there."

"Maybe if you want to go blind," Keyes replied.

"Vodka is Russian," Rayburn said.

"They got it here too," Wierzbowski said before looking uncertain. "Right? Hey, Sergeant, what the hell do they drink in Hungary?"

Washington came to sit in the shade with them. "Probably whatever they can."

Rayburn and the others laughed.

Up on the road, Doc finished looking over the Hungarian kid and sent him and his mother on their way.

After a few minutes Eichmann still hadn't returned so Rayburn lay in the grass, staring up at the cloudless blue sky. He listened to the banshee wail of artillery and the deadly thunder around him. He had just drifted into sleep when Keyes nudged him awake.

The whole company gathered up around their captain who half-climbed the grassy slope to the road to address them all. It was an impressive sight, a Marine company in full combat gear gathered on the eve of battle. It made Rayburn's chest tense with anticipation.

"Italians are cutting east here," the captain said. "First Battalion is going to be doing river crossings to establish a bridgehead. We're going north. Into the city."

Rayburn saw the worry in the captain's eyes and felt it echoed in his own heart.

"Looks like OpFor has dug themselves in and we need to screen the crossings, make sure they don't get crushed." He paused as the Marines absorbed this information. It wasn't good news, but that was just their lot in life, wasn't it? Rayburn knew that urban operations were a special tier of hell, one he'd hoped he wouldn't have to experience. "We'll be moving out in one hour. Once we go in, make sure you're ready to rock. This is the real shit." He said no more and made his way back down the hill.

"Ain't this already the real shit?" Keyes asked, bewildered.

"City fighting's totally different," Rayburn said. "Three dimensional war. Bad guys in front, behind, above and below."

"Shit," Keyes muttered.

"We call that a 'target rich environment'," Wierzbowski replied. "Line em up and I'll knock em down."

As the Marines formed up and moved out again, Rayburn looked up at the roadway, watching the Hungarians fleeing, leaving behind their homes. Those same homes were about to become a brutal killing ground. It was strange to think about, so he tried not to. Instead he shouldered his rifle and joined the company.

15

Bulgaria had folded like a house of cards. It was mind boggling how quickly almost fifty years of communist domination had come crashing down. Jean knew that the collapse of the People's Republic left behind a tremendous vacuum waiting to be filled, one which would likely be filled with chaos and hardship. Still, she reasoned, chaotic freedom had to be better than orderly slavery.

"They're not going to go for it," Pete said, walking briskly beside her as she made her way downhill, toward the bank of the Danube River. He sounded worried. That was typical Pete. He was always the pragmatic one but, God love him, he had guts.

"They will," Jean said, confident in the outcome because she refused to accept any other possibility.

They moved steadily downhill in the fading dusk, passing beneath the boughs of shade trees and weaving through brush growing on the slopes of the hill which overlooked the river. Beyond them, on the reverse slope, a Grecko-Bulgarian army had gathered with amphibious vehicles, pontoon bridges, and assault rafts, all the tools necessary to force a river crossing. Jean wasn't a soldier, but she'd seen enough of war to know what a terrible human cost would be paid by such an operation, hasty as it was.

NATO seemed to think that speed itself was a virtue, refusing to countenance a halt or a consolidation here. They drove on, and on, and on, ever north, ever into the heart of the enemy. She supposed it made some sense. If they stopped or slowed, the enemy might recover, stop flailing long enough to land a blow of their own. She was glad she didn't have to make these kinds of calls.

Trailing close behind her and Pete were Cristos and Boris, her Greek and Bulgarian interpreters respectively. Boris had been a lucky find, a member of the old government's limited trade bureau. They were her trump cards and the other reason she was sure she could worm her way into the impromptu peace delegation.

"Maybe they won't," Pete pressed.

"Oh come on, Pete," she gave him an exasperated look. "When have you known me to be wrong about something like this?"

Pete was wise enough not to answer directly. Instead he said, "maybe you shouldn't try."

This drew her short. The interpreters came to stop awkwardly beside her but she sent them on with a gesture, continuing down to the river. Jean stared at her cameraman, hands on hips. "Why not?"

"Jesus, Jean," Pete said, sighing. "I mean... what does it matter? Who cares if you're on the fucking boat to go over and talk to the Romanians? We don't even have an exclusive. This is all just archival stuff."

"It matters to me," she replied sharply. "And don't—"

Pete cut her off. "Jean, this war is ending." The harshness of his tone, the anger in his voice drew her short. "Don't you see that? It's all coming down. This war is ending and I want to live to see it happen." Anger smoldered in his eyes for a moment before softening to concern. "I want *you* to see it. Why are you doing this?"

The sudden rush of emotion she felt caught her off guard. Anger and despair clashed in her heart. Through sheer force of will, she managed to keep these feelings bottled up, swallowing them down. "I have to do it," she said finally, "so that it means something. So that..." she thought of Dario, their Croatian interpreter before he'd been killed. "So that what we did matters. If I get killed, then I die, Pete, but if I'm there when this happens then I'm *there* forever. You see?" She tried to put a confident smile on her face. "Me. Jean Carson. When they write the history books they'll have to put my name on that delegation, they'll have to read my stories, have to see your videos. People will know all this happened because *we'll* show them."

Pete said nothing, looking at her with unwavering concern. Finally he shook his head, snorting softly, a stifled laugh. "You're really messed up, you know that?"

She tried to smile back. "Yeah. But that's why I have you around, right?" She touched his arm, a fleeing gesture of affection, the most she would allow herself. "Now, I want to get on that boat."

With no more argument, Pete went with her down to the river's edge where two small knots of people stood awkwardly arguing through middlemen. Greek and Bulgarian continued on ancient fights with words, hammering out the details of this delegation one painful detail at a time. Cristos and Boris injected themselves into the discussions automatically. How could they not? Lacking a common tongue, they each interpreted to Jean who likewise naturally inserted herself into the middle of the conflict.

"Just hear what they have to say," Jean said to Cristos, relaying the Bulgarian demands. "No shelling, no threats, just talk to them."

A pair of Greek colonels spoke angrily with Cristos. "If we are fired on, we will fire back."

Jean repeated it to Boris who repeated it to his own leaders, and so the argument went until finally, painfully they sorted out an agreement. The Bulgarians—with Jean's support—got their way. They would go to the Romanians as friends first.

"Let me come," Jean said as the soldiers readied an inflatable raft with an outboard motor.

The Greek colonel selected to lead the delegation looked at Cristos, bewildered as he translated for Jean.

"He says you can come if you keep quiet," Cristos said apologetically. "And your cameraman must stay here."

Jean looked at Pete whose expression made it clear he was vetoing that idea. She looked north and the hilly green land on the Romanian bank of the Danube. "Alright. Fine."

"Jean!" Pete protested.

"Relax, that thing has zoom, right?" she teased. It felt less funny when she was made to put on a ballistic vest and helmet. After boarding the bobbing, unsteady raft she clicked on the Dictaphone in her pocket, feeling the tape start turning as it recorded.

At a word from the colonel the raft set off, engine buzzing noisily.

The rolling waters of the Danube sparkled orange in the late afternoon, the heat and humidity of earlier in the day was just beginning to tail off. Jean sat toward the back of the raft, just beside the engine. She was grateful for the occasional cooling spray of water from the river's surface.

After going about halfway across, the driver killed the engine at a word and the colonel stood up and handed a megaphone to his own interpreter, a Bulgarian army soldier. Nervously, the young man stood, shaking slightly on the pitching raft and called out in Romanian, his voice booming to the far bank.

The answer was a burst of gunfire.

Jean ducked for all the good it would do, everyone if the raft went low, nearly toppling their interpreter into the water. He shouted frantically into the megaphone, a plea. There was no more gunfire. After a minute a human voice shouted back to them.

The Bulgarian translated to Greek and Cristos translated to English. "They say we may come ashore."

Jean nodded, heart still hammering in her chest. Her mouth tasted like battery acid from fear.

The engine throttled up and then closed to the far bank where a trio of Romanian soldiers in khaki uniforms and steelpot helmets emerged, weapons trained on them. One of their number stepped forward and spoke to their interpreter.

"They say they do not trust the Bulgarians," Cristos whispered to her. "They will only talk with the Greeks."

This was beginning to feel like the river crossing puzzle to

Jean, trying to make all these ethnicities and nationalities play nice.

"Can I say something?" Jean said, standing up and drawing everyone's attention.

The Greek colonel rolled his eyes in exasperation and sat back in the raft.

"English?" Jean asked. The Romanians looked at each other blankly. "Shit... English?" She asked the Bulgarian soldier serving as their Romanian interpreter.

He shook his head.

Jean sighed. "Cristos, tell him. He can tell them, okay?" This message telephoned its way to the Romanians who acquiesced with a shrug. "We're not here to conquer you," she said finally. "We're here to help you be free, like the Bulgarians." She gestured demonstratively, waiting for the translation chain to catch up. "We want to help you. Friends."

"They say that once we come we won't leave," Cristos said. The Romanian's faces made it clear enough that they didn't trust either Greek or Bulgarian not to become the new boss, same as the old, or maybe act on some ancient territorial claim.

"Oh for God's sake," Jean blurted. "Look, do you like the Russians?"

She didn't need a translator to understand their emphatic answers. "Right. Neither do we. So, what can we do to help you get rid of them? Can we help you fight them?"

The question took longer to answer than she would have thought. She wasn't sure what the hold up was until she became aware of the distant popping of gunfire. It came from further north, deeper into Romania.

"I think," Cristos said finally. "That they've already started."

16

It was a strange homecoming. As Lieutenant Adamcik watched the German countryside become Czechoslovakian countryside he could not help but notice the wreckage of two separate border crossings, the first from East to West, the second—the tide coming back in—from West to East. Both were primarily marked by destroyed Eastern bloc vehicles. They dotted the roadside like mile markers. Those from the initial invasion were blackened and dead, those from the more recent return smoldered and sometimes still burned. Not all belonged to the Warsaw Pact. Among the ruins he saw German Marders and Leopards.

The T-72s and BMPs of the Czechoslovak Legion passed through the triple coil of razor wire which marked the Iron Curtain, fanning out to pass along the same corridors they had come over almost one year ago. Adamcik recalled vividly the sleepless terror he'd felt in their midnight border crossing. The minefields of the Iron Curtain had been opened by engineers, the way marked by infrared lamps.

Adamcik shook his head to clear it from that strange sense of deja vu. No, this time was different. They were not going as the thrall army of conquerors. They were coming as free men, as liberators.

Once the tanks of his platoon cleared the open corridors of the minefield, Adamcik toggled on his radio.

"Tiger One Six, combat dispersal."

The NATO organizational structure, while still novel to him, had been drilled into his head in their brief refresher training. Adamcik was intensely aware of the existence of a fourth tank in his platoon as he directed his vehicles to maneuver and advance. It gave him more freedom of maneuver than they'd had with three. This way he could split into pairs where before splitting up had always meant one tank going alone.

"Copy, Tiger One Six?"

"Acknowledged," Adamcik said. He listened to the voices buzzing in his headset and watched the ground slope up into the hills of the Sudeten. His heart beat hard and steady, eyes sweeping the ground ahead of them. He sometimes caught glimpses of the lead recon element of the battalion. It consisted of Soviet-made armored cars mixed with American Humvees. These scouts picked their way ahead, crawling open ground or weaving through pockets of woods.

The blue, white, and red banner of Czechoslovakia fluttered from the radio aerial beside him. He still felt it made them an unnecessary target but supposed at least this way no one would mistake them for a Soviet tank.

"Infantry ahead," Spider, the recon element reported. "Village at two kilometers."

"Tiger Six copies," Captain Vesely responded over the company command frequency. "Confirm infantry. Are you certain?"

A long pause. "No. Negative. Not certain."

"Those may be our people," Vesely said patiently. "I will not kill anyone who does not need to die. Close range and confirm. I will have Bear Two provide infantry support."

"Acknowledged, Tiger. Spider out."

Adamcik watched as the BMPs of Bear's infantry complement accelerated past him. Their treads threw rooster tails of soft earth behind them as they raced to join Spider ahead.

Soon they had an answer.

"Tiger Six, this is Spider Six," the recon unit commander came back a moment later, sounding subdued. "Negative infantry. I repeat, negative hostiles. These are civilians."

Adamcik felt a surge of relief mixed with horror. What sort of massacre would they have perpetrated on their own people if they'd followed the old methods of war? How many had they killed under their old leadership? Adamcik preferred not to dwell on it.

"Affirmative Spider. Good job. Tiger One, move up to support Bear. Sweep the village."

"Tiger One copies," Adamcik said. A moment later his driver shifted course slightly, the tank rocking across uneven ground as it moved back onto the road and closed in on the village. Once they were within a kilometer, he saw the village's inhabitants clustered outside their homes on the edge of the town. They watched in blank confusion as this armored force bore down on them. He wasn't sure if fleeing didn't occur to them or if they were simply unwilling to leave their homes.

"Slow," Adamcik told his driver, angling the tank into the village center. They passed slowly by rows of people who soon clustered around his tank, forcing him to slow further until he finally had to come to a complete stop.

"Clear a path!" Adamcik called out from his turret hatch, waving his arm. "Move aside."

An older man looked from the flag to Adamcik and back. "You're our boys?" he asked.

"Yes," Adamcik said, feeling suddenly foolish for being so blase about this homecoming. "We've come home to free you," he said.

The crowd rippled with voices, murmurs and exclamations. Some people cheered, hugging together, others wept openly, unable to process what was happening.

"Free us?" the man repeated. "God... my God... it is a miracle, a miracle! Bless you. Bless you, son."

Adamcik's heart softened at that moment. He couldn't help but smile as the people of the village celebrated, fanning out to greet each vehicle of the Czechoslovak Legion, heedless of their apparent haste.

"We have to get through," Adamcik said. "We are here to fight the Russians."

His driver opened open his hatch as a woman hurried over to

the tank, bearing a basket of warm bread.

"Bless you! God bless you all!" She said, tears streaming down her face.

"The Russians have gone," the man beside the tank said, shaking his head and wiping his eyes.

The BMPs of Bear Platoon stopped short of the village, dropping their ramps and disgorging infantry who soon gave up trying to clear aside the villagers and instead welcomed hugs, drinks, kisses, and posed for photographs.

"Gone? Gone where?" Adamcik pressed.

"East," the man pointed. "In a hurry. They are withdrawing to Prague."

"Prague, you are sure?" Adamcik asked.

The man shook his head. "No. But that is what I heard."

Rumor and hearsay was better intelligence than no intelligence at all.

"Thank you," Adamcik said. "Now if you will please clear off, we must proceed. The Russians will not wait for us."

At last their countrymen managed to rein in their exuberance and clear from the road, moving back onto yards and sidewalks. A path opened ahead of them, pointing deeper into Bohemia.

The Czechoslovak Legion put themselves back in gear and proceeded. As *Milacku* got underway, Adamcik flipped on his company frequency. "Tiger Six, this is One Six. I've heard a rumor that the Russians are retreating to Prague. Over."

"Only a rumor?" Vesely asked.

"That's all. But I see no sign of the enemy here." Adamcik gave one final glance around the village, grateful he didn't have to blast his way through it. "They've certainly gone."

"Affirmative. Spider is moving ahead. Follow at a distance and be wary of an ambush."

"Captain, we might catch them if we hurry," Adamcik said. "If the Germans move ahead we might be able to pin them before they reach Prague."

"The last time the Germans entered our country in tanks they did not leave willingly," Vesely said.

Adamcik knew that. It had been widely repeated by the battalion's commissar when he had served the Communist Party.

"I understand, but if we move rapidly we still may catch them," Adamcik pressed, more interested in being pragmatic than being diplomatic. Germans, or Czech, or Slovakians made no difference to him as long as *someone* killed the enemy.

"People have not forgotten. It is best that we handle this ourselves," Vesely said, unwavering. "Besides, the Russians are more interested in running than fighting. We will let them run. Every kilometer they run is one less kilometer to fight over. In any case, we must be cautious. If we allow ourselves to be destroyed in haste, then who will free our people?"

Adamcik saw the logic in it. They had a purpose here, one greater than simply obeying orders. If Czechoslovakia was to be a nation again, then that nation would need an army and that army would need precedent, tradition, heroes. It wasn't just today they were fighting for, but tomorrow as well.

Milacku rumbled along, deadly muzzle trained ahead, the wind in Adamcik's face. He looked back over his shoulder and saw Ambroz's platoon following close behind, the rest of the company trailing like an iron snake slithering across the countryside. It was a fearsome sight, one he imagined would only grow more fearsome as they continued deeper into their homeland, gathering up deserters and growing in number. Each day they would grow stronger and their enemy would grow weaker until one day—maybe tomorrow—the Russians would fail.

"Understood. One Six out."

17

The Soviets were keen to drive the NATO spearhead crashing against them into Berlin. That was reason enough, Vance thought, to resist that attempt with everything they had. So Cutthroat Company broke from the highway, spreading into a line of battle, and advanced over the broad plains of East Germany toward the northern end of Dresden. The horizon was dotted with columns of black smoke and gray-white clouds of recent munition bursts.

Vance and his company neared the source of one of those towers of smoke, a burning Soviet tank. He couldn't make the exact model through the thick, noxious smoke pouring off of it, but it was unmistakably the enemy. It was likely picked off by one of the innumerable airstrikes which came in around the clock. He watched paint blacken and peel, consumed by heat as they rolled past. Craning his neck and peering into the morning sun Vance saw no sign of NATO's roving tank killer teams, but he knew they were there. A-10 Warthogs and F-111 Aardvarks prowled the skies above, searching for targets on the ground.

As he looked, Vance saw the white streak of a SAM launch far to the east. The missile climbed skyward, pursuing an unseen fighter. Within minutes a Wild Weasel team was on station and punished the enemy SAM battery for its impudence. A pair of air-to-surface missiles flashed in and exploded. A minute later another column of smoke joined the others ringing the horizon.

Crocodile Tears reared up, throwing Vance back as it tore into a hedgerow which bisected a field. The brush gave way and the tank fell flat again, crushing an opening in the tangle of vegetation. Now he had a clear line of sight across a huge grain field, watching his tanks move in a staggered line.

"Air Force isn't leaving much for us to do here," TJ said, his voice buzzing on Vance's radio.

Vance adjusted his microphone. "I'm not going to complain about that. I'd just as soon let them kill them all."

"Slippery red bastards are running faster than we can chase them," TJ muttered.

"Good problem to have," Vance returned.

A missile launched from ahead, wobbling on an unsteady course like a bumble bee as it closed on one of Vance's tanks. An enemy anti-tank missile.

"Shit!" Vance ducked down into his turret and pressed his face to the periscope just in time to see one of his Abrams struck on the flank. There was a muffled bang and the tank jolted to a halt, smoke leaking from its wound.

"Contact right, ATGM team," Vance said, speaking with forced calm. All the same his voice wavered with nerves. Animal instinct wanted to fight, kill, or run, anything but sit and watch and relay orders.

A second missile launched before Second Platoon's tanks came to a halt, turrets pivoting to deal with the threat.

The Americans fired before the missile found its mark. Shells burst in the treeline and the missile wobbled away as the gunner lost the target—or his life.

A heartbeat later the tanks fired smoke grenades and reversed. Without any real cover, all they had to rely on was movement and concealment, and their own armor.

"Cuttrhoat Six to Sable Six, enemy ATGM team ahead, I think they might be dismounts. We're suppressing them but I want infantry to clear the trees ahead, copy?"

"Solid copy, Six!" Kelly replied. "Sable moving."

The M113s leaped past the Abrams, zigzagging across the field as Vance's tanks kept throwing shells at the unseen enemy. Working in tandem, the APCs were able to cross the distance at speed and unmolested.

"Cutthroat One, keep pressure up, cross in the open to the left and cut off any retreat. If they try to bug out, nail the bastards," Vance said, not blinking as he watched Sable's infantry close on target.

"Copy! One Six Out!"

First Platoon hooked to the north, edging around the trees where the enemy were. On a hunch, Vance called a fire mission on another thick stand of trees further ahead which had clear lines of sight over First Platoon's new movement. If he were going to lay an ambush, he'd put something there.

A minute later friendly shellfire ripped into the woods, felling trees by the score. Through his periscope, Vance saw each concussive blast blow the leaves from the treetops, sending them fluttering down in a shower of green. Trunks shuddered like stalks of grass in a breeze.

Kelly's men reached killing range of the ATGM position and deployed, infantry sprinting toward the target. Compared to the solid, armored boxes they traveled in and the deadly power of the main battle tanks backing them, the dismounted infantry seemed so vulnerable, so naked. Flesh and blood versus steel.

Vance heard the sound of rifle fire only as distant pops. It wasn't just his men firing.

Second Platoon poured more shells into the woods, blasting them blindly while Kelly's guys worked closer, laying suppressive fire with their own machine guns. When Kelly's men finally reached the edge of the ruined woods and pushed in, Vance's tanks held fire.

"We're clear, Cutthroat," Kelly said a moment later. "Wasted em. Lotta dead Russians."

"Nice work, Sable. We'll leapfrog past you. Get your guys mounted up again."

Kinney put *Crocodile Tears* back into motion and they cruised up, passing the Abrams which had taken an ATGM hit. Vance popped his hatch and called out to the crew he saw dismounted. "You guys all good?"

He got a thumbs up from the tank's commander. The vehicle looked like a loss, at least until the recovery teams could get to it.

Vance didn't really care about that. He was more worried about the men inside. It was a small miracle they were all unharmed.

Vance returned the thumbs up and they continued on, calling in the tank loss for a salvage vehicle. With some luck it would be repaired and back on the lines within a week or two. Time would tell.

Beyond the open fields, Cutthroat Company reached the highway which fed into Dresden, severing it. He saw the road was lined with half-finished fighting positions, shallow trenches and sandbag emplacements. All of it was abandoned alongside some civilian construction equipment.

A BTR sat silent in the middle of the road.

"Gunner, BTR on the highway," Vance said. "Make sure it's empty."

"Sabot!" Waxman said, pivoting the tank's turret to acquire this target. After Patterson loaded the gun Waxman fired. The round punched easily through the nose of the APC and tore out the back. Smoke began to curl up from its hatches. Definitely dead now.

Feeling relief, Vance contacted battalion HQ. "Cutthroat Six to Hammermill, we're over Highway Four past Dresden. Only token resistance. Everyone else bugged out."

"Copy Cutthroat, nice work. Reform your company and wait for Assassin to join you. We're going north. Brigade is going to try to cut Berlin off from the Oder River. Might be a chance to bag a whole lot of bad guys."

That sounded good to Vance. "Cutthroat Six copies. Make sure Assassin brings up some fuel trucks, we're close to E."

"Will do. Hammermill out."

18

From the roof of the highrise which served as Strelnikov's headquarters in Potsdam, he watched as a company of East German infantry dug fighting positions to the west. Shovels and picks rose and fell as they worked to shouted commands from their officers. Earth flew in the fading daylight and a pair of bulldozers hastily shaped it into a parapet for a trench. They worked diligently under close supervision of Soviet engineers. Strelnikov could not help but wonder how many of those Germans would still be holding those positions by the time the enemy arrived.

Turning away, he circled the roof, now looking north toward a ribbon of highway running to the east.

It was full of vehicle traffic, an army in retreat, fleeing for the safety of the Oder River one hundred kilometers to the east. They moved under the safety of a carefully constructed SAM umbrella. Everything from powerful BUK missile batteries to shoulder-launched Strela's—like those carried by sentries posted around the roof—watched the skies. He had no doubts that NATO could penetrate such a defensive screen if they really wanted to, but they could only do so at great loss. All that he really had to fear jeopardizing this orderly evacuation was the enemy's stealth bombers. There was nothing which could really be done about them despite desperate claims of frequency switching and boosted radar gain. Fortunately, the enemy only operated their limited stealth bomber fleet in the dead of night for maximum effect. For now, his men were safe.

When Strelnikov finally turned away from this sad sight, he saw a junior officer hovering anxiously by the open stairwell door, afraid to approach.

"Well?" Strelnikov demanded.

"We have confirmed that Rostock has been lost," the lieutenant said, not mincing words. "An Anglo-Dutch force is pressing for the coast as we speak."

With the enemy breaking through first at Dresden and now at Rostock, his reinforced position at Berlin between them was in grave danger of being pinched off. All his efforts, all his men's lives spent to funnel the enemy had come to nothing. He'd made the right call by withdrawing from this place, but that didn't mean he liked it.

Strelnikov had given serious thought to holding here, or leaving behind a force with more resolve than the East Germans. With some advanced preparation and resolute determination they could turn Berlin into a new Stalingrad, defend it to the very last as the Nazis had done a half century ago. It was a fading dream. For all the Soviet propaganda otherwise, NATO were not the Nazis, they were not driven by motorized hatred and lust for power. They would not easily be suckered into a pointless urban brawl. Anything he left here would likely be bypassed and starved out. A waste of men, material, effort, and time.

Strelnikov nodded at the messenger who turned to leave. "What of Prague?" he asked, halting the young man.

"I-I have heard nothing."

Lukin was too proud to come mewling back to Strelnikov at every setback. He would command independently to the very end. That meant Strelnikov would have to check in with him.

"Raise Comrade General Lukin," he said. "Make it known that I wish to speak with him urgently."

The lieutenant saluted and bustled off.

Strelnikov took one more look around at the suburbs of Potsdam and the abortive attempts being made to defend it. All a waste.

When he could bear no more he left the rooftop behind and then left the building entirely, pacing through the rapidly emptying motorpool of his headquarters. He walked past one of the innumerable anti-aircraft guns tasked with its defense when he saw his courier returning. "Have you reached him?" Strelnikov asked.

The lieutenant nodded affirmation so Strelnikov followed him back to the mobile HQ, finding a waiting radio on a table between two parked BTRs. Strelnikov picked up the handset. "Lukin?"

"Yes, Comrade General," Lukin's tone was grave.

"We have lost Dresden," Strelnikov said.

"I had heard," Lukin replied. "This puts the enemy in my rear."

"Soon," Strelnikov agreed. "If nothing can be done. Can you gather your front and strike north? if you can pinch that salient off then we might be able to force them to pull back."

There was a long pause. "If I am to do that I will have no one to hold the lines. The enemy presses us from west and south."

"Can you use the Czechoslovakians?" Strelnikov asked.

Another painful pause. "They have ceased to be reliable."

No surprise. All of the Soviet Union's Warsaw Pact allies were proving to be fickle, if not outright treacherous.

"With Bratislava in enemy hands I fear that Czechoslovakia cannot be held," Lukin continued. "I will obey my orders to the last, Comrade General, but if I may, we would be able to fight longer if we withdraw northeast into the Sudeten highlands on the Polish border. From there we can screen the southern flank of the Oder river and draw a new line."

Leave them to fight and die or surrender more territory. It was a painful choice, suboptimal either way, but what other purpose was there in a buffer zone if it could not be willingly traded to the enemy for time?

"Very well," Strelnikov said, "Withdraw what you can and leave the Czechoslovakians and Poles to slow the enemy. Do not delay any longer." He worried that it might already be too late. In modern war Strelnikov had learned that breakthroughs often developed quicker than commanders could manage them. By the time he was even aware of a breakthrough, NATO might have driven in dozens of miles. At the height of Soviet power, he would have had plenty of mobile, modern forces at his disposal to counter these penetrations and drive them back. Now he could barely scratch together then men needed just to hold the line.

"And Lukin," Strelnikov said. He paused. The order he wanted to give stuck in his throat. It was unmilitary, unprofessional, he told himself. It was not a logical command but an emotional one. A year ago he would have vehemently protested the receipt of such an order. Much had changed in a year. If he could not defeat the enemy, then he would have to settle for hurting them.

"When you withdraw from Prague," Strelnikov said, "destroy it."

He expected even the stalwart Lukin to protest. Instead, Lukin chose to escalate. "Am I free to deploy chemical weapons?" he asked. "We have a persistent mixture on hand which would render the city uninhabitable for a week at least."

Strelnikov surprised himself by not answering right away. He imagined the streets of that ancient city filled with deadly, invisible gas, smothering all who would dare to enter it. Turning it into a necropolis and choking off a vital logistical hub. Only the thought of imagining the same done to his own cities in return stayed his hand. "No. Not just yet. It would do nothing to change the balance and would likely only harm us in the long run."

"Understood," Lukin said without emotion.

"We are abandoning Berlin," Strelnikov said. "Conserve what strength you have. We will trade space for time and then when the enemy is weak and we are stronger, we will attack." He couldn't doubt it. Strelnikov had to believe what he said was true. If he felt there was no hope, then who in his army would?

19

Gradenko was all too aware of the eyes of the gulag's criminals on him as he worked. Even in the sweltering humidity of the plant, he always felt a cold tickle in his belly. He considered it a phantom pain from the shiv he'd jammed in that gangster. Unlike Dragomirov, that gang member had been given at least basic first aid by the on-site infirmary. Now his men watched Gradenko, eyes gleaming hungrily, waiting for a chance, waiting for revenge.

When it came there would be no warning. Much like the war the Soviets had unleashed on Europe, it would come suddenly and without remorse. Gradenko might have considered it poetic justice in a sense if he wasn't so near to his goal of escaping this place.

Gradenko hefted a sack of wood pulp off the train and shouldered it awkwardly along, moving down the work line toward the rendering vat. Sweat beaded down his forehead and his breath came hard and fast. The work here wasn't making him stronger, only weaker. Each step was a struggle, the weight of the pulp in the sack felt like Atlas's burden on his shoulders.

He passed a gang member in line. The young man's eyes bored into him like searchlights.

Gradenko glanced anxiously at his hands, seeing they were empty. It only took a moment...

At the end of the line he dumped the sack into the vat and staggered back from the heat rolling off the boilers. When he turned around he saw two guards facing him, both had their clubs in hand. They looked unhappy, nervous.

"Citizen Gradenko, come." One gestured with his club. The

other took a half step back, watching closely as if he expected Gradenko to run.

There was no chance. Gradenko could hardly walk. Without option he bowed his head and followed, sandwiched between the two men as they escorted him from the plant and into the cool, dry air outside.

He had hoped they were taking him to the administration building or the gate, but instead they veered him to the south, toward a line of chemical sheds. He'd seen prisoners taken there from time to time. None ever returned.

He glanced left and right. There was nothing but open muddy ground in all directions terminating in a towering fence crowned with razorwire. He would maybe get a dozen paces before a guard in a tower would cut him down. So he walked numbly on, shambling toward his death.

At the sheds, the first guard fumbled with a key and padlock before getting it open. The interior was dark.

"Inside," the guard barked.

Gradenko stepped inside and closed his eyes. He wondered if he would hear or feel the gunshot before it killed him.

Nothing happened.

He heard the door close behind him.

"Get inside."

Gradenko opened his eyes in confusion. He was already inside. Then he saw a black, plastic tarp on the ground. It was the length of a man, split by a zipper. A body bag.

"Inside," the guard repeated again, clearly agitated.

Gradenko glanced at him. He had a hundred questions but resisted voicing any of them. Before he had thought they were going to shoot or club him, now he was more worried about being incinerated or buried alive. Of those options he preferred the quicker death but... he had to have faith.

Clumsily, Gradenko got on all fours and then wormed his way into the bag, laying down on the cold concrete floor.

One of the guards unceremoniously zipped the bag tight, shutting out what little light made it into this place.

"Not a sound," the other guard said, kicking his legs. A test.

Gradenko winced but remained silent. He listened as both guards left the shed. Then he heard the door close and the padlock latch in place.

Panic set in. This body bag was nearly airtight. He felt each breath accumulate in it, hot and deadly. In his fear he only breathed quicker, hastening the end. His head felt light, dizzy.

Gradenko squeezed his eyes shut and willed himself to be calm, forcing his breath to come slowly. He felt his heart hammering in his chest, pulse thudding in his neck.

In the suffocating darkness there was no time, everything seemed to go on forever. He was left here to die, the cruelest death he could contemplate. Strelnikov's final insult to him.

Screaming or struggling would be useless. No one would come. No one *could* come. He kept breathing slow and steady.

Then he heard a key rasp into the padlock.

Gradenko lay very still as the door came open.

"Jesus, they killed him," the voice was American.

Someone muttered in a language he didn't know. He didn't recognize the speaker until they said, "come. We move him." The Dane.

The POWs hoisted Gradenko awkwardly, one carrying the body bag by the head, the other by the feet.

"Let's go," the American said from his head. His knees thumped against Gradenko's head with each awkward step until they got out of the chemical shed and started across the yard.

"I wonder why," the American said.

"It is impossible to say. At least he is out."

"I kind of liked the old bastard," the American said.

"A Russian is a Russian," the Dane replied coldly.

Gradenko could hardly blame him. He tried to stay as limp as he could until finally they reached their destination. He heard a series of doors open and close, voices in Russian directed the POWs with harsh, simple commands.

Finally they laid him on a heavy metal table. Or he thought it was a table until it slid suddenly with a rattle of metal. Then a heavy hatch closed behind him and all was silence.

A morgue.

His only chance to prove he was alive and he squandered it on the dim belief that the guards were working for Mishkin.

With the excitement of the trip over, all he could focus on now was the beat of his heart and his own breath. His heart began to race madly, lungs pumping hot, humid air.

He tried to take a deep breath but was all too aware of sucking in his own exhalations. Even if he got out of this bag he was locked into a steel coffin. If he did not suffocate he would freeze. Panic set in all over again.

Gradenko fumbled against the inside of the zipper with his fingertips, trying to find the little slide to release himself. Eventually he located it just above the tip of his nose. He pulled, tugged, yanked, but it would not budge. The tab on the outside had to be pulled in order to move it. It was locked in place.

"No," Gradenko whispered, pulling harder. He was going to suffocate. He was going to die in here. The heavy plastic bag was smothering him. He needed to get out! He needed—

The door unlatched and he froze. The tray slid back out. Finally, mercifully, the zipper came down.

A young army lieutenant peered down at him, seeming almost surprised to see him. His surprise vanished quickly. "Come. Get out," he said, stepping back.

Gradenko managed to wriggle free. "What—"

The lieutenant shushed him, finger to his lips. He glanced nervously at the morgue door. The two of them were alone here.

The lieutenant pulled open another morgue drawer, this one containing a body bag. The paper label affixed to the drawer said **DRAGOMIROV, N.**

"Help me," the lieutenant whispered, picking up the body.

Gradenko only hesitated for a moment. Together they lifted Dragomirov's body and shifted it onto the tray where Gradenko had laid. Then the lieutenant moved Gradenko's empty body bag onto Dragomirov's empty tray. "Get in." A body switch.

Gradenko started to, but hesitated. He couldn't make himself get back in the bag, back in the drawer.

"Quickly!" the lieutenant hissed, glancing at the door again. "Quickly or it is too late."

Buried alive for freedom. Gradenko as he had once been could have never done it. He thought of his dead wife's face. He thought of Dragomirov's plea.

If you ever escape this place, make sure that bastard Strelnikov answers for this.

Gradenko climbed back into the body bag and watched the lieutenant zip it up. This time he left a small hole above his face, enough to breathe through.

"Now be silent," he said, gently pushing the drawer back in and locking Gradenko inside.

"He is dead," the lieutenant said loudly. Beyond that Gradenko heard nothing distinct. He laid in dark and quiet for an indeterminable amount of time. Maybe an hour, maybe two or three. It felt like a day.

Finally the locker door was thrown open and his body bag dragged out with him in it. He was carried a short distance and tossed onto a concrete floor, landing painfully. He ground his teeth to avoid crying out and forced himself to lay at the strange angle he'd landed at. Then footsteps left.

From the ashy smell that filtered in through the tiny unzipped hole he imagined he was in a crematorium.

The door opened and booted feet approached. Something soft landed beside him.

"You are safe now."

Gradenko relaxed at the sound of Mishkin's voice. The bag was unzipped and he practically sprang out.

General Mishkin stood nearby wearing the uniform of a captain. He pointed to a pile of civilian work clothes beside Gradenko. "Change."

Gradenko thought about telling Mishkin the hell he'd just gone through, but what would be the point? It was over. He changed quickly, ignoring the pain in his joints and the ache in his back. It was trivial compared to all he'd endured so far.

The two of them left the building through the main entrance, no one gave them any second glances. Still Gradenko did not dare look up until they boarded an army truck and left the gulag, driving east.

"Are you alright, comrade?" Mishkin asked.

Gradenko could hardly believe that he was out. Even the sight of the ramshackle city of Arkhangelsk rolling serenely by did not convince him. He thought of his wife again.

"I am free," he answered finally, clearing his throat.

Mishkin nodded. This seemed to be the most he could expect from him.

"Where are we going?"

"The train station," Mishkin replied.

"To Moscow?"

Mishkin shook his head. "No. The Zagreb Guard still hold that place. They are loyal to Strelnikov, not to me. Most have been sent on to Warsaw, but not all. If you return they will arrest you straight away."

Gradenko's spirits fell. How could he expect to change anything without access to the governmental apparatus? "Where then?"

"We must find loyal men," Mishkin said. "Men who will help us."

"Who? Where?"

"Leningrad, to see Dmitriyev," Mishkin said. "General Dmitriyev."

Gradenko was surprised to recognize the name. He knew his father. He was part of the Communist Party, the part which Strelnikov had purged.

"He will help us?" Gradenko asked.

Mishkin frowned slightly and looked away. "I hope so."

20

As the men and machines of the Czechoslovak Legion closed on the southern outskirts of Prague, Adamcik could see that there would be no celebratory entry into the city.

Prague was burning.

He watched, dumbstruck by the scale of the destruction, as Soviet artillery fire plunged into the heart of the city with banshee wails. Muffled thumps and booms echoed back. Pillars of smoke and dust climbed into the sky as the shelling went on and on.

Prague was too large a city to be destroyed by such a comparatively paltry barrage, but the damage would be horrific on the ground. Adamcik had seen firsthand what shrapnel and high explosive shells did to buildings and vehicles—what they did to human bodies...

Milacku's treads rattled over the highway bridge spanning the Vltava River. It was part of a cloverleaf-style exchange. The east-west route was empty aside from the vehicles of the Legion. The north-south route was a jam of traffic, cars, trucks, vans, and buses. They were bumper to bumper, trying to flee out of the city. Some had either given up trying to drive in that tangle or never had a vehicle to start and simply walked or biked along the shoulders or weaved in and out of traffic.

Adamcik turned his head as they passed over and by these people—his people.

"Maybe they are targeting the factories or the train yards," Janco suggested. The road noise and growl of *Milacku*'s engine were too loud for him to be heard save over Adamcik's headphones, though he was scarcely two meters away in the gunner's hatch.

"The train yard is ahead," Adamcik said, gesturing. "There are no factories downtown."

"Maybe they are attacking the road network. They want to jam the roads with rubble," Janco tried again. His face betrayed only confusion.

Adamcik wasn't confused at all. "They are punishing us," he said, voice cold and certain. "They are punishing us for disobeying. They want to show us the cost of freedom."

Janco looked subdued. Even after everything they'd seen and done, he couldn't seem to accept the darkness in the human heart, even as it stared him in the face.

"Tiger Six to all platoons," Captain Vesely's voice came into Adamcik's ear. "Spider reports enemy anti-tank positions to the south east. Continue east, leave the highway and push into those suburbs. Confirm."

As the platoon leaders chimed in, Adamcik looked back over his shoulder at the T-72s of the company, rumbling along in a haze of exhaust. Ahead, the highway curved south. It ran in a sort of valley-like depression, likely funneling straight into the enemy emplacements their recon unit had discovered. Ahead, up a grassy slope, were the suburbs of Prague, a sprawling sea of homes.

"Tiger One Six confirms," Adamcik said, relaying the command to his platoon. "One Two, lead us in. One Three will follow at fifty meters."

"Copy, Six," Sergeant Coufal replied. He didn't seem to mind being used as bait, though surely his life would be the cost if those houses were also an ambush.

The BMPs of Bear Company growled by, accelerating to pass the tanks and press into the suburbs. They wouldn't be much better at identifying an ambush, but at least their infantry—those who survived the opening salvo—would be better suited to clear houses than Adamick's tanks.

Milacku's treads crashed over an aluminium guardrail and bit into the soft earth of the highway embankment. The tank lurched back, engine revving as it climbed. Adamcik fought the urge to duck into the illusive safety of the tank hull. He stood a better chance of surviving if he spotted the trap before it sprang, and he had a better chance of *that* if he kept unbuttoned.

Beside him, Janco lowered himself back into the tank to man the gun. The autoloader carousel fed a shell into the breech with a hiss and whine of electric motors and hydraulics.

The tanks leveled out. Coufal's vehicle led the way, proceeding along a quiet side street, treads furrowing the pavement.

A distant bang echoed through the air followed closely by another. Adamcik took the silence afterwards to be ominous.

"Enemy maneuvering, Tigers," Vesely said. "Spider has driven them into the open. Advance and engage."

Adamcik pressed his mic close. "Gunner, load sabot."

"Already done," Janco replied.

No ambush lashed out at them from the quiet houses and soon they passed through a small commercial area. The shops were all looted, windows broken in. Beyond that, they found a broad, open park.

"Contact!" Adamcik blurted, seeing tiny shapes moving across They were BRDMs—Soviet scout vehicles, or tank hunters in this case. Each carried an array of anti-tank missiles on their roof. He dropped into *Milacku*'s armored interior and pressed his face to the periscope, finding the vehicles.

"I see them, Six," Coufal said. "Three armored cars moving in the open."

"Are they ours?" Adamcik said. Spider platoon was also using BRDMs. The downside of being equipped with castoff Warsaw pact gear was that friend and foe was harder to ascertain at a glance.

"Negative. No markers," Coufal said, "No markers."

Adamcik found them with his sights around the same time Janco did.

"We've got range," Janco told him.

The BRDMs must have spotted them because they turned away, belching black exhaust and accelerating.

"Hit them. All fire."

Janco fired first, Coufal a moment later. Both sabots struck true. The first BRDM exploded in a flash, burning road wheels flipped away and bits of metal cartwheeled through the air. The other lurched with the impact and rolled to a stop, flames licking from its hatches.

Adamcik watched this second one closely for survivors. None emerged.

One by one the tanks of Tiger passed the dead armored cars and pressed into another cluster of houses.

"Tiger Six to all platoons," Vesely said, sounding more subdued than normal. "Spider platoon has been confirmed destroyed. I am working to find a recon element to guide us in, but for now we are on our own."

Adamcik swallowed, feeling a tense knot of fear in his gut.

"Bastards," Janco said of Spider's killers.

Suburbs alternated with stands of trees, the tanks of Tiger company forging through each of these with determined caution. Occasionally Adamcik caught sight of Bear's APCs following along with them or the other tanks of Vesely's company, but at times the platoon was totally isolated. Only the steady drumming of shellfire on Prague of course the rumble of their engine gave any sign there was a war on.

"Contact ahead!" Coufal said.

Adamcik looked forward and saw Coufal's tank rounding a curved street and approaching a wooded park running along the side of the road. As *Milacku* followed behind, he saw that the park was dotted with enemy fighting positions, foxholes and trenches. All were visible from the large earth spoils piled around them. Before Adamcik could call targets, he saw there were almost none.

Almost.

A platoon of infantry approached, hands over their heads. A single platoon had been left to hold this ground against a full regiment on the attack. They'd never stood a chance.

Standing up to get a clearer view, Adamcik rested his hand on the DsHK machine gun mounted to *Milacku*'s roof.

The infantry wore Soviet-pattern uniforms and body armor. They weren't Czechoslovakians, Hungarians, or Germans. They were Soviets.

"Prisoners?" Janco asked.

Adamcik didn't think about it. He swiveled the machine gun, sighted it on the Soviets and opened fire. The banging of the gun deafened him almost immediately. The first burst of shells chopped down a Soviet in the middle of the group.

The others froze, paralyzed with fear and confusion.

Adamcik did not hesitate. He swept his machine gun across them, firing continuously. Spent casings danced and skipped across *Milacku*'s top, tracer rounds flashing briefly through the air before punching into flesh and bone.

The Soviets tried to flee—fighting back wasn't an option as they were unarmed. It did them no good. In a few heartbeats they were all dead. Adamcik swept them with fire once more to be sure.

Milacku grumbled closer, never stopping. It passed close by where they lay dead in the grass.

Adamcik's heart pounded in his chest, blood pumping.

He felt something touch his sleeve and jerked away in surprise, seeing Janco looking at him, bewildered and shocked. "What have you done?" he asked.

Adamcik stared back at him then shook his head. What *had* he done? He looked back at the dead. As he did, he saw another T-72 approaching quickly—one of theirs. He didn't wonder who it was long as the hatch came open and Lieutenant Ambroz emerged, red-faced and angry.

"Adamcik!" he shouted, hopping from the tank before it had completely stopped.

Before he knew what he was doing, Adamcik pulled off his headset and leaped from *Milacku*, landing hard and meeting Ambroz in the open ground between the tanks.

"What is the meaning of this!?" Ambroz demanded, gesturing to the dead enemy.

"I killed them," Adamcik replied, feeling strangely detached from it all.

"Why? For what reason?"

Adamcik gave him the only reason. "Because this is our home."

This answer did nothing to mollify Ambroz. He grabbed Adamcik by the lapels of his uniform. "This is murder! You understand that? This is war! We have orders! Rules!"

Adamcik's ears were still ringing with the report of his gun. He felt a rising fury to match Ambroz's. He knocked the other's hands off him. "Murder?" He asked. "What is it they are doing to Prague? To our people?"

Ambroz stammered but Adamcik cut him off.

"I want you to think about who the *real* murderer here is," Adamcik replied, prodding Ambroz's chest. "I remember Nuremberg."

Ambroz's eyes flew open, his jaw dropped.

"Why should I follow your orders to kill civilians and spare the enemy? Why should *they* surrender while they slaughter our people?"

Another tank pulled up to this gathering—one from Adamcik's platoon. Adamcik eyed it and then looked back at Ambroz who was cowed to silence. "Think about *that, comrade*." He turned away and scaled his tank, hands shaking, heart pounding. "Let's go," he said as soon as he'd pulled his headset back on. "The enemy is waiting for us."

21

The suburbs of Budapest seemed endless to Rayburn as he walked the deserted streets with his Marines. Multi-story apartment buildings were intermixed with much older structures housing shops and stores. It was an uncanny fusion of the elegant and old with the spartan and new. Imperial-era buildings butted against Stalinist high rises.

The Marines moved along the edges of the road in two parallel columns, single file. Each column was flanked on one side by the stone and concrete walls of buildings and on the other side by row on row of parked cars. *Decimator* brought up the middle, trailing behind them by almost fifty meters.

The built up area refracted and set sounds echoing in strange ways. The thunder of artillery was mostly muffled, just dull thudding sometimes heard over the bass rumble of *Decimator*'s engine. More pronounced were the shrill cries of rounds passing to and fro overhead, like an argument between spiteful and powerful deities. It sounded like most of it was directed south, toward the Italians crossing the Danube. "Man, they're really catching it," Rayburn said, his voice nearly a whisper.

"Don't feel too bad," Keyes replied softly. "Gonna be our turn next."

The Marines reached a T-junction in the street where it ran into a broad park, grassy, open, and dotted sporadically with trees and benches.

The Marines spread out and took cover, sighting their weapons across this open ground. It would make for a great ambush spot.

Lieutenant Eichmann stepped into the open, waving a hand at

Decimator, gesturing for her to stop before she exposed herself to this killing ground.

Rayburn's eyes darted back and forth, checking the park, the buildings, and the empty windows frowning down on them from all sides. Not far away, a machine gun chattered. It was met with a smattering of rifle fire.

"Dunner, Hart," Eichmann called, gesturing ahead.

The two selected Marines rose into a hunched walk and moved forward, jogging across the street to take shelter behind wide tree trunks. When no fire met them, Eichmann moved the whole platoon up. He was on the radio a moment later.

"Blackmark this is Buzzsaw, Gesztenyeskert is secure. Over." He only stumbled a little on the name. Eichmann's eyes scanned a laminated map as he spoke. This park had been marked as a helicopter landing zone, a place to bring in supplies and take out wounded. Now that their objective was secure, they would be moving on.

Soon another pair of platoons joined them, moving to the far ends of the park, securing all approaches. A couple minutes later, a team of engineers arrived and began cutting down trees and laying flares, converting a recreational space into a functional landing zone. The Marines moved on again, creeping north.

Rayburn saw movement ahead a moment before Dunner called out. "Contact front!"

The Marines ducked down, taking firing positions to either side of the road. No one fired because they all saw the white flag.

A lone figure carrying a white towel in one hand walked slowly toward them.

"Friend!" he called in accented English. "Hungarian!"

Lieutenant Eichmann rose up and beckoned him closer. "Come on, keep your hands up."

The Hungarian wore dirty civilian clothes, a denim jacket and ratty work boots, but also an old-style Soviet steel pot helmet, a green strip of fabric tied around his arm, and webbing carrying magazine pouches. He had no weapon. After a brief frisking by Hart, he was waved over to Eichmann.

"I am Toth," the man said in heavily accented English. "We are friends. We fight the Russians."

Eichmann seemed unsold but didn't argue. "What do you need, Toth?"

The Hungarian turned, pointing down the road the Marines were following. "There is Russian ambush ahead. Past this turn."

Eichmann's eyes widened slightly. "An ambush?"

"Yes, maybe ten men. A missile launcher for your tank," he pointed to the AmTrac.

"ATGM?" Eichmann asked, the acronym meaningless to Toth. "What kind of missile?"

"I do not know English word. Malyutka."

"Malyutka?" Washington repeated.

"That's a Sagger. ATGM," Eichmann said. "How do you know all that?"

"They make us fight. Try make us fight. We only want surrender," Toth said.

Eichmann eyed Toth's equipment. "Seems like you want to fight."

Toth's expression hardened, eyes sharp as he caught his meaning. "Yes, I fight."

"Okay, so show me." Eichmann produced his map and went over it with Toth. It became clear that the Soviets were blocking the American advance into Budapest where possible, focusing on a few well-placed ambush spots and defensible hardpoints.

"Let's start flushing them," Eichmann said finally. "If I give you a fire team, can you lead them around and clear out the Russians?"

"Yes," Toth said. "I do that."

"Sergeant, take a team with Toth and see if you can clear the way."

"Yes, sir." Washington pulled his team, including Rayburn, and followed the Hungarian fighter off on a perpendicular street.

"We must be careful," Toth said as they walked. "Try not destroy buildings. I ask you please be careful."

Washington seemed unswayed by his concern. "We'll do what we have to," he said. "I'm more worried about saving lives than saving buildings."

"Lives, yes," Toth agreed. "Russians not let us evacuate. Save lives."

"The fuck you mean 'didn't let them evacuate?'" Washington asked.

"People in these basements. Underground. Kept here for..." Toth couldn't think of the phrase.

"Human shields?" Rayburn asked, horrified.

"Yes," Toth said unhappily.

"Jesus Christ," Keyes muttered.

Rayburn looked around again at the "empty" buildings with a newfound anxiety.

"This way," Toth said, breaking from the road and instead guiding the Marines through alleyways and backyards. They vaulted a few flimsy wooden fences until he gestured for them to keep low. Creeping along the backside of a fence, they left the suburbs and came into sight of a sprawling rail yard where dozens of parallel tracks held long parked trains of box cars and flatbeds.

A series of explosions rang out from the far end of the yard. Booms reverberated periodically and plumes of smoke and dust rolled up.

"Russians destroy what they cannot take," Toth said. "Missile is there." He pointed out a cinderblock structure on the edge of the yard.

"Let's stop their fun," Washington said. "You have any men?" He looked at Toth.

"Yes, but not here. Busy helping."

Rayburn understood. With his city burning there was too much to do and not enough hands to do it.

Washington eyed the train yard again, studying the layout. "Lotta open ground," he said finally. "Toth, you take us along the edge here?" He gestured along the perimeter of the yard which was marked by a rusted chainlink fence and sporadic undergrowth.

"Yes, I do that," Toth said.

At a word, Washington followed the Hungarian, circling around the anticipated ambush point. The Marines kept low, hunching along, making sure to keep as much brush and yard equipment between themselves and the Soviet position. As they drew slowly closer, Rayburn saw the Soviet plan more clearly. The ATGM team was established in a building which rose above the others. It looked sort of like a stunted air traffic control tower. Barely three stories tall, it still loomed over the rest of the yard, providing a clear vantage for engaging hostile vehicles.

An anti-tank guided missile attack from that position would stall out any approach long enough for the Soviets to pack up, escape, and do it all again a couple kilometers away.

"There," Toth pointed as the fire team crouched in a brush-lined ditch.

Washington risked standing up for a better view. The tower betrayed no movement, but the windows were all broken out.

"Missile in that building."

"You're sure?" Washington asked.

Toth nodded. Sure as anything.

"Right. Wierzbowski, set up here and in sixty seconds, start hammering them," Washington said. "Keyes, Rayburn, with me. You too," he pointed to Toth and then started off, pressing through the brush.

Rayburn followed behind as they prepared to ambush the ambushers. Taking cover along a parked flatbed train car, they crept along its length and cut across a gap between cars. Rayburn stepped over the couplers carefully, too focused to be afraid. They were nearly on top of the tower when Wierzbowski opened up. The bark of his machine gun was met with the whistle of bullets over their heads. He walked gunfire back and forth over the upper windows of the building.

Washington's team was close enough to hear panicked shouts and commands. They took position, sighting weapons on the ground floor doorway.

Rayburn's heart pounded as he caught a flash of movement—a green uniform. He opened fire and a dead Soviet flopped out. More rifle fire ripped into the doorway and sporadic return fire banged back.

"Grenade out!" Keyes yanked the pin and pitched a grenade with perfect precision straight into the doorway.

It skittered inside and burst, silencing the enemy gun.

"Cover me," Washington said.

Before anyone could object he dropped his rifle, letting it hang by the sling as he sprinted forward, arms pumping.

"Shit, what the hell is he doing?" Keyes asked, firing another burst at the door.

Washington pulled the pin on a grenade and tossed it inside before ducking against the wall by the door. The grenade exploded inside but he wasn't satisfied. Backing up for a better vantage, he pulled the pin on another grenade and lobbed it up, sailing it into the upper story where it exploded with another flat bang.

This time there was only silence.

Eventually everyone stopped shooting.

"Was that it?" Rayburn asked, licking his lips.

A trio of Soviets dashed out of the building on the far side. He only knew they were there from the sound of feet pounding gravel. No one in Washington's team could see them.

No one but Wierzbowski. He adjusted fire and scythed them down like wheat with ripping bursts of his M260. After another minute they were all dead.

The Marines cleared the building, finding only mangled bodies and a destroyed ATGM launch system.

Decimator emerged from the city further back, clattering along in the open, trailed by the rest of the company.

Rayburn looked over the dead, faintly aware that he could end up just like any of them if he wasn't careful. Memento Mori. It didn't frighten him exactly, it was just something to be aware of. He imagined it would only frighten him once he got out of this. If he got out of this.

"Man," Wierzbowski said, coming over to join him, looking over the dead. "This is just for the train yard. This isn't even the main line."

Rayburn looked at him. "It's not?"

"No, dude," Wierzbowski said. "Listen."

They did, hearing the sounds of heavy fighting not far away. Machine guns barked back and forth, tempo and pitch rising and falling, but never ceasing.

"This is gonna be fun as hell," Wierzbowski sighed wearily, hefting his gun.

Washington shook Toth's hand. "Thanks for the help. You want to tag along? I think we're going your way."

Toth eyed the APC and nodded. "Yes. I think so."

Rayburn fell in with the others, sparing a single glance back at the failed Soviet ambush. It seemed like the show was only just beginning.

22

Gradenko and Mishkin arrived at Dmitriyev's headquarters in Leningrad still in disguise. Traveling in the Soviet Union was difficult enough in peacetime, but in wartime it was nearly impossible. Gradenko travelled as a workman under forged papers—an industrial boiler specialist from Novgorod—for obvious reasons, while Mishkin maintained his ruse as a mere captain simply to keep a lower profile.

Their arrival in Leningrad was unceremonious. The grand, white, tsarist structure of the Moskovy Railway Station was busy —crowded with soldiers. Many of them were wounded, broken, and spent men from further north. They'd returned from the deadly marshes of Finland and the fierce battlefields of Sweden and Norway as fresh troops arrived to replace them, though "fresh" was a relative term.

Gradenko eyed them as they gathered in Vosstaniya Square outside the station, filling that huge, open space in a milling sea of drab green. Their uniforms were moth-eaten and fit poorly. Much of the equipment they had been issued looked like it might have also been issued to their fathers and grandfathers. They carried rusted, ill-maintained Kalashnikovs slung on their backs. Their faces were grim, lined with exhaustion. There were no young men among them. All those had already been sent to more vital fronts or already expended. The men here were reservists in their thirties and early forties. They were men who had been living mostly contented civilian lives just weeks ago, now violently pulled back into the cruel embrace of the army.

Their officers stood on the hoods of vehicles and addressed them with bullhorns, barking directions, instructions, and information.

"Assemble by class! Body armor will be provided once it is available! Questions of terms should be directed to your company officer!"

Cattle to the slaughter.

How many generations would the Soviet Union burn on the battlefields of Europe to maintain its pride and prestige before it decided it had enough? Whatever the answer, it was too many.

The men here looked sick to death of it. Angry and afraid, they did not cooperate willingly with their half-drunk, aging officers. They seethed with impotent fury, fear coursing through them as they were cajoled into motion.

"Comrade, this way," Mishkin said, holding open the door of a waiting army truck.

Gradenko took his eyes from the grotesque display and climbed into the passenger seat, riding through the city. Compared to the more "Russian" Moscow, Leningrad was distinctly European. Its broad boulevards and baroque building facades could almost almost fit into the Parisian suburbs.

Electrical lines for the city's trolleys crisscrossed overhead. There was a surprising amount of foot traffic here, despite—or maybe because of—the military marshalling taking place not far away. The whole city felt balanced on a knife's edge, teetering just between order and chaos.

Dmitriyev's headquarters building was unremarkable. A red Soviet banner hung above the doorway and a pair of armed sentries checked Mishkin's papers before admitting them. They seemed far more concerned about the disorder of the nearby plaza then they were about an unassuming captain.

It had been no object for Mishkin to arrange a private audience with Dmitriyev. Though Dmitriyev commanded the entire Leningrad Military District, Mishkin was understood to be Strelnikov's regent in his absence. If his captain's uniform confused the staff at the headquarters, they hid it well, nor did they ask questions about the unkempt civilian in his company.

After being admitted they waited in a spacious, sparsely

decorated office. Gradenko stood by the window gazing out onto the city while Mishkin sat and fidgeted across from Dmitriyev's desk. He bolted to his feet when Dmitriev blustered into the room.

Before the war, before Yugoslavia, Dmitriyev had a reputation as a dandy, a summertime soldier who was more interested in a fine uniform than in the military sciences. His playboy smile was long gone, replaced instead with a hardset frown.

Gradenko turned, regarding him from the window.

"Comrade General," Mishkin blurted, "I am glad you agreed to see me."

Dmitriyev's staff may have been fooled by their thin ruse, but he was not. He dragged his baleful gaze from Mishkin to Gradenko and then circled around his desk, ignoring Mishkin's greeting. He thumped his palms down on his desktop as he leaned over to glare at both men. "I should have you both shot."

Mishkin gaped, blinking rapidly.

Gradenko was too far beyond fear of such idle threats and did not react.

"I should tell General Strelnikov of all this," Dmitriyev continued angrily. "You have the nerve to come to me here like this? To place *my* life in danger."

"C-Comrade, we only—" Mishkin stammered but Gradenko stepped forward to spare him.

"We are here to speak with you about ending the war," Gradenko said calmly.

"No," Dmitriyev snapped back. "You are here to inspire me to treason. You will ask me to march my army on Moscow and declare you tsar in Strelnikov's place," Dmitriyev said, meeting Gradenko's gaze.

Gradenko didn't correct him.

After a moment of painful silence Dmitiyev shook his head and sighed. "I am sympathetic to what you want," He said finally. "I hate this war. In truth I desire nothing more than peace, but what you want, I cannot do." The general gestured to the window past Gradenko's shoulder. "The enemy is just there, over the border. Our corridors through Finland must be held to keep our armies in Sweden fed and supplied. The Finns have rejected this arrangement and now make us pay for our arrogance and lack of imagination. My soldiers—" he stopped, laughed and shook his head. "The soldiers here are boys and old men. They do not obey me. No doubt you have seen the mob they have sent me as reinforcements. If I cannot make them leave this city, then I cannot make them march on Moscow, even if I wanted to do so."

While Gradenko's face remained a careful mask, Mishkin wore his emotion on his sleeve. He was crestfallen. "You will do nothing?" he asked.

Dmitriyev cast an unhappy look at Mishkin and then sat. "Yes," he said. "I will do nothing but follow my orders. I will not arrest you... but I cannot help you." He stared at his hands, laid flat on the desk. "I will simply pretend as though I have not seen you." He opened his desk drawer and produced a stack of paperwork and a pen before starting to work his way through it. "I can only wish you luck," he said finally by way of dismissal.

"Outrageous," Mishkin blurted, his meek patience at an end. "Dmitiyev, we are comrades!"

"*Comrades*?" Dmitriyev replied venomously, eyes flashing as he looked up again. "I do not know the meaning of the word. It has lost any value to me." His anger faded again to pity and then he looked away. "Farewell, General Mishkin. Gradenko."

The two conspirators traded a look. They had no leverage. They'd come as beggars and as beggars they would leave. Reluctantly they did just that, turning to the office door. Gradenko made it to the doorway before Dmitriyev called out to him.

"Gradenko." He waited until the old general secretary turned and then said, "My father was arrested with the Assembly." A pause. "What has happened to him?"

Gradenko felt a faint pity for Dmitriyev but he could only give him the truth, unsoftened. "I do not know."

The thin hope in Dmitriyev's eyes faded again. He hung his head, looked down, then continued on with his paperwork.

Mishkin took Gradenko's arm and led him downstairs. They left the building unmolested and found themselves standing in the muggy, humid air of Leningrad again, breathing car exhaust as a column of army trucks rumbled by.

Gradenko had always loved coming to Leningrad with his wife. It was so utterly unlike Moscow, but no less storied in its history. Now it felt more foreign to him than Bangladesh or Zimbabwe. He looked around at the surrounding, white stone buildings and the crowded streets, and felt despair.

"What now?" Gradenko asked, not daring to dream of the future. He was happy to leave that burden to someone else.

"We will have to find an army officer with a field command who is sympathetic to our cause," Mishkin replied, looking just as lost as Gradenko, maybe moreso. It had been his hope that Gradenko could wave a magic document and resolve the war tidily. The realization that things might not be so simple was crushing to him. "Perhaps in the Caucasus."

Gradenko mulled over Mishkin's words on the drive back to the train station. Dmitriyev was sympathetic to their goals, but even he would not help them. If *he* wouldn't join them then no one would. Any officer they might find who *was* willing to topple Strelnikov's rule would do so only for personal gain. They would replace one dictator with another, the next in an endless procession of praetorian usurpers.

Exiting the truck, they found the train station even more jammed as a fresh train of reservists arrived. More reservists and inductees crowded into the square, nearly leaderless.

"If we cannot fight, then we must flee," Mishkin said finally, having to speak up over the clamor of voices and growl of megaphones. "A government in exile. Perhaps in Austria or Switzerland... China." A hopeless dream.

Gradenko ignored him. His attention was focused on a growing crowd of reservists loudly protesting their deployment. They raised voices in anger against their officers who were trying impotently to control them with the bullhorns. It had no effect. If anything, the officers themselves were beginning to doubt. The younger among them faltered, some standing idle and simply watching in shock as their control over this vast body of would-be soldiers slipped.

The fact was that the upper echelon of Soviet officers were out of touch with the common man, too indoctrinated in a system which meant little to the rank and file. The gulf between a captain or a major and a private was insurmountably wide.

The demands of the protestors were simple enough. They were not afraid to fight, they were willing to die, but they were not willing to die without reason. Their weapons and equipment were inadequate, their leaders inept, they refused to have their lives thrown away for nothing.

These people were angry, frustrated, but in a way they were still cattle, bellowing unhappily, but soon to be whipped back into shape.

"Comrade?" Mishkin asked, seeing Gradenko ignoring him.

A megaphone lay on the ground beside a parked army truck, abandoned or forgotten. As Gradenko stared at it, a strange recollection sprang to his mind, a realization. He remembered that he was more than just a bureaucrat. He started forward.

Mishkin looked startled. "Comrade? What are you—"

Gradenko picked up the megaphone and climbed onto the hood of the truck, staring over the sea of men, feeling a latent energy within him. He did not know what he would say until he said it. He just knew that he had no more fear.

"My friends," he said, voice booming out of the bullhorn. "My friends," he repeated again.

His words and tone were so strange that they could not help but draw the attention of the soldiers. When they looked, they saw a thin, gaunt man with a long beard and flowing gray hair frowning down at them.

"We have been mistreated. We have been lied to. We have been used," Gradenko said.

Behind him, Mishkin looked around nervously. He was too principled to flee outright, but unhappy with all this sudden attention.

"They call you 'comrade', but you are not their comrades," Gradenko continued. "You are not fodder for their guns, you are not slaves to be driven. You are men! You are the people! The people for whom this nation was built, for whom the Communist Party serves!"

This time, instead of blank confusion there was an echo of agreement. He saw fists and rifles raised in support. The furor of the crowd died down as a hundred separate angry voices fell silent, drawn in by one clear voice speaking directly to them.

"Yes!" Gradenko said, shouting into the microphone, his voice amplified a hundred times, echoing through the square. "I say 'whom the Party serves!' For it is the Party which serves you!"

The soldiers murmured, ripples running through the crowd as they gravitated toward this demagogue in their midst. The truth was such a rare commodity in the Soviet Union that it was nearly a delicacy, especially when served publicly.

They were gradually coming to terms with the fact that they had power. This power had always been within them. The power to collectively stand up and say "no." They had anger, but no leader. No one was willing to rise above the others and make himself a target, but Gradenko was different. He had nothing left to lose.

"Too long we have suffered the yoke of tyrants," he said. "Too long we have sweat, and bled, and died for tsars!" Gradenko's blood roared in his ears. His heart raced. He vented all the rage and fury which he'd so tightly bottled inside. He channeled all this feeling into his voice, into his words, and into these men.

The officers of this unruly unit, those who still remained, gave up, quickly. They filtered away before any retribution might be dished out.

Now the protesting reservists were joined by other soldiers stationed to watch them and the trains of newly arrived conscripts. Their numbers swelled and grew. They'd had a taste of truth and wanted more. They *demanded* more. Gradenko gave it to them.

"You are not afraid to fight, so fight! Our enemies are not

in Helsinki," he said. "Not in Stockholm. Not in Washington or London. No! They are here! Right here! Our enemy is tyranny! Stalinist overreach! Bonapartist despotism! Militant imperialism! The enemy of the people is the man who draws his sword against his family and places his boot on their necks and says 'serve me and die!'"

A hoarse cheer erupted from the men, short but powerful, leaving Gradenko's ears ringing. He couldn't stop now even if he had wanted to.

"How can we be expected to achieve true communism when our leaders guide us not to progress, but to ruin?"

They cheered again, longer and louder, all eyes fixed on this strange, wild prophet.

He pointed back at the train yards. "I will board this train and I will take it to Moscow," he said. "I will march on the Kremlin and I will tell the bastards there that this war must stop! That this fighting must stop! Honorable peace must be made! If they will not agree to that, then I will show them why the tsars were right to fear the people! I hope," Grandenko said finally, "that you will join me."

The soldiers erupted with cheers and now moved eagerly back to the trains.

Gradenko had found his army.

23

Something Wicked and the rest of the F-1117 Nighthawk stealth bombers flew the night skies of East Germany, invisible to radar and nearly so to the human eye. Far below, scattered fires burned like inverse constellations, a vision of hell.

Captain Harry "Wizard" Welles, felt like an avatar of Death as he surveyed the apocalyptic scene below. Maybe that was a little dramatic, but it felt like the moment called for it. He'd lost count of the number of sorties he'd flown, how many bombs he'd dropped, but this one felt especially important. This time, instead of just hurting the enemy, they had a chance to destroy them.

As usual, the bombers in the strike group flew in radio silence. Emit and die. Too slow and awkward to run and totally unarmed, their only chance of survival was simply not to be seen.

The Soviet air defense network was a pale shadow of what it had once been. Radar coverage was patchy, their stockpiles of advanced SAMs reduced. The worse things got, the more pressure NATO could bring to bear on them. Cascade failure—a term Welles was hearing a lot of lately and starting to see first hand. The stealth design of their aircraft was almost unnecessary at this point. Almost.

He eyed his radar warning receiver as it flashed intermittently. Enemy waves brushed his craft in the dark, caressing it, searching for it. He tried not to let it worry him.

Breathing hard behind his oxygen mask, Welles switched his attention to the television camera feed for his laser designator.

He flew straight and level, low enough to get a good look at the ground through his black and white infrared camera feed. The Soviets were on the run. Roads were clogged up with trucks and tanks. They usually moved in the daytime. It wasn't safe for them at night—a fact Welles took no small degree of pride in—but they were getting desperate.

Any part of this snaking convoy would make for a juicy target, but he had something special in store.

Adjusting his flight slightly, Welles saw the broad, dark snake of the Oder River. The Soviets had their backs against it. Welles wasn't a soldier, but he understood that an army with its back against a river was an army waiting for death. Only a handful of lifelines connected them with relative safety in Poland.

Here was one of them.

He spotted the sharp peninsula of land where the Warta River flowed into the Oder. On the northeast bank was the town of Kostrzyn nad Odra. The town was dark, likely by military orders, but the heat signature of idling vehicles was unmistakable.

Welles nudged his stick gently, putting *Something Wicked* into a slow orbit of his target below. Now came the dangerous part. With a press of a button he opened his bomb bay doors, giving his Nighthawk the smallest of radar signatures. Nearly invisible, but not quite. While he was like this he was vulnerable.

Working quickly, he adjusted his laser designator and put it on the middle span of a bridge crossing the river. It was packed with trucks trundling east. He released weapons.

Breathing hard, he kept up his slow orbit, keeping the laser on the bridge, praying for a hit.

Anti-aircraft guns started banging away below him. Arcs of golden tracer rounds sprayed into the sky, sweeping the night. Someone had seen him. He swore under his breath a moment before the bomb smashed powerfully into the bridge. The explosion whited out his TV display for a moment. When it cleared he saw burning trucks, chunks of concrete showering the water, and human forms dashing around. More importantly, he saw the bridge was down.

Bingo.

A pair of shells punched into his port wing, juddering the Nighthawk.

Welles swore louder and closed his bomb bay doors. Jamming his stick to the side, he turned his lazy orbit into a hard, banking turn. He throttled up and raced south, praying that it was just bad luck he got hit.

If it was, it didn't let up. The aircraft vibrated again, a hit to the tail stabilizer maybe. His right rudder pedal went mushy. An angry light flashed on his console about hydraulic pressure.

"Come on, come on, girl," he muttered, starting to sweat.

More tracers cut the sky in front of him, then they stopped and he was away.

Welles exhaled, breathing deep from his oxygen supply as he relaxed slightly. *Something Wicked* shuddered, vibrating from time to time, the hydraulic warning light stayed an unhappy amber. But he was alive.

He'd worry about landing when he got back to base.

More importantly for the consequences of the war, he'd closed off a gateway to Poland. Other aircraft were doing the same along the Oder. They'd be followed in the morning by conventional strike craft hunting for Soviet pontoons. If they played their cards right then they would trap the Soviets against the river and annihilate them.

Something Wicked sailed away into the gloom.

***

Even Strelnikov had to sleep. It came fitfully and irregularly, but it was a function as necessary as eating or breathing. He awoke before dawn to the throaty sound of diesel engines. It wasn't that which woke him, that was an expected and constant sound in and around his headquarters. No, he woke to the sound of voices outside his tent.

Strelnikov sat up on his cot and rubbed sleep from his eyes. When he stood he felt a painful crick in his neck. He was not as young as he used to be. He rolled his head and rubbed his shoulder, trying in vain to relieve it. Finally resolving himself to the presence of his pain, he dressed. He pulled on trousers, shirt, and coat, before stepping out of the tent.

Nearby, General Rastayev whispered in conversation with one of Strelnikov's staff.

"What is it?" Strelnikov asked.

Rastayev looked startled at first, then his eyes darkened. "We've lost the bridge at Kostrzyn," he said. He was too tired to be afraid of Strelnikov's fury.

Strelnikov rubbed his eyes again. "To the north?"

Rastayev nodded.

Strelnikov grunted. He couldn't do much about that now. He looked at his aide. "Find me some breakfast," he said, "and coffee." He wouldn't be getting back to sleep.

"Yes, Comrade General!"

"Tell me," Strelnikov said, now fixing Rastayev with all his attention.

Rastayev's uniform was frumpy, his eyes shadowed with exhaustion. From the stubble on his chin he hadn't shaved in days. "The entire 62nd and 19th Motor Rifles divisions are trapped on the west bank," he said. "The bridge was destroyed over an hour ago."

"What?" Strelnikov's heart missed two, maybe three beats. Two divisions trapped? Not just that, but two of his best? "Trapped how? Can they not bridge the river?"

"They're trying but the Americans have bombed the pontoons twice."

"Where is their air defense?" Strelnikov growled.

Rastayev only shook his head.

"The British are pressing from the north as well," Rastayev said. "A reconnaissance overflight saw at least a division preparing to sweep down the river." From bad to much worse.

Strelnikov let out a low growl and started for his headquarters tent. Rastayev followed obediently behind. "Where is the 55th Tank? They are in reserve in that area, are they not?

"On paper," Rastayev said quietly.

Strelnikov stopped and rounded on him, eyes flashing.

When his general did not speak, Rastayev continued. "They are combat ineffective, Comrade General. They do not have the fuel or vehicles to mount more than small scale attacks. Now we cannot get them fuel because the bridge is gone."

Worse to much worse. Nearly catastrophic.

Strelnikov continued on into the headquarters, spreading open a map and studying it, searching for a solution. "We must pull those divisions south," he said finally and reluctantly. "They will have to cross here at Frankfurt an der Oder." He tapped the map. It was suboptimal, the crossing here was already crowded, choked with the volume of men and material trying to cross it, but it was well-defended with redundant pontoon bridges already being set up.

Pulling back his trapped divisions was easier said than done, especially with the enemy closing on them. "We have a Polish motor rifle division here," Strelnikov said, reading the map. "They will move to act as a rearguard."

"Comrade General," Rastayev said apologetically. "That division... it no longer exists. There are not enough men in its ranks to function."

Strelnikov's eyes drifted close as he felt despair wash over him. It should have been no surprise that the Poles weren't reliable anymore. He would have to sacrifice his own men. "Give orders to the 55th Tank and 19th Motor Rifles to hold position and defend the crossing. The 62nd will withdraw south."

Rastayev nodded, looking only slightly relieved. He was probably just glad to have someone else tell him which men's lives to sacrifice.

"But this situation with Poland cannot be allowed to continue," Strelnikov said. "I want you to issue new orders to all units entering Poland."

Rastayev looked at his commander with a mixture of curiosity and apprehension.

"Any town or village caught harboring deserters or any place which resists attempts to restore these men to uniform is to be razed."

"Razed?"

"Burned to the ground," Strelnikov clarified. "And any civilian strikes or protests are to be met with immediate, overwhelming, and deadly force. No half measures. Is that understood?"

"Yes, clearly," Rastayev said. "But with our numbers stretched so thin—"

"We must rely on brutality to force obedience," Strelnikov replied. "What worked in Warsaw before will work again now."

Shortly after Rastayev left to see to this, Strelnikov's breakfast arrived, two thick slices of buttered bread topped with healthy hunks of sausage. He ate ravenously and chased it with bitter, black coffee. As the sun rose, activity in his headquarters increased. His evacuation proceeded well, beating off repeated NATO attacks despite mounting losses.

Rastayev returned later in the day, bearing news that the 62nd Motor Rifles had extricated themselves from the trap to the north. He brought no news of the other two divisions.

Strelnikov couldn't bring himself to say 'good' or 'excellent' and so he said nothing. One of his staff brought him a slip of paper, a dispatch from Lukin. Prague had been lost. It wasn't a shock, but it was unwelcome news, coming much quicker than he would have liked.

"Rastayev."

"Yes?"

"Once the 62nd is over the Oder, I want you to shift them south toward Wroclaw to act as a second line. We are in danger of being outflanked there and we will need to stabilize things if we are going to bleed out the West. Poland will be the battlefield."

Rastayev acquiesced. He lacked the imagination to do anything else.

Following this, Strelnikov reviewed the broader picture of the war, reviewing each front with his staff and accepting the news coldly. The situation was grim, but he saw hope.

By giving ground in Turkey and Scandinavia and falling back

to more easily defensible ground he could concentrate his army in Poland.

The Warsaw Pact was dissolving before his eyes, hemorrhaging men at an unsustainable rate. Worse, the soldiers that left often took up arms for the enemy. Whole divisions of Czechoslovakians, Bulgarians, Hungarians, and soon Poles would be rallying against them. The technical term was 'Lanchestrian Collapse.' The surety of mathematics. Only if war were simply a product of math then his tanks would be in Paris now. Factors beyond numbers mattered. A painful lesson that the Soviet military had paid for in blood.

Strelnikov had gathered what Soviet troops he could in Poland to counteract this. It was a start, but he needed veteran troops, a strong unit which could serve as the nucleus of a reserve to be used delivering punishing counterattacks to any possible NATO breakthrough.

His eyes fell on Moscow. "My Guards," he said. The 121st Zagreb Guards Motor Rifle Division had occupied Moscow since the coup which brought him into power, their skill squandered on occupation duty. Perhaps though that was now a blessing in disguise. These men were rested, fed, and well-equipped, ideal for the task he had to give them now. Beyond that, he could rely on them. These were men who would never quit.

"Bring the 121st here," he told a junior officer. "I am sure we can put them to good use."

24

If there was a Hell, Rayburn thought it might be a lot like Budapest in the Summer of '93.

"Alright, go!" Washington slapped his back.

Rayburn took two short breaths, puffing and jumping through the shattered, ground floor window and into the open. He ran as fast as he could across the street, feeling glass shards grit on the pavement beneath his boots. He breathed hard, seeming to fly. Across from him, sheltering in the doorway of the opposite building was Lieutenant Eichmann. Keyes, and a few others from the platoon hunkered further back in the dark interior of the building.

Rayburn reached the doorway just as he heard the bang of a rifle. Bits of brick sprayed beyond him, a near miss.

"I see him! Third floor, right side!" one of the Marines on the opposite side of the street shouted.

The platoon opened fire, those who were in a position to do so, anyway.

Wierzbowski knelt in the open doorway, gunfire chopping at the half-glimpsed Soviet sniper.

"You alright?" Eichmann asked, grabbing Rayburn by the arm.

"Yeah. Yes, sir. All good," he said, feeling like his heart was beating so hard he was going to die.

One of the Marines in the far building tossed a smoke grenade which hissed and started filling the street with dense, gray fog.

"Alright, let's go," Eichmann called, beckoning Washington and the remaining men over.

They crossed in ones and twos, dashing through the smoke.

The sniper, unsilenced, fired at random into the smoke,

banging away in frustration. Rounds zipped through the air or caromed off the pavement with cracks. Once all the Marines were across Eichmann called for *Decimator*.

"We're through," he said. "Move up and hit the building straight ahead. White facade, about ten stories, copy?"

Rayburn didn't hear the reply, but he didn't need to either, he saw the results.

Decimator rounded the corner and started belting grenades into the sniper's nest, advancing confidently through the smoke as it plastered the building.

Budapest's streets and alleyways had become firing lanes for snipers, guided missiles, and machine guns. Moving in the open wasn't safe, typically only done as a last resort.

The upper stories of the enemy apartment building caved in under *Decimator*'s relentless assault. The whole structure collapsed like a house of cards, burying the sniper, hopefully forever.

Rayburn couldn't help but poke his head out the doorway to watch the building come down in a shower of dust. It wasn't something you saw every day. He was so captivated by the sight that he didn't see Toth come up until he turned to see him talking with Eichmann. They were reviewing a map together.

"Right," Eichmann said. "We'll do it." He gestured to a nearby Marine. "Jones, find a way forward. Sergeant, we ready? Is that everyone?"

"Yes, sir."

"Super. Let's go."

The Marines were a small part of a larger NATO force snaking and worming their way through Budapest even as the rest of the army swept the flank, attempting to bypass the city. Despite that, Rayburn couldn't shake the sensation that they were fighting this war all alone. The backdrop of echoing gunfire felt like nothing but the soundtrack to their struggle.

"Rayman?"

"Coming." Rayburn followed the Marines.

They burrowed through the walls of the building like

termites. They used explosives where they had to to blast narrow holes so they could crawl through them rather than risk going outside.

"We're gonna blow the wrong wall one day and bring all this Soviet brutalist shit right down on us," Keyes said after they'd blasted just such a passage.

Rayburn's heart sank. "Really wish you hadn't put that idea in my head," he muttered. He followed the platoon through a deserted apartment lobby and to the far side of the building.

"Ah shit," Keyes said.

More open space greeted them, this time a small park with a few trees in it, totally ringed by buildings. "Can't go over it, can't go under it, oh no! Gotta go through it," Keyes said.

"Volunteer?" Eichmann asked.

After a long pause, Wierzbowski raised his hand.

Eichmann shook his head. "No. Someone else." They needed the machine gun.

Rayburn glanced over at Rivers, the other corpsman for the platoon and swallowed nerves as he raised his hand.

Eichmann looked at him curiously. "Rayburn?"

"I'll go," Rayburn said.

Eichmann considered it then relented, beckoning him over with a wave of his hand.

"Get it, Rayman," Keyes said encouragingly.

"Don't get shot," Wierzbowski added.

Rayburn moved up to the doorway, wondering why he'd volunteered. Eichmann was probably wondering the same thing.

"That tree," the lieutenant said, pointing into the park. "Get up there and check the coast." By that he meant 'see if anyone shoots at you.'

"Yep," Rayburn said, adjusting his grip on his rifle. "Right." Before he could think about it any more, he ran for the tree. He didn't stop until he collided with bark, nearly knocking the wind out of his lungs. He crouched on his heels, rifle shouldered, checking the buildings around him for any sign of the enemy.

Nothing happened. The mutterings of war echoed around him but this park was an oasis of calm.

Rayburn relaxed slightly and gestured to Eichmann. All clear.

The Marines moved into the park by fireteam, advancing slowly forward.

Sergeant Washington was dead before Rayburn realized what had happened. His body went limp, strings cut as he collapsed onto the grass.

Enemy gunfire poured down on them from two angles, fireteams hidden on the upper floors of the building to their right.

"Man down! Corpsman!"

Rayburn stared at Washington, mouth agape. He hadn't realized the sergeant wasn't immune to harm until the moment of his death, and he *was* clearly dead. Facedown and motionless, he'd taken a round to the heart probably, unconscious almost instantly, dead in seconds.

"Corpsman!" A Marine called again, firing angrily up at the enemy.

Rayburn took aim, teeth clenched, and fired up into the building, targeting muzzle flash in the gloom. No corpsman on this Earth could help Washington now.

Eichmann directed a grenadier in the platoon to pop the windows one by one with grenades from his underslung launcher. It only took three before the surviving Soviets bugged out, fleeing deeper into the city, but at least leaving the Marines alone.

Rayburn went to Washington's body, finding him still and limp. Kneeling, he turned him over gently.

"Shit man, they got him?" Keyes asked, coming beside him.

There was no question that they had.

"Dead before he knew it," Rayburn confirmed, drawing his hand down Washington's face, closing his eyes. There was nothing more for him to do. He stood up and took a few shaky steps away, leaning on a tree to try to catch his breath.

Behind him, Eichmann marked Washington's body on his

map for later recovery. Like Rayburn, there was nothing else he could do. For now, they had to leave him.

Toth led the way forward, away from Washington's grave and on to an unassuming stairwell sat in the middle of a sidewalk. It plunged down into the ground. The metro. "Here," he said, after checking the street signs again.

Eichmann eyed the darkened hole warily. "You sure?"

"Yes."

The lieutenant nodded and then proceeded down, leading the way, apparently unwilling to ask for a volunteer this time.

As they descended into the dark, their eyes adjusted, aided by a multitude of candles and battery-powered lanterns set up down here. They were far from alone. After just a few bends they came to a train platform choked with humanity. The citizens of Budapest—men, women, and children—sheltered below as their city burned above.

Rayburn stared, looking over these miserable throngs as they stared back. They were exhausted, afraid. He remembered what Toth said, that they hadn't been allowed to evacuate. He thought unpleasantly of the apartment *Decimator* had demolished. He hoped to God that one had been empty at least.

The civilians weren't the only ones down here either, dozens of armed Hungarians met the Americans, conversing quickly and quietly with Toth. They were Hungarian resistance fighters, many of them deserted soldiers, others simply proactive citizens.

"The way ahead—the tunnel—is clear," Toth said, translating to Eichmann. "It lead straight under river. The Danube. You come down the tunnel and come behind the enemy."

"Cross unopposed?" Eichmann repeated.

"Yes, unopposed," Toth said, relishing the new word.

As Eichmann, Toth, and the Hungarians laid out the details of the plan, Rayburn wandered nearby, moving among the civilians. He came upon an elderly man sitting on a bare mattress with what Rayburn assumed was the rest of his family—an adult man and woman and a pair of children, both no older than ten.

The old man stood out because his left shoulder was wrapped in a bloody towel and dried blood crusting the left side of his face.

"Sir?" Rayburn said, kneeling beside him. "Can I see?" He gestured at the wound.

The old man's family gripped him protectively, looking at Rayburn with alarm.

"I'm a corpsman," Rayburn explained, realizing that didn't translate well. "Doctor."

The Hungarian word for doctor must have been radically different since they didn't react any better.

He opened his medical bag and showed them some bandages. "Doctor," He repeated, pointing to their grandfather's injury. "Can I?"

Reluctantly they let go, moving aside so Rayburn could see.

The wound wasn't fresh. He moved the towel aside, willfully ignoring the man's grimace as sticky blood peeled away. It looked deep. The head wound was superficial but it was a miracle this one hadn't hit something vital. Rayburn thought it was from an artillery or mortar splinter, but couldn't be totally sure. Without much light he couldn't assess it all that clearly. It was just as well, he didn't have the equipment to do more than stabilize.

"This will sting," Rayburn explained uselessly before sterilizing the wound.

Grandpa hissed in pain and his family reacted with shock and outrage.

"Yeah, I know, I'm sorry," Rayburn said, carefully re-bandaging it. He took a packet of painkillers from his bag and looked around for Toth. "Toth!" He called, gesturing the fighter over when he saw he was free. "Please tell them to have him take these pills for the pain," he said. "And let them know that he will still need to see a doctor as soon as he can. Otherwise the wound should be cleaned with soap and water and the bandages changed once a day. Clean sheets if they can."

Toth quickly translated, and the concern and fear in their faces faded somewhat.

"*Koszonom*," grandpa said, echoed by his family.

"Thank you," Toth translated.

Rayburn forced himself to smile at them. "No problem." He stood up when one of the children grabbed his leg, hugging him. He froze, staring down at her in surprise.

"*Koszonom!*" The little girl said, seeing her grandfather apparently saved by this stranger.

"No problem," Rayburn said again. When she released him he left, walking back for the stairwell they came in through. It was deserted and quiet.

Rayburn sat down. Without warning he felt a rising tide of emotion within him. Fear, anguish, and grief. Alone, he buried his face in his hands and wept.

25

Gradenko's army of rebels and mutineers ought not to have made it as far as they did. That they reached Moscow at all was a testament to the shaky foundations of Strelnikov's empire. At every junction where they might have met resistance, it either melted harmlessly away or—more often—joined them. The watchers, the guardians of the Soviet Union, were so preoccupied with matters on the frontlines that they neglected entirely the business of home governance. Strelnikov had thought he might trust that to Mishkin. That was proving to be a dangerous oversight.

As the trains carrying the mutineers rolled into Moscow, Mishkin now worked directly in opposition to Strelnikov. He was the warning bell meant to ring if anything went out of control and he was resolutely not ringing.

The end result of this was that when Gradenko moved on the Kremlin, he was followed by an army. It had begun as a mob of disillusioned soldiers but soon others had flocked to them. Now he marched at the head of a sea of men in denim jackets and army fatigues.

A brisk wind fluttered the crimson Soviet banners the mutineers flew, reclaiming the symbol of socialist progress from the Bonapartist Strelnikov. At their head marched Gradenko and Mishkin—the military and civil arms of the government working hand in hand to restore the rightful leadership.

It was an echo of Gradenko's street protests of months earlier—those which had led to Karamazov's downfall. It was a parallel he tried not to dwell on since that particular uprising had been doomed to failure.

The scene could not have been more perfectly staged if it had been directed by a Soviet propagandist. A river of humanity flowed towards the Kremlin, clogging the streets, chanting and waving Soviet flags. The people united.

The absence of the Zagreb Guards was fortuitous, beyond providence. Had those battle-hardened elite troops remained here, then this bloodless coup would have become a terrible nightmare instead.

Though Gradenko had an army, they were an army of individuals of singular purpose, carrying nothing more than rifles or their own two hands. Against tanks and artillery and fighter jets they wouldn't stand a chance.

The Bolshoy Moskvoretsky Bridge, the last obstacle between the mob and the Kremlin, was crossed. Strelnikov's tanks had crossed this bridge nine months before and so it seemed poetic in a way that Gradenko's homecoming would take him along the same course.

The guard posts at the Spasskaya Gate were empty. The red brick clocktower over the gatehouse still remained stuck in time, its face damaged by stray autocannon fire, the hands frozen at the hour of Strelnikov's assault on the Kremlin.

The crowd advanced slowly but surely. There has been plenty of time for men to assess their true loyalties. None who Strelnikov left behind were willing to sacrifice their lives in his name.

What they had done—seemingly all they had managed to do —was park one of their armored vehicles crosswise in front of the gate in an abortive effort to bar access to the mutineers.

"Clear this!" Mishkin barked at some nearby soldiers. They obeyed instantly, one of them clambering inside and starting the vehicle to drive it aside.

Instead of passing through the gate, Gradenko changed course, moving straight for the armored car.

"Comrade?" Mishkin looked puzzled.

Gradenko ignored him and tried to climb atop the vehicle. His knees were weak and his body protested. He was not a young man anymore and a life of privation in the gulag left him weakened.

A dozen helping hands came from all directions. People boosted him, lifted him, and pulled him up on the armored car. When at last he stood atop it he looked out over an ocean of faces, all turned to him, all anxious, all watching, listening.

He only had to reach out his hand before a megaphone was pressed into his grip. He held the microphone to his face and spoke.

"Comrades, we have arrived. The Palace of the People has been returned to the People."

The ocean roared back in approval, surging like the tide. Boisterous current ran through them. Soviet flags fluttered and waved as his audience fought for better vantage points. Abandoned cars lining the road made small hills of people, light posts were climbed, heavy with humanity. He saw cameras trained on him, snapping photos and recording video. History in the making.

"This is a new chapter," Gradenko continued. "A new chapter in socialism and progress. Today, the people reject militarism and embrace peace. Together, my comrades—my friends—we claim the future!"

More cheering, deafening, battered him. Gradenko stood, blinking in awe, his fear shed like scales falling from his eyes. This was the power of the Soviet Union and it always had been. How men like him had forgotten that—turned away from it—baffled him. What purpose did power serve if it was not used in favor of the people? It was a lesson, a realization, that Gradenko would carry to his dying days. He handed off the megaphone again and—with helping hands—got back off the APC.

Mishkin waited anxiously for him in the shadow of the Kremlin's gate. "What now?" he asked, resolute but unfocused.

"We take back what is rightfully ours," Gradenko responded, continuing into the Kremlin proper. He left the spreading sea of mutineers to fill Red Square and lap at its edges, threatening to overflow into all parts of the city.

No one stopped him, the guards had all gone.

Gradenko walked the familiar halls, hunting—he realized—for someone whose surrender he could accept. As he did so he passed an ornate mirror hanging in the hall and paused, seeing himself for the first time since he had been disappeared. With his beard, long hair, gaunt features, and bright eyes he could think only of one name. Rasputin.

"There is no need for violence," a familiar, subdued voice said.

Gradenko and his escort turned to see a lone man standing in the hall. Ozerov.

"The city is yours," Ozerov said. "There does not need to be any fighting here."

Gradenko didn't think that was up to either of them.

"It is not mine to take," Gradenko replied coolly. "Or yours to give. The people have spoken and must be obeyed."

Ozerov looked taken aback. The courage he'd mustered to speak with what he took to be Moscow's despoilers was commendable, Gradenko thought, but misplaced. Too little and too late. "What you say is true, Comrade..." As Ozerov waited for a name, Gradenko realized just how unrecognizable he had become.

"Gradenko," he said.

"Grad—" Ozerov's eyes widened in surprise and recognition. "Gradenko?" He'd seen a ghost, a man back from the dead.

"The demands I bear come not from me, but from everyone." Gradenko said, undaunted. "We have come to reassert control and take back what the military has stolen. Will you join us?"

Again, Ozerov looked surprised. He was a dinosaur, a relic of a darker time of the Party's past. He was a bureaucrat, an instrument. But Gradenko knew that bureaucrats had their uses.

"I..." he looked at Mishkin and then back to Gradenko. "Yes."

"Carry word to all the soviets, the General Assembly is to reconvene. Those who have been illegally arrested by Strelnikov's regime are to be released at once. We are to decide—legally—what will happen next."

"Yes, comrade."

"And bring me a representative of the Foreign Ministry," Gradenko said. He would have to get a diplomatic cable to the governments of the West to start negotiations as soon as possible. A ceasefire would have to be arranged. There was no time to delay. Every day created more mourning mothers and grieving widows. His son, abroad in Cuba, could be relied upon as a courier for these messages. "We must put an end to this vicious and pointless fighting."

Ozerov was reeled by bombshell after bombshell. "An end to the war?" He sounded incredulous, like Gradenko had suggested putting out the sun.

Gradenko forced a smile. "All wars must be ended, don't you think so?"

"Of course," Ozerov replied.

"And," Gradenko said, almost as an afterthought. "I will need to be taken to Programme One. I must make a broadcast."

26

Slubice, on the Polish side of the Oder River, played host to Strelnikov's headquarters and now provided his grim vantage point to watch the last of his soldiers crossing over from Germany. He stood silent in the early evening and watched truck after truck racing over. Each was laden with men and material desperately clawed away from NATO's oncoming armies. When the last of them had made it over, his rearguard crossed. These were hardbitten men, Rastayev's exhausted soldiers riding on tanks and APCs. They were few in number, far fewer than they had been some days ago when they'd made a gallant attempt to blunt NATO's armored spearheads. They'd suffered under endless airstrikes and sharp action with the enemy, their strength whittled away until only these remained. Heroes, all of them.

As was always true in war, there was simply no award worthy of these men, Strelnikov thought. Not enough Orders of Lenin could—or ever would be minted to properly show them thanks. Their only reward was blood and suffering.

He was reminded uncomfortably of his bitter withdrawal east across the Rhine River less than a year ago. The fortunes of the Soviet army had been grossly reversed. They'd been driven from the very gates of France to halfway across the Eastern Bloc. The pressure to perform a miracle was great and Strelnikov felt it as a crushing weight which rested squarely upon his shoulders.

After an hour, as darkness claimed the skies, Strelnikov finally spoke. "Is that all of them?" he asked Rastayev.

"All but the final vanguard," Rastayev said, subdued. He was a broken man, commander of a division which now existed only on paper. His men had been left dead and dying across the plains of East Germany. "They have arrangements to ford the river with amphibious gear."

Strelnikov doubted if any of them would ever find that chance. NATO ruled the nights and if they had not escaped by now, they never would. More likely they weighed the odds and would take their chances with surrender over a death ride back for a nearly hopeless opportunity to cross a river under fire in the dark.

"Then destroy it," Strelnikov turned away from the sight.

The bridge which they had so painstakingly defended from NATO air attacks had been carefully rigged by his engineers the day before. Explosive charges rippled across the structure and sent it plunging down into the black Oder below. The crossing between Slubice and Frankfurt an der Oder had been the last bridge across that river. Anyone still left on the western side would have to make their own way.

"Gather your men and leave a battalion here," Strelnikov told Rastayev. "NATO will attempt to follow right on our heels. If you cannot stop them here then make them pay for it. With ATGM teams in the suburbs you can cover your flanks and with RPGs along the banks of the river you can prevent any amphibious crossing."

"Is there no one else?" Rastayev protested. "Comrade, my men have been fighting nonstop for weeks. We must have relief."

There was no one else. Not yet. No one Gradenko trusted. "When the Zagreb Guards arrive then your men can be rotated back for refit," he said. "Until then, stand to your guns."

Rastayev's dim hope faded, his expression fell, but he knew his duty. "Yes, Comrade General."

Strelnikov left him, marching up the muddy bank of the Oder and into the edge of Lubice. A few high rise buildings along the river edge were darkened. He saw movement in one of the windows. Some of Rastayev's men were setting up a machine gun nest to overlook the bridge.

Walking past a glass bus stop shattered by a NATO bomb,

he circled the crater and the charred ruin of an anti-aircraft gun. Just ahead he found his headquarters APCs in a parking lot behind the apartments. They'd been covered with plain blue tarps, disguising them from the air so they were not obviously military vehicles.

Strelnikov wondered just how effective that was.

He was lost in thought as he passed by a military sentry and found a map table. Strelnikov had always loved maps, even as a child. His father had owned a travel map of Ukraine and he'd studied it endlessly, tracing the roads and rivers with his eyes, imagining what it must be like to travel those paths.

He held no joy in his heart as he studied this map, dotted with markers showing the rough positions of military units. So much of it was illusory. Whole divisions existed only on paper. Virtually none of their allies could be counted on. The Poles, the East Germans, the Czechoslovakians, all seemed to be melting away like snow in the sun. At least with the Oder secured he could by time. Time to make a miracle.

Nearby, he saw his staff officers gathering around a folding table set up just inside an entryway to the apartment building. A civilian radio was set up there and they were all listening intently. Their expressions were drawn, haunted, like they'd seen a ghost.

Strelnikov forgot the map, forgot his troubles, and made his way over. When he drew nearer he heard the radio announcer speaking in Russian. It was Programme One. What he said was unclear, but as Strelnikov came to stand by the others he heard a familiar voice speaking clearly and calmly.

"Good evening, comrades. Today is an auspicious day in the history of the Soviet Union and the history of mankind. Today is the day which we reject the shackles of authoritarian imperialism."

Gradenko.

Strelnikov's jaw dropped. He was aware of the uncomfortable glances the men here were sending his way, but he forced himself to stand and listen.

"Today marks the end of the illegal coup which swept the old government from power and an end to the bloodshed which has marred our great country. Today we place blame and call to justice the one responsible for such chaos. Pyotr Strelnikov."

Strelnikov's eyes widened and he jerked as if shot.

Gradenko's voice continued. "Strelnikov, who murdered General Secretary Karamazov and General Tarasov in an illegal coup, who has ruled our country by decree against the will of the people, who even now desperately prolongs the war which sustains his power."

"No," Strelnikov whispered, horrified. He was undone.

"I am formally reclaiming my title as General Secretary of the Soviet Union from Minister Ozerov who has voluntarily stepped aside, and hereby formally reconvene the Supreme Soviet that we may restore the rule of law and civilian control of the government. An emergency session of the Soviet General Assembly held just tonight has voted to declare Strelnikiov a traitor and an enemy of the people. I call at once for his arrest and removal from power that he may stand trial and face justice. All those still loyal to the communist party and the Soviet Union —"

But Strelnikov had heard enough. He fairly staggered away from the radio, hurrying back for his headquarters. His mind raced. Betrayed. Failed. Ruined. Mishkin, Ozerov, they had failed him. His Zagreb Guards had been called away and now no one was there to maintain control over Moscow, over the bureaucracy which he needed to maintain his war here. If he could not restore order, and quickly, then the war was lost, and if the war was lost...

At the map table he quickly studied the ground, the disposition of units. So many had been called from Russia and sent to the front, so few could he count on. He would need to resume command of the Zagreb Guards if he was to crush this rebellion quickly. Only they had the strength, proximity, and most importantly, the numbers. He muttered to himself and glanced at a nearby lieutenant, hovering anxiously in the shadows of his headquarters. "Get me General Rastayev," Strelnikov barked. "Quickly."

The lieutenant hurried away as Strelnikov made plans. He could pass word to the Zagreb Guards to return to the city at once and take control. Then he would have to ascertain just what had gone wrong, and how bad the damage to the governmental apparatus was to have failed so catastrophically.

Rastayev arrived some minutes later, looking grim.

"Comrade," Strelnikov said. "We are betrayed. Enemies on both sides. I need a company of your best men, men you can trust," he said.

Rastayev said nothing.

"We must—" Strelnikov drew himself short as he saw General Turgenev arrive behind Rastayev. He led a gaggle of junior officers, all of them armed. "What is this?" Strelnikov asked, eyes narrowing.

"Comrade General," Rastayev said, drawing in a shaky breath. "You are under arrest by the command of the Soviet General Assembly."

"Ridiculous," Strelnikov spat. "What do you think you are doing?"

Rastayev looked unsure of himself. "What choice do we have?" he asked. "We have our orders."

"Damn your orders!" Strelnikov spat back. "What about the Soviet Union? What about the war? What about victory!?"

"Enough," Turgenev moved closer, a Makarov pistol leveled at Strelnikov's stomach. "Shut up." He looked at the nearest lieutenant. "Arrest him."

With only a moment of uncomfortable hesitation, the lieutenant moved forward, handcuffing Strelnikov as gently as he could.

"Pigheaded fools like you will cost us this war!" Strelnikov spat, seething with rage at this blind incompetence.

Turgenev smiled back. "Be glad, *Citizen Strelnikov*, that I *am* a slave to my orders, otherwise I believe I would shoot you myself."

Strelnikov fell silent, fuming.

"What do we do now, Comrade General?" Rastayev asked, resolutely avoiding Strelnikov's harsh stare.

"As we are commanded," Turgenev said. "Prepare a train. We will take him back to Moscow."

27

The tanks of the Czechoslovak Legion left the sacred soil of their homeland, forging northeast into Poland in close pursuit of the enemy. It was bittersweet to leave Czechoslovakia again so soon after having returned, but war called.

The rolling, forested hills of the Sudetan fell away, blending seamlessly into the flat Polish countryside. Adamcik's tank led the way, the Czechoslovakian flag fluttering proudly from his radio aerial, camouflage be damned.

The crossing had been fiercely contested, Soviet tank and rifle units fighting over every kilometer of the Sudetan highlands. Losses were significant. Adamcik had lost one of his tanks, Ambroz had lost two, but they carried on, leaving the dead to burn in their gutted tanks. Now that they were through this more defensible ground, the enemy fell rapidly back, abandoning vast swaths of Poland.

"Probably leaving for the Oder," Vesely speculated over the company frequency. "But remain vigilant."

Adamcik had no intention to do otherwise. He knew the cost of complacency.

Their first objective of consequence was Lubawka. Aside from a small train depot here, the town was unremarkable, or seemed so from a distance.

People watched the tanks rumbling through town with mute shock, eyes and cheeks wet with tears. Adamcik wasn't sure if they knew whose side they were on, he wasn't sure they cared.

The Czechoslovakian tankers drove with care, paying attention for ambush or betrayal, but the Poles simply watched. Women clutched their children close and the elderly stood by, apparently resigned to fate.

"Where are the men?" Janco said.

There were no men, certainly no military-age men anyway. They discovered why as they passed the train depot.

The men of Lubawka lay in heaps around the empty train tracks. They'd been gunned down en masse after being brought here. They had their hands bound with white plastic ties that stood starkly against their dark clothes and blood.

"Driver, stop," Adamcik said, standing up higher in the turret. *Milacku* rocked to a halt, nearly pitching Adamcik out of the turret hatch. He stared in disbelief at the scale of the slaughter here. Not one, not a dozen, a hundred. Maybe two hundred or more dead lay like a great carpet of corpses. This, he reasoned, was the cause of the locals' shock and horror.

Janco swore, a mix of anger and horror. "They killed them all."

Nearly all of the dead were civilians, but mixed into their number Adamcik saw a handful in Polish uniform. Deserters.

"The bastards," Janco growled, pounding a fist on *Milacku*'s roof. "The bastards!"

The tanks of Tiger company rumbled by, commanders and crew craning their necks to gawk at the murder on display.

Ambroz's tank slowed to a stop nearby and he likewise stared at the dead.

Adamcik looked at him pointedly, as if to remind him who the real murderers were.

Ambroz met his gaze, but only for a moment before looking away and continuing on.

Adamcik got back inside the tank and toggled his radio. "Tiger One to Tiger Six."

"Go ahead, One."

Adamcik swallowed. "All the men in Lubawka are dead," he said, voice trembling with anger. "Over."

The radio hissed silence. Vesely didn't ask for him to repeat, he knew it was true. "Copy, One. We will notify battalion command. Please continue on and maybe we can stop more of this."

"One copies. Out." Adamcik said through clenched teeth. He flipped on his intercom. "Go."

The driver went, tank lurching into gear and back onto the road.

Things were not better outside of Lubawka. Just past the town limits they found a trio of dead women, their clothes scattered in the field around them. Beyond them was a cow pasture, the animals all dead on their sides save one which limped around, bellowing in pain, blood running down its flank.

Adamcik's knuckles were white from gripping the tank hatch as they reached the next dot of human habitation, Przedwojow.

The village was in flames. Fire climbed the sides of houses, spreading from one to the next. A handful of people loitered in the fields outside of the town. Some wailed, some wept, others stood by in shock. There were not as many of them as there should have been.

There was a cluster of houses and shops at their next objective, a crossroads.

"Tiger One Six, mines ahead," Coufal said. He sounded shaken.

"In the town?" Adamcik asked.

"Everyone is dead," Coufal replied, a non-answer.

Adamcik arrived and saw that it was so. Artillery-deployed mines lay scattered across the roadways and the town. The inhabitants were likewise scattered and motionless, hastily killed by the retreating Soviets. The gas station was a blackened shell, its underground tanks had apparently been touched off all at once.

Two nasty words explained all this destruction though they couldn't adequately capture the human cost of such an inhuman policy.

Scorched earth.

If the Soviets couldn't have it, then no one would. They were burning Europe to the ground as they withdrew.

"Tiger Six, this is Two Six," Ambroz said over the radio. "The crossroads has been mined, over."

"Affirmative Two Six. We will have the Germans bring up

mine clearing engineers. Is the road north clear?"

"Yes," Ambroz said.

"Affirmative. Proceed north and circle around the minefield. The fields should be clear."

"Two Six copies."

"Tiger One will support," Adamcik added, directing his platoon to follow behind Ambroz.

The T-72s of the Legion went offroad, plowing great ruts across wheat and rye fields. They churned the earth to mud as they groped toward a distant treeline and the open road beyond.

A sabot round caught Ambroz's only remaining platoonmate in the engine. There was a flash of flame and it ground to a stop. The crew scrambled free of the narrow hatches, throwing themselves to the earth and crawling away.

"Enemy ahead!" Ambroz said. His tank fired smoke grenades, spreading them around to form a gauzy screen.

"Move to engage," Adamcik told his platoon. "Coufal, go right!"

"Affirmative!"

The tanks wheeled and advanced in a cumbersome, muddy ballet.

Adamcik tried to scan for targets through the haze from Ambroz's smoke screen. He saw nothing amidst the green hedgerow hundreds of meters distant. "Tiger Six, contact ahead! Enemy ambush, enemy armor and—"

Another round screamed by. Adamcik felt its passing before he realized what had happened. It felt as if death itself had just glanced at him. He couldn't think. All that went through his mind was the thought of escape, to leap from this tank and run for safety.

"Target!" Janco cried triumphantly. He fired and *Milacku*'s main gun boomed.

Something exploded in the tree line, but now more enemy fire came at them. An ATGM buzzed bumblebee-like toward the Czechoslovakians before veering away at the last minute as Ambroz fired a high explosive shell at its launch point.

Vesely was buzzing in Adamcik's ear but he couldn't think

straight, fear gripped his mind. He acted on instinct. They were caught in a killing ground. "Reverse! Driver reverse! Tiger One, deploy smoke and withdraw!"

They would be lucky to escape. T-72s could not shoot with any accuracy on the move, and so couldn't run and fight at the same time. To stay would be death, to run would be death.

Janco fired again to no result as *Milacku* started grinding laboriously back the way they'd come.

They were all going to die here.

Adamcik caught a glimpse of Ambroz's tank in the smoke, still motionless, turret tracking. It fired and something else exploded in the treeline ahead. He toggled his frequency to Ambroz's channel. "Withdraw! Ambroz, Tiger Six gave order to retreat!"

"Save yourself, Adamcik," Ambroz replied. He sounded distant, calm. "I will hold them." His tank boomed again to punctuate his words. A moment later his gunner and driver clambered out of their hatches and set off at a run, leaving Ambroz alone in his vehicle, immobilized but able to fight on by virtue of his autoloader.

Shellfire started to fall like a sprinkle before a thunderstorm. Adamcik wasn't sure whose guns were firing because it fell indiscriminately. Rounds burst in the treeline and among the tanks of Tiger Company.

"Ambroz!" Adamcik shouted, knowing his old lieutenant would not obey him.

"I will show you," Ambroz replied, voice strained. "I will show you a true soldier." His tank spoke again for the last time. A round ripped into the turret, setting off the ring of shells within. Ambroz was dead in an instant. His tank's turret flew into the air, propelled on a jet of flame.

Adamcik jammed the smoke launcher button and in seconds lost sight of Ambroz's burning tank, concealed by a curtain of smoke. He sat back hard, stunned, drained. In that moment he realized Vesely was still talking, his voice desperate, harried, struggling to bring any semblance of order to the fight.

"One Six," Adamcik said. "Ambroz is dead. He saved us." The

smoke ahead glowed red with the fire of burning tanks. "Tiger One is withdrawing."

28

Walking through Budapest's deserted, black metro tunnels was like venturing into some ancient and forgotten catacomb. Rayburn's boots crunched gravel, his feet occasionally striking the rail, causing him to stumble and swear.

The Marines walked through the dark, guided only by a single, red-lensed flashlight. It was enough light to vaguely see their path and continue forward, but not enough to keep from tripping.

Aside from the occasional oath or soft command, no one spoke. They were all imagining the same thing, a Soviet platoon lying just ahead, watching them with rare—but not non-existent—Soviet-made night vision goggles, painting them with invisible infrared beams. Their fingers squeezing on triggers as the Americans obligingly blundered straight into a fight, blind and helpless.

It was a small consolation that they wouldn't be dying alone. Eichmann's platoon led nearly a full company of Hungarian resistance fighters armed with an eclectic mix of Soviet gear, most of it a generation or two out of date.

As if that wasn't enough, Rayburn kept thinking about the fact that they were walking beneath the Danube River. What if a shell were to plunge through the water and shatter the ceiling overhead? What if these black tunnels were to fill with thousands—millions of gallons of icy water, drowning them in the dark? Rayburn wasn't sure that was even possible, but his mind wanted him to be aware of the mere possibility.

"Man, I wish we had some NVGs," Keyes whispered, seeming to read Rayburn's mind.

"What do you think this is?" Rayburn asked, "the Army?"

"Marines make do," Wierzbowski said from behind both of them.

Ahead of them Eichmann hissed for silence.

Over the sound of feet, Rayburn became aware of distant rumbling. Dust sometimes filtered down from the ceiling as a heavy shell burst overhead nearby. He realized then that they were beyond the Danube and now on the opposite bank.

"This platform will take us to the surface," Toth whispered to Eichmann, pointing ahead.

"Hold up," Eichmann said, holding up a fist.

The Marines all took a knee. The Hungarians drew short around them.

Toth was about to ask why until he saw it, flickering red light ahead. "Civilians," he whispered. "Refugees."

Eichmann shook his head. "That's a flare."

Rayburn's adrenaline began to pump through his veins, driven by fear and the feeling that they were about to be in the shit.

The lieutenant gestured silently and brought his Marines up. "Get in close, no sound. Quiet." He peered at each of them in the dark. "They have no idea we're here."

"What if it's Hungarians?" Rayburn asked.

"Then we don't kill them," Eichmann said. "Let's go."

The Marines advanced with as much quiet as they could muster, moving in two parallel columns, one at each end of the subway tunnel. By following the cold concrete walls they were able to move without any light save the dim flickering ahead.

In a few moments Rayburn heard voices. He couldn't tell Hungarian from Russian, but it sounded hurried. Tense. A group of men working.

He moved up with his squad, crouching and peering over the lip of the platform.

A platoon of Soviet infantry were here, some carrying flares, others carrying canvas satchels. Two groups of them were talking heatedly, the others milling around nervously. One of those waiting glanced toward the platform and locked eyes with Rayburn.

The Soviet gasped and was cut down by rifle fire.

"Kill em!" Eichmann shouted as his Marines laid into the unsuspecting enemy.

The platform strobed with light as muzzle flash competed with the sputtering flares the Russians dropped.

The Soviets, to their credit, reacted quickly, firing wildly back or diving for cover. They fought hard, but even so didn't stand a chance.

In seconds it was over.

"That all of them?" Wierzbowski asked.

Keyes jumped up onto the platform and started checking the dead, kicking them and flipping them over. "Wasted," he said.

Rayburn and the others climbed onto the platform, bringing the Hungarians up. "The hell were they doing down here?" Rayburn asked.

Eichmann pulled open one of their satchels and withdrew a bundle of plastic explosive. He set his jaw, realizing that if they'd tried this just a few minutes later they might have been buried alive down here. "Closing the barn door after the cows got out." He put the explosives back carefully. "Let's get the fuck out of here."

This movement wasn't conducted in a vacuum. The under-Danube attack was timed to coincide with a helicopter assault across the river and a demonstration to fix the enemy's attention.

Rayburn and the assault force stormed out of the metro and spread out like poison in a vein, quickly securing a foothold so that more infantry could be brought over. The Marines cleared building after building, establishing a safe zone near the half-demolished Erzsebet Bridge in the heart of downtown Budapest.

Rayburn crouched beside a baroque apartment building, watching as a bridge-layer closed the gap over the missing span and opened it to a flow of armored vehicles.

"That gottem!" Keyes called triumphantly.

The Marines cheered as the cavalry arrived, racing into Budapest to drive the last vestiges of the Soviet army from this place.

The enemy wasn't content to go quietly.

Artillery howled down.

"Cover! Cover!" Eichmann shouted.

The world came to pieces.

Rayburn felt himself get thrown into someone else, knocking them flat. He tried to get back up when a second wave of overpressure hurled him into a wall. He curled into a small ball, screaming silently as artillery fire systematically demolished downtown Budapest in a desperate bid to hit the newly-prepared bridge.

The barrage could not have lasted longer than a minute before tailing off dramatically, silenced or surprised by NATO counter-battery fire or loitering attack aircraft.

Rayburn lifted his head and saw Keyes clutching his side and rolling on the sidewalk.

"Corpsman! Goddamit!" Keyes shouted through clenched teeth.

Rayburn reacted instantly, scrambling over to his friend, ripping open his medical bag. "I got you, I got you."

"Doc," Keyes said. "I'm hit bad, is this it? Is this it?" He was surprisingly lucid for someone whose intestines were being kept inside only by his blood-slick hand.

Rayburn was surprised by this. He was also surprised that he didn't feel sick. He thought maybe he was too scared. "Shut up," he said, saying the first thing that came to mind. "You're fine."

"Fine?!" Keyes repeated, equally shocked and pained.

This time Rayburn ignored him, quickly treating the wound, probing around for split and perforated capillaries and veins, spilling blood across the ground, dark and bright.

"Oh fuck," Keyes groaned, laying back his head as shock began to set in. "Oh fuck, I'm gonna puke."

"Wake up," Rayburn shouted. "Wake up! Stay with me, Keyes."

"Oh God," Keyes pleaded.

Rayburn had stopped most of the bleeding and was now struggling to pack the wound with gauze. "Almost done," he said, then he heard the howl of a fresh wave of artillery. "Ah shit." He hunched forward, covering Keyes's body with his. There was nothing more he could do. Keyes was one of his Marines, and he would be damned if he let him die.

Shells burst nearby, smashing into buildings and splashing down in the river. One exploded overhead and whipped a beehive of shell splinters down the street. Rayburn heard someone cry out at the same time he felt pain streak across his back. He then realized he was the one who screamed. The sharpness of the pain subsided quickly, leaving a throbbing red burn which seemed to radiate, filling him like a fluid. "Shit," he said. When the shelling stopped he reached around and touched his back, feeling both pain and wet. He felt suddenly dizzy and slumped to his side beside Keyes. "Corpsman!" Rayburn's voice gave out. "Corpsman..." his vision began to dim and his hands felt tingly.

Suddenly Rivers was there. "I'm here. I'm here, Rayburn."

"Doc's hit," Keyes said, speaking through clenched teeth. "Saved me."

Rayburn felt River's hands on his back, felt the icy sting of anti-septic and the painful pressure of bandages. He tried to cooperate but kept crying out. Rivers was saying something comforting, but he couldn't focus on it. Only when Rivers finished did his sense return to him.

"Gonna be alright, Rayburn," Rivers said. "I think this one's sending you home."

"How bad?" Rayburn asked.

"You're in one piece," Rivers assured him.

Nearby, someone else called out in Hungarian, drawing Rivers away.

Rayburn and Keyes lay side by side on the sidewalk. Keyes on his back, Rayburn on his side. They watched Italian armored vehicles crossing the bridge one by one.

"Made it to the end," Keyes said.

Rayburn hurt too much to say anything. He closed his eyes and counted every agonizing second before he could be carried out of this godforsaken hellhole.

29

Strelnikov thought that his captivity might almost have been bearable if he did not have to share a train compartment with Turgenev. That smug, smirking bastard had always had it in for him since the early days in Germany. He'd always resented Strelnikov's passion and ability. As a stiff-necked product of the machine he hated to see a maverick surpass him. Now Strelnikov's only recourse was to stare silently out at the muddy Belorussian countryside as the train chugged steadily eastward, packed mostly with severely wounded men returning home.

Strangely, he had no fear. No fear of judgement or repercussion. The Soviet Union was not well known for having fair courts or a robust legal system, but Strelnikov believed in the court of public opinion and he knew he would be vindicated wholly. If it came to a contest between Gradenko's faux populism or Strelnikov's celebrity with the common man he had no doubts where a war hero would rank against a disgraced politician. All that bothered him was the lost time, the wasted effort, and Turgenev's damned smirk.

The train car clicked rhythmically and rapidly as its wheels crossed the gaps between rails. Normally it was pleasant, but Strelnikov was in no mood to feel pleasant. It grated on him.

The train neared Biyalistock. Through the window, verdant fields gave way to suburbs, homes, telephone poles, and apartment blocks. Soon the industrial waste of a train yard rolled by.

As Strelnikov looked outside, he saw the train pass by a main battle tank parked beside the tracks. Its crew watched the train glide by from their open hatches. Then they passed another tank. Then another, and another. A whole platoon watching the rails. As the train passed by, Strelnikov thought he saw one of the tanks spew exhaust and rumble forward to drive onto the track behind them.

He pressed his face to the glass, trying to look back but he lost sight of it.

The train blew its whistle and brakes screamed. The whole car lurched.

"What is that?" Turgenev blurted, grabbing onto the overhead luggage rack for stability.

"I do not know, Comrade General!" The staff officer sharing the cabin with them said.

"Go find out!" Turgenev retorted.

The lieutenant staggered from the car, struggling to stay on his feet as the train rapidly decelerated. The train shuddered, continuing to slow to a halt in the station. Strelnikov saw more and more soldiers and military vehicles gathering in the yard around them.

Men lined the tracks in combat gear, weapons ready. These were men Turgenev obviously wasn't expecting to be here by the look of fear on his face.

Rebels? Strelnikov couldn't be sure. But when the train finally hissed to a stop, he saw junior officers bark commands and infantry squads stormed onto the train, rushing out of view as they boarded it.

As he watched he saw one of the nearest tanks was a new model T-72BU. He knew of only one division which had been issued these new weapons. The Zagreb Guards.

A rifle report rang in the train, once, then twice. Turgenev went for his sidearm just as the cabin door was thrown open. Lying in the aisle outside was his lieutenant, dead. Standing over him was a sergeant with a scowl and an AK-74 levelled at Turgenev.

The general blanched, hand frozen on the handle of his Makarov.

"Draw that weapon and die," General Sidorov said, stepping

past the sergeant. He reached out and drew Trugenev's pistol from its holster. Its former owner could only stand chagrined.

"What do you think you are doing?" Turgenev blurted.

Sidorov ignored him and looked to Strelnikov. "We saw the broadcast," he said. "We heard the traitor. When I found out you were being taken by rail I set an ambush."

Strelnikov could hardly believe it and so he only sat mutely, staring back at his subordinate. Sidorov the Loyal.

"I would sooner die than see you hauled off in chains, comrade," Sidorov said, extending the pistol grip first, toward him.

Strelnikov rose slowly and accepted the weapon, feeling its deadly weight.

"Mishkin has betrayed us," Sidorov continued. "He is working with the traitors."

This came as a blow even more severe than his arrest. Strelnikov could scarcely believe it was true. Mishkin, his oldest companion, the man he had trusted with everything.

"It's all unravelling," Sidorov said. "We must stop it."

Strelnikov looked over at Turgenev who frowned deeply at him.

"You cannot fault me for following my orders," Turgenev said sharply.

"Unlike you, Turgenev," Strelnikov said. "I make my own orders." He raised his pistol and shot the general between the eyes. The gunshot was deafening in the confines of the train cabin.

Turgenev's body fell back limp, shivering and twitching spasmodically where he lay on the seat. His bright blood oozed out to stain the seat and drip onto the carpet.

Strelnikov waved the pistol dismissively. "Get him out of here."

A pair of soldiers moved forward to drag the dead general from the train.

"Should we kill the others?" Sidorov asked, meaning Turgenev's men.

"No," Strelnikov said. "They were following orders. Unlike Turgenev, I cannot fault them for that. They will join us or they will be forced to obey orders and face the consequences."

"Very good." Sidorov accepted the pistol when Strelnikov handed it back to him. "What now?"

"Now we must reassert order. Clear the train and board your men. Everything which can be boarded by rail must be taken. We will need it all. Have we heard from any of the others?"

Sidorov shook his head.

"Send word to Rastayev to hold the Oder at all costs. I want Kozlov to assume command of the Danube front. Lukin must return to Moscow with whatever force he can spare, a rifle regiment perhaps. Who else do we have?"

"Dmitriyev in Leningrad," Sidorov said. "He reported a force of new inductees and reservists mutinied and joined with the traitors."

"Dmitriyev," Strelnikov repeated thoughtfully. "He will have to bring everything he can and meet us in Moscow."

"Surely we can handle the traitors alone," Sidorov said.

"I will not underestimate my opponent again," Strelnikov replied, moving past Sidorov and walking the aisle of the train. It was packed with his men who crowded aside, watching with awe as he passed. "We must return to Moscow, dissolve the General Assembly, purge it of traitors and Western lapdogs." He thought unhappily of his friend Mishkin. "All loyal soldiers in the district must congregate there at once before it is too late." He stopped at the head of the train car and turned back to Sidorov who tailed him loyally. "Gather your men. We march for Moscow."

30

"The general secretary's son?" President Bill "Hoss" Dewitt asked, glancing up from the memo in his hands. Behind him, clear, bright summer light filtered into the oval office from the windows.

"That's right," Alan Hart, his secretary of state replied. "We flew him in from Havana by way of Guantanamo Bay."

"Top secret," Dewitt's chief of staff broke in.

"Top secret," Hart agreed. "Hush hush. All because of a telex we received from Moscow."

"Moscow," Dewitt repeated, still grappling with this information. His presidential ambitions had never been secret. The Senate was nice, but he'd wanted more. Now he had it, a gift handed down unexpectedly by Bayern before he ran off to play sailor in the Mediterranean. Granted, his elevation from Vice President to President hadn't been quite as unexpected as Bayern's had been, but it still left his head spinning and of course now he felt a bit like the cat that caught the canary. Maybe this was why Bayern was so quick to hand back the reins. "And Gradenko's the guy in charge now? I can't keep all these damn Ruskies straight. Too many 'Skies,' 'Ovs,' and 'Evs,' and 'Enkos.'"

"We thought so," Hart continued, rubbing the back of his neck ruefully. "Only they keep shifting things over there. He took over after Karamazov but it looks like the Premier—General Strelnikov—is calling the shots."

"Democracy in action," Dewitt mused sarcastically. "So the old man sent his kid? This some back door diplomacy or what?"

"Looks like it," Hart agreed. He sat on the arm of a white upholstered couch which dominated the center of the room.

Across from him stood Dewitt's chief of staff and an anxious, pasty-faced Russian translator, part of the state department sworn to secrecy and ushered in here at the last minute.

"Alright," Dewitt said finally. "Reckon we'll play ball. Send him in."

For all his time in politics and his lofty office, Dewitt had never met a Russian before, not a real one anyway. He wasn't sure what to expect exactly, but it wasn't the meek, round-faced young man escorted into the Oval Office by an unsmiling Marine guard.

The man—the Soviet—seemed extremely uncomfortable, trying to look everywhere at once and constantly wringing his hands.

Dewitt stood and rounded his desk with a warm smile. "Dewitt," he said. "Friends call me 'Hoss.'" He offered a hand.

The translator relayed all this automatically in rapid Russian, startling the young man. He blinked first at the interpreter and then at Dewitt before clasping the hand and shaking firmly.

"Horse," he said, failing to hide his bewilderment. "Good. I am Vlad. Vladimir Gradenko. I speak English good enough, I think." He gave an apologetic glance at the interpreter who in return looked questioningly at Dewitt who shrugged.

"Works for me, have a seat Mr. Gradenko and why don't you tell me what it is you're doin here and why it's gotta be you with this message."

Vladimir sat, but looked no less confused. "Me?" he repeated.

"Y'all've got a whole embassy staff," Dewitt returned placidly. "If they hadn't all run home they'd be the ones with this message. Why'd your daddy send you?"

"Only I can be trusted," he said, deadly serious. "I am here because to show you that this is genuine."

"What's genuine?" Dewitt continued. He'd heard the rumors of course, the protest in Moscow, but hard news was rare. He wanted to hear the words.

"Peace," Vladimir stammered. "The peace between us. The end to war. We wish now to negotiate an end to this foolishness."

Dewitt looked at Hart, his polite smile frozen on his face. "Hell of a lot of folks died. Don't know I'd call that 'foolish.'"

To his surprise, Vladimir didn't mince words or back down. "That only makes it more foolish, yes? You do not want this war. We do not want this war."

Dewitt caught Hart shifting uncomfortably out of the corner of his eyes but he spoke for everyone. "If you didn't want it then you didn't have to start it."

"A mistake," Vladimir said, not yielding. "A mistake we make. And I think you make mistakes too."

Dewitt thought of Bayern's bomber raid on the Soviet shipyards and couldn't argue with it. "So what are you asking for? In concrete terms."

"Cease fire," Vladimir said. "Freeze the battle lines and then negotiations. We may make peace."

"You're going to have to pardon me for being skeptical," Dewitt said. "Seems like these peace jitters are coming out just as soon as we're making real ground in Europe. Way I see it, this war's ending whether you're ready for it to or not."

The shock and horror in Vladimir's expression was unmistakable. "But... this war is mistake."

"Vladimir," Dewitt said patiently. "I hope you won't take offence, but you Russians like talking outta both sides of your mouth at once."

At Vladimir's confusion, the interpreter supplied a few words of Russian and the young man blanched. "Yes... but..." After a moment of stammering he found some new well of resolve within himself. He looked down at the carpet, clenched his jaw, and finally looked back at Dewitt. "We want to change. It is time for change. Time for..." he was lost for a word and spoke quickly to the interpreter. Dewitt only caught one word. "*Glasnost.*"

"Transparency," the interpreter supplied.

"Transparency," Vladimir repeated. "To be new. To make a new start." Before Dewitt could speak he added. "Please."

Now that was a word Dewitt had never heard come from the mouth of a Soviet or one he remotely associated with their diplomatic style. He swallowed his next automatic reply and spent a moment in thought. He had to remember that millions of lives hung in the balance here. A mistake, a misstep would ruin countless lives.

"Please," Vladimir said again, seeing the effect the word had. "We want no more war between us. No more death. My father, my people, we want peace."

"That may be true," Dewitt said finally. "But... even if I believed you, there's a big obstacle here."

"Obstacle?" He understood the word, but didn't follow Dewitt's meaning

"Strelnikov."

The word made Vladimir grimace, teeth set in dismay.

"Let's say I sign a treaty with your daddy. It isn't at all clear he'll be the one sitting in the Kremlin by the end of the summer. I don't have to tell you that it would look really bad for both of us if we make a deal with the loser. A deal that no one honors."

"Strelnikov is traitor," Vladimir said, confused. "He is be arrested."

"That's not what my intel says," Dewitt replied coldly. "Sounds like your boy Strelnikov cut himself loose and is raising Cain, making a play of his own and by our estimation, he's the one with all the tanks."

Vladimir looked sick.

"Look," Dewitt said with a heavy sigh. "I wish I could make a deal with you, Vlad. I really do. The sad truth is that until your daddy can prove he's the de facto ruler of the Soviet Union then we're going to have to assume that he isn't."

Vladimir could not argue with the logic, no matter how much he wanted to. The remainder of his visit was short and perfunctory, but when he left, Dewitt found himself suddenly thinking less about the war and more about peace.

"Can we trust him?" Hart asked, looking uncertainly at his chief.

"Probably not as far as you can throw him," Dewitt answered, staring at the door that Vladimir had just passed through. "The whole thing stinks of commie intrigue. But..."

"But," Hart agreed. "We've got a big push going in on the Oder today. They make it across and this whole ceasefire thing might be a moot point."

Dewitt drummed his fingers on the desk. "We'll have to play wait and see."

31

The brilliant warm day was marred by the thunder and crash of shells dropping on the east bank of the Oder River. NATO artillery barrages were short but sharp, highly concentrated like an explosive crescendo.

Vance watched from a distance, aided by the magnification of his tank's optics. The shells mostly airburst with puffs of gray and black, scything the air with splinters. This first volley was followed by a second flurry of high explosive rounds. These bloomed with fire, ripping into the earth, digging for enemy entrenchments.

Beside him, Waxman licked his lips nervously, eyes fixed on his own sights as they watched. No one spoke, the only sounds were the high whine of the engine and the rumble of the guns.

Crocodile Tears sat hull down, half-hidden by brush on the west bank. To their left was the tumbled ruin of a house, to their right, a shrapnel-riddled tractor lying on its side by the crater they sheltered in. The rest of the company was arrayed in either direction, all of them out of sight, ready to move up at Vance's word.

At first, he had been worried the enemy might spot his tank lurking at the edge of their vision, but as the bombardment tore into them that fear faded. The Soviets had their hands full.

Vance let out a shaky breath, eyes searching the dust and smoke for any sign of the enemy. Cutthroat Company stood ready to attack, knowing that their lives were in his hands and depended on his judgement made his pulse race his hands clammy. He was intensely aware of the armored walls of *Crocodile Tears* closing around him.

Vance swallowed. He saw something burning on the far bank, flames licking up from what he'd taken to be a clump of foliage at first. From the dark, oily smoke pouring skyward it must have contained a vehicle of some sort.

"How we looking?" Waxman asked, his voice a whisper. He was well aware of Vance's responsibility here and maybe felt the need to remind his commander of his job.

Vance saw nothing. Nothing saying he should go in, and nothing saying he should not. It was his call. Well, it was partly his call. His orders were to cross here and attack unless the bombardment seemed ineffective. He saw no evidence that it *wasn't* effective.

"Sir?"

Vance didn't answer. He checked his radio frequencies, verifying he was connected to battalion HQ. "Cuttrhoat to Hammermill, Effect looks good. I see one vic burning. Drop smoke, over."

"Copy, Cutthroat, wait one."

Two minutes later more shells whistled in. Instead of exploding, these bloomed in puffs of white, gauzy smoke. The smokescreen settled like a veil over the enemy, erasing them from sight and likewise hiding Vance's men.

It was time.

"Sable," Vance said. "Go." His voice cracked. "You're clear to attack."

"Sable copies, rolling!" Captain Kelly returned.

Vance looked left and watched the lozenge-shaped M113 APCs crawl out of cover like primordial monsters. Their engines roared as they crossed in the open to the Oder.

The enemy was ready. A Soviet artillery barrage answered the American one. Shells peppered the ground, bursting across Vance's front. Most found nothing. One landed directly beside an APC which juddered and came to a stop, smoking and riddled with splinter holes.

Vance swallowed but kept his eyes fixed on Kelly's men.

They reached the river and surged into it. The APCs threw

up water and slowed dramatically, their tracks turning to chug them unsteadily across.

The smoke was clearing. The Soviets sighted their quarry and opened fire. Tracers danced over the water, splashing down around the APCs dangerously.

"Sabot!" Waxman called to Patterson.

The loader jammed the shell into the breach. "Up!"

Waxman fired, blurring Vance's optics for a moment. He tried to ignore his gunner and loader's work, focusing on the company as a whole.

The tanks of Cutthroat hammered away, blasting the enemy, seen and unseen. It was a desperate bid to protect Kelly's men from harm.

It didn't work.

An M113 exploded in a flash of flames the moment it touched land. Another was shot full of holes and began aimlessly circling in place, infantry and crew bailing out of it.

Most of his company made it ashore. Kelly's infantry surged forward, dashing through the open to take what cover they could, clawing out a toehold on the east bank of the Oder.

"Hammermill, Sable is across. Requesting fire support on secondary positions," Vance said, voice high and tense. "Bring it quick."

More shells came, these falling further off, landing on suspected Soviet fallback and reserve positions.

If Kelly's men could eke out a grip, they could bring up reinforcements, expand the bridgehead, and put a pontoon crossing here. After that, Vance's tanks could come over and they could slash across the open Polish countryside.

It wasn't going to happen.

Enemy artillery and mortar fire fell like rain on Kelly and his men. Infantry went down as bursts of shrapnel raked the fields. APCs burned and exploded.

Close range enemy fire kept them pinned, plastering them with machine gun fire and RPGs.

Vance could only watch in horror as his men were

slaughtered.

"Cutthroat, Sable," Kelly called over the radio, fuzzing out slightly as he shouted. "We need a lot more fire support! We're taking fire fro—"

He cut out at the same time an ACPC erupted in flames.

"Kelly? Sable? Say again?" Vance spoke automatically, knowing it was hopeless. Kelly was dead. "Sable," Vance said again, staring at the burning wreck as more shells came in. He closed his eyes tight, breathing hard, refusing to give in to panic. Not this time. When he opened them again he spoke clearly. "Cutthroat Six to all Sable units, deploy smoke and fall back. repeat, deploy smoke and fall back." He gave orders to his tanks to cover the retreat, banging away at the enemy while the scant few surviving APCs ferried back across the river under fire.

Once they'd all returned, Vance noted with horror that some of his infantry were still on the far bank, fighting and dying, unable to come back.

"Cutthroat to Hammermill," Vance said, voice hoarse, feeling nauseous. "Sable's combat ineffective. I've pulled them back across, over."

Esposito responded quickly. "Any chance you can push them over again? If Brawler supports?"

"Negative," Vance said firmly. "No chance. No chance at all. It's a slaughterhouse."

A long pause.

Vance wiped unshed tears from his eyes, hands trembling.

"Hammermill copies. Fall back and regroup. We'll have to let someone else take a crack."

For now, the line was stable. The Soviets held.

32

Many—though not all—of Gradenko's original crop of mutineers from Leningrad had brought their weapons and gear with them. Helmets, bandoliers, grenades, and rifles. When coupled with the wave of disaffected protestors from across Moscow it was enough show of force to cow the scattered defense Strelnikov had left in his absence. The city had been liberated with a minimum of bloodshed. Now though, Gradenko had no illusions about how much blood would be spilled.

"We have already stripped the garrison depot of everything," Mishkin said, walking beside Gradenko as they paced across the open yard of the vehicle pool. The term "vehicle pool" was used loosely here. It was an expansive pavement and gravel lot devoid of everything save for a few ancient and decrepit tanks, trucks, and APCs. Virtually nothing here was in any condition to be used for anything but scrap and parts. The few examples which were close to running condition were being desperately and frantically poured over. a rust-eaten T-55—which hadn't likely seen action since Kruschev was general secretary—sputtered and growled to life. It belched thick black exhaust as the mechanics coaxed breath into the steel beast.

"Heavy weapons," Mishkin continued as they walked. "Tanks, mortars, artillery, anti-air missiles, anti-tank missiles, we have almost none of these things."

Gradenko's eyes were heavy, tired, sunken deep and ringed with black fatigue. He said nothing. Past the empty motor pool was a Stalinist-era building—the depot's armory. It hosted a mob of men, most in civilian clothes, clamoring for weapons.

A few harried NCOs and reservists passed out AK-74s and

magazines. Enterprising bands roamed the halls of the depot's abandoned buildings, scrounging up whatever semblance of kit they could. Some had found old steel pot helmets, the lucky among them even managed last generation body armor, but there was almost none of this. Most wore denim jeans, windbreakers, work jumpsuits, police uniforms, or secondhand fatigues.

"We're distributing what we can," Mishkin said. He paused his relentless march, glancing around in the fading summer light. "But we are going to be crushed."

Gradenko knew it in his heart, but to hear Mishkin say it aloud was brutal all the same. He had no more fear of death, but he had hoped to at least make a lasting change here, something to make a difference.

"The Assembly has issued its edicts, given command to what forces remain but..." Mishkin trailed off.

"But Strelnikov is free," Gradenko said. "And the army will go to him."

"Yes," Mishkin hung his head slightly. "Everyone is afraid to oppose him."

"Not everyone," Gradenko corrected, nodding toward the rag tag group arming themselves and hurrying back to the city on appropriated commuter buses and the handful of army APCs they had at their disposal. "They will fight."

"But most who would join them were already arrested or purged out," Mishkin pressed. "These are... they are civilians. Few weapons and worse leadership. We have no officers."

Gradenko looked at Mishkin, gaze level. "We have you."

"Then we really are without hope," Mishkin replied, shaking his head bitterly. When Gradenko only stared coolly back at him he sighed, running his hands over his face. "Strelnikov's army is now at Krasnoznamensk. Just forty kilometers from the city center. He has tanks, planes, helicopters, and artillery. We cannot win. It cannot be done."

"The tsar was toppled with less," Gradenko returned.

"The tsar was not Strelnikov," Mishkin countered. For all his desire for peace, he could not shake his image of the man. He could not bring Strelnikov off the pedestal he placed him on. Mishkin sighed and studied the scene again, hands clasped behind his back. Beneath his peaked cap, his eyes narrowed and were hard, calculating.

He had been an unassuming staff officer when Gradenko had first met him—a toadie. He had since become something else. A leader. A general. Gradenko hoped that when all this was over, Mishkin would serve as a bridge between the old guard of the military and the new Soviet state he was trying to build.

"We can contest him," Mishkin said with a sigh. "Fight for the suburbs, conduct a delaying action as he draws near to the city. He won't dare to shell Moscow itself. Not even Strelnikov would be so cold. But once he comes across the Moskva River it will all be over. Just as it was done the first time, it will be done again."

"There is hope that the West will agree to the cease fire still," Gradenko said, hoping to bolster his spirits.

Mishkin flashed a humorless smile. "I had always heard that politicians were skilled liars."

"I will make an address to the people," Gradenko said. "This is the last weapon available to me. For all his tanks, bombs, and guns, if Strelnikov does not have the will of the people, then he has nothing."

Mishkin made no reply. He'd seen the "will of the people" crushed beneath tank treads time and again. He held no illusions about how well it would fare this time. "I will lead this army," he said finally. "I will fight this battle." He said the words as if he were convincing himself. When he finally looked back at Gradenko, his eyes shone with tears. "If there is any justice in this world: it will be my last." He snapped his heels together and saluted Gradenko. "Comrade Secretary, if you will excuse me."

Gradenko inclined his head in a slow nod and then watched Mishkin retreat, marching sharply toward a waiting truck. He was to face his old friend and commander on the field of battle in a hopeless defense. That Mishkin fought at all spoke more to the quality of his bravery than a thousand battles in Europe.

Gradenko had his own service to perform. He turned away from the rapidly emptying depot and got into a waiting car, going back to the city. The broadcast studio of Programme One was little different from any other high rise in Moscow. What was different was the city itself. The stakes were clear. Unlike Gradenko's cultivated guest worker protests, no one would sit out this time. The streets were full of people busily erecting barricades, parking buses and trams across wide boulevards and piling benches, cans, cinder blocks, and trash into obstacles to slow the enemy.

Gradenko was guided into the office and taken to a broadcast studio. When he saw the desk and nondescript background he shook his head. "No. I will not sit. I will stand."

The staff of the studio exchanged bewildered glances, but made no argument. His backdrop would be the office itself, the desks, computers, chairs, tables, and staff of this place. They all gathered in curiosity to watch, to hear him speak.

Gradenko did not wear his suit. He wore the plain jumpsuit of a worker still—the clothes he had been given when freed from the gulag. It suited him and his purposes better now. This was not a time for suits and ties. He was counted in and the recording lights came on.

For a heartbeat Gradenko stared at the camera. He had prepared no notes. He'd had no time. Instead of thinking, he spoke straight from his heart. The first word was easy enough. "Comrades." He paused. No, it needed explanation. "I call you all comrades and I mean it in the truest sense. It has become a title, but it did not used to be so. We are all comrades here. Comrades in arms, comrades in purpose, united in belief of a better world. Our nation has long stood against the will of the world, opposed at every turn by fascism, imperialism, and capitalism. Now we face despotism at home." He paused again. "Comrades, this war is unjust. This war was a mistake. I saw the truth at the beginning but I did nothing. I acquiesced to fate and pressure and inertia. 'Stronger men,' I thought. 'Stronger men control the fate of this nation. Not I.' It is perhaps how many of you feel now."

He stared into the black glass lens, willing himself to see the faces of the men, women, and children watching this broadcast. "I was wrong. You are wrong. There is no one stronger. There is only us and only what we do now. This war burns our people and it only serves to destroy. It must end, but for it to end we must remove those who seek to continue it. Those who wish to climb to glory on a stairway of corpses. Comrades, the future is unwritten."

He felt it bore repeating. "The future is unwritten. What happens next could be the gateway to a beautiful socialist future—the promise of true communism." This time Gradenko lowered his voice, speaking coldly. "Or the death of the nation under Bonapartist militarism." A long silence fell over the studio. No one dared utter a word in that painful quiet. "The future lies now with you, comrades, and what you choose. If you do nothing, if you look away, then Strelnikov will have his way. He will turn this country into a military camp and he will fight until there is no one left to fight his war. He will bury his failures beneath mountains of the dead." Gradenko shook his head. "I cannot make you act. I can only tell you what I believe will happen if you do not. How many of our sons, brothers, husbands, and fathers must die before we have had enough? What is the price of prestige and how many souls will satisfy honor?"

He had no answers for these questions. He wasn't sure anyone did. "I cannot tell you what to do," he said again. "I will just tell you what I will do. I will fight, Comrades. I will fight if it is my final act." Gradenko stared out, through Programme One, at the population of the Soviet Union itself. "I will fight." He glanced at the studio director and gave a curt nod. He was done.

The camera went off, the broadcast went out. There was no cheer. There was nothing to cheer for. The history of the Soviet Union—of Russia and those people which fell under its banner—was nothing if not a tragedy. It did no good to see the end coming. "There is a barricade being built outside of this place,"

Gradenko said, speaking to the staff of the studio. "Will you come with me to build it up, comrades?"

33

A persistent sense of deja vu clung to Strelnikov and made him grind his teeth unhappily as he squinted into his binoculars at the suburbs of Moscow. It wasn't snowing, it was hot, but his men idled in a long column along the highway, pointed like a knife at Moscow. It was much the same as the last time he'd come here in anger, the pieces lined up just as they were. But not quite.

This time they were opposed much more methodically, the resistance was armed and organized.

Through his binoculars he saw spots where heavy machinery —bulldozers and excavators—had gouged channels into the highways. Telephone poles were hacked down and lay across the road. Abandoned cars sat arranged into obstacles. It was a path of organized destruction laid out like a carpet all the way up to the city itself.

His men were already at work—engineers laying bridges and plowing obstacles aside. It would slow them, but it would not stop them.

Strelnikov lowered his binoculars and looked back down his column. In the dim light of dawn he saw his best men arranged here. The 121st Zagreb Guards Motor Rifle Division—what was left of it anyway. They'd joined with other units, a handful of regiments and battalions who had flocked to his banner but it wasn't everyone. It wasn't enough.

Strelnikov scowled to himself. Too many people were playing wait and see. There was no reward for "runner up" in politics, and in Soviet politics it was better not to run at all than to finish second.

Strelnikov dropped his binoculars, letting them hang from a

strap around his neck, and started back down the column of tanks. To his right, a quartet of self-propelled artillery pieces arranged themselves and elevated their muzzles, readying the first shots of the preliminary bombardment on the outskirts of the city. It would be a start, but shelling alone couldn't with the day. He could not make a desert of Moscow and call it peace. His legitimacy as a leader depended on taking the city as quickly and painlessly as possible.

Strelnikov found a gap in the waiting line of tanks and crossed the road, ignoring the wide-eyed stares of his soldiers. Ahead was Lukin's headquarters—a parked BTR surrounded by staff. Strelnikov heard the high buzz of a radio set playing over open speakers.

"Lukin, you must withdraw your men before it is too late." It was a familiar voice made alien by its tone. Mishkin, Strelnikov's right hand, now standing opposed to him. His words were cold, voice pleading. "Tell your men to retreat, Do not do this," Mishkin said.

Strelnikov stopped within sight of the radio. He saw Lukin leaning over it, his face a mask of grief, eyes as sharp as the edge of a knife while he listened.

"No matter what happens next, you and I will both die," Mishkin pressed. "What is the point of all this? Who will win? You understand that everyone will be killed. Withdraw your men. Have pity for their mothers. Have pity for all your men. Withdraw."

Lukin drew a hand across his eyes, wiping away tears and uncertainty. When he looked up again, he caught Strelnikov's glance. Without looking away he toggled on his microphone. "I cannot give that order."

"Lukin," Mishkin pressed. "With all my heart I hope that you live through this, but you should leave. Just turn around and leave. If you come here, come as a guest. Let us talk."

Lukin hardened himself, looking away from his commander. His brow furrowed in anger. "I have no choice. I have my orders, and I will obey them." He cut the radio off before Mishkin could make a reply and buried his face in his hands, lost in grief.

Strelnikov moved to stand beside him.

When Lukin looked up again he turned his face to Strelnikov. "Will you speak with him? Ask him why he has betrayed us? Try to make him surrender?"

Strelnikov shook his head. "He will not yield." He did not understand why Mishkin had turned on him, but he knew him well enough to know that his old friend's mind was set. "He is a soldier like us." There was no room for argument there.

"What now?" Lukin asked. For all his merits, for all his bravery, he did not have the strength to give the command he knew came next, the one that Strelnikov now had to give. This was why it fell to him and no one else.

"We will attack. Ready your men."

Lukin nodded, looking momentarily stunned. He shook his off quickly and barked orders to his staff who went instantly into action.

"We have a rare blessing," Strelnikov said finally. "All of our enemies are gathered here now in the open. It will be as it was in Warsaw in 1989. We can secure our position with one sweep of the saber. Go to your men and lead them in."

"Yes, Comrade General." Lukin saluted and Strelnikov returned it.

He watched his subordinate mount the APC as it roared to life. All around them the tanks and tracks of the 121st Zagreb Guards girded themselves for war. Moments later Strelnikov's artillery began to speak. Coughing booms echoed back from the suburbs ahead where shells burst, demolishing outlying buildings and scattering erstwhile resistance. As the rumble of the guns increased, the tanks and APCs set forward, advancing on the Third Rome.

34

Ash fell like snow. Smoke blanketed the skies over the city, transforming the summer streets of Moscow into a hellish wintry scene. The Shelepikhinsky Bridge which spanned the Moskva didn't have the storied past of the Bolshoy Moskvoretsky at Red Square, but was no less vital. In an ordinary situation, this bridge could have been demolished to deny it to the enemy. But this was far from an ordinary situation. The fact was that the pro-Assembly forces had no demolition charges and even if they had, they had no engineers to set them.

Mishkin didn't need binoculars to see the suffering of his men on the southern side of the Moskva. People were gunned down in the streets like animals. Artillery fell among them like rain. Bursting shells blanketed the open road, smothering everything in clouds of dust, smoke, and beehives of shrapnel.

A handful of stunned, wounded men staggered clear of this nightmare only to then be chopped down by automatic fire.

Strelnikov's tanks emerged from the smoke like demons crawling out of hell. A Soviet banner—shredded by shrapnel—fluttered from the radio mast of the lead tank. Its coaxial machine gun chattered as it spat fire across the river at the next defense line.

Mishkin pressed the radio receiver tight to his ear, shouting over the return fire from the men around him.

"Affirmative, all combat units withdraw north of the Moskva! The enemy is here. Expect a crossing within five minutes."

A few weak acknowledgements came back. More damning was the silence. So many fighters already lost. It was a miracle they fought on at all, but what other trait was the Soviet fighting man blessed with but a superhuman ability to endure the unendurable?

Mishkin handed the radio back and looked around at his staff, such as it was. A handful of lieutenants and a reservist captain. "We have done what we can here." It was the truth, but that made it no more comforting. This bridge was the right flank of their lines. Now everything was undone. Strelnikov's tanks could plow a path straight down the broad thoroughfare of Kalinin Prospekt and be at the Kremlin within minutes. "We have done what we can," he said again. "Withdraw back. Slow them if possible, but sell your lives dearly."

A muttering of agreement dismissed the men. His whole headquarters evaporated quickly. Soldiers gathered weapons and equipment and filtered back, away from the river.

Mishkin stayed. From the parking lot before a high rise on the river he watched the lead elements of Strelnikov's force crossing.

A machine gun resting on the hood of a car abandoned on the road stitched a line of fire across Strelnikov's loyalists. Small figures on the bridge ducked and scattered for cover.

An enemy tank replied, blasting the car and the gunner to ribbons before continuing on.

"Let's go," Mishkin told the few men who remained with him. He picked up a carbine from nearby and moved on foot, jogging along a side street, moving parallel to Strelnikov's axis of advance. The men who moved with him, barely more than a platoon, were mutineers—army conscripts and reservists who still wore their uniforms.

Upon coming to a narrow intersection, Mishkin looked left. He saw Kalinin Prospekt running perpendicular at the end of a tree-shaded street. He saw the small forms of Assembly militia manning barricades there.

He grit his teeth, then turned and started to hurry for the barricades. After all, where else was there to go?

What truly surprised him was when the ragtag group he travelled with turned to follow him.

He stopped himself on the edge of a small park and looked

at them with bewilderment. "This is the end for me," he said. "I release you."

The men exchanged confused looks. "Comrade," one with an RPG on his back said, "you are our officer."

Mishkin might have argued more, but shellfire whistled in, bursting across the mouth of Kalinin Prospekt. If they would fight with him, he would not question that.

Ducking low, they dashed across the street, using a line of parked cars for cover before coming to the main barricade being built up along a bulwark of city buses.

The barricade was held by a thin line of men with rifles and machine guns, banging away at the half-glimpsed enemy.

Many others here—unarmed civilians—formed a human chain, passing more material for the barricade like worker ants. Others dragged away the wounded or ferried in ammo and grenades.

"General Mishkin!" A lieutenant on the barricade waved him over.

Mishkin joined him.

"What news, Comrade General? reinforcements?" The lieutenant asked, eyes wide and desperate. The hope in his voice was painful.

Mishkin looked back at the platoon he'd come with as they fell into place along the barricade. "Yes," he said. "Yes, we are to hold this place at all costs. There is nothing behind us." The lieutenant stared at him blankly so Mishkin put it in simpler terms. "We will fight here and we will die here."

Though the lieutenant didn't speak, the cacophony of battle grew only louder around them. A machine gunner nearby fired off a long, constant string of rounds, the barrel of his weapon smoking.

"I understand," the lieutenant said, taking a moment to rouse himself before seeing to his men.

The tanks came on, moving in a staggered line and spraying gunfire. Molotovs and petrol bombs rained down on them from the buildings above but didn't stop them. Armored vehicles wrapped in cloaks of fire and smoke charged on, crushing abandoned cars beneath their treads.

The Assembly fighters went down in twos and threes, blown apart and cut to pieces. For as brave as they were, they were not unbreakable. Many of them began to melt back.

Mishkin sighted his rifle across the avenue and fired in staccato bursts, trying not to think about the fact that the men he was so desperately trying to kill had been *his* men only days ago.

The soldier with the RPG rose to his knees, shouldering the weapon before dropping it with a grunt and rolling off the barricade.

Mishkin ducked down as return fire ripped into the bus and debris around him.

Burying fear, he crawled to the dead man only to see he wasn't dead. The wounded soldier clutched his face, blood spilling down his cheek. He looked at Mishkin with his remaining eye, wide, afraid, hurting.

Mishkin picked up the RPG and risked a glance over the parapet.

Strelnikov's tanks moved steadily closer, falsely assured of their own invincibility. Mishkin stood, aimed, and fired the weapon. The rocket lanced out, spiraling towards the enemy.

At this range even the tank's armor couldn't save it.

Its ammunition cooked off all at once, the vehicle exploding in a concussive fireball.

A mortar shell burst behind Mishkin and pain flared through his body as he was perforated with shrapnel. He swore and fell onto his back. He only had a few moments of pain before a creeping numbness overcame him. He lay on his back, failing to draw breath as he watched Strelnikov's tanks breach the barricade one by one, crawling over it undeterred. There was no time for regret.

Then he was dead.

35

Helicopters thundered over the smoky Moscow skyline, orbiting the lead elements of the 121st Guards as they probed, like fingers, toward the city's dense downtown.

Strelnikov did not ride at the head of his columns, he could not, but he rode among them all the same, head and shoulders above an open hatch on a BMP grumbling along a corpse-strewn boulevard. The once-pristine faces of the buildings to either side were marred by combat. He'd seen it before in Europe, as had many of his men. A modern city in turmoil no longer shocked him. What was more, he'd seen worse. When he'd seen entire cities laid to waste at a word, a few broken shopfronts did not bother him.

Or it should not have.

A T-80 at the front of the column rammed a city bus which rolled onto its side with a shower of broken glass and a shriek of metal as it was nudged gracelessly aside. The path into the city was paved with the bodies of those who had dared oppose them. Mutineers, rebels, malcontents, revisionists, traitors, terrorists, thugs, radicals, and mercenaries. Strelnikov sneered pitilessly down at them even as he wondered how these people—his people—could betray their nation in the time of greatest need. What stilled him, what bothered him, was that these men had given their lives in service to a desperate and futile cause. Surely they'd known how hopeless resistance would be. So why then did they bother?

The city rang with gunfire, rattling rifles and the reverberating boom of tank guns. It was a fraction of the true firepower at his beck and call. Strelnikov had enough rockets and artillery shells to flatten this city so it would be no different from any of the open-air tombs dotting central Europe behind him.

Kalinin Prospekt was a charnel house, painted with grit, dust, and blood. The rebels of the General Assembly had paid dearly for their attempt to hold him here. But no matter how many barricades they erected, Strelnikov had enough ammo to blow through them.

Ahead, the boulevard narrowed to a single street. High above framed by the buildings, Strelnikov saw the Soviet national flag fluttering against a blue, smoke-streaked sky. Ironic, he thought, that both sides of this abortive civil war claimed the same flag. Maybe if the rebels had lasted longer they might have been forced to adopt a different symbol.

Strelnikov shielded his face from the heat of a tank which was now a funeral pyre for its crew. His men were paying a steep toll for their rapid advance, but it couldn't be helped. If they delayed any more than necessary, the rebels might only grow in strength. What was necessary was a show of raw, brutal power. Really, Strelnikov thought, he might be grateful to Gradenko for obliging him with a willing face to stamp on.

"Comrade General, we have driven back the enemy from the Bolstoy Moresvky Bridge," Sidorov's voice buzzed in Strelnikov's ear.

The news was good, another vital artery to the heart of the city opened up. What troubled him was who delivered the news. It was Lukin's regiment tasked with that objective. He'd been holding Sidorov in reserve.

"What of Lukin?" Strelnikov asked.

Sidorov did not mince words. "Comrade General Lukin is dead. He was with the lead battalion which was eliminated taking the bridge." The shock barely had time to register with Strelnikov before Sidorov continued. "I have moved the reserves up to exploit the gap."

The news of Lukin's death was grim, but Strelnikov could taste victory. The city, he thought, had seen enough death. It was time to end things.

"Press on then," Strelnikov said. "Once the Kremlin is secured we can see about rounding up the rest of the vermin."

A hand tugged lightly on Strelnikov's trouser leg. He looked down into the BMP and a staff officer inside reached up, offering a hand-written message. Strelnikov took it and read quickly, lips skinning back from his teeth. Finally, some good news.

"Comrade Dmitriyev's division has reached the train yard at Khimki and is now deploying," Strelnikov read aloud for Sidorov's benefit. One division would likely be enough to crush the remaining Assembly forces, but more would be needed to maintain order and pry out the lingering malcontents.

"We have them in a vice," Sidorov said, echoing Strelnikov's sentiments. With Dmitriyev coming down from the north and his own forces pressing from the west, they could scissor the city and claim victory.

"I will coordinate with Dmitriyev, provide the disposition of our forces and direct his attack. Focus on securing the Kremlin."

"Yes, Comrade General."

Strelnikov crumpled the paper into a tight ball. It was time to end this. It was time for the final push. It was time, he thought, for a reckoning between Gradenko and Strelnikov.

36

Working the barricade was little different than working in the gulag, at least physically.

The novelty of working alongside the General Secretary of the Communist Party was short-lived for the people in his work gang. Fear was their main motivator now. Fear and hope.

Gradenko was one small part of a long human chain busily passing building material up to the madmen acting as engineers. These special few scrambled along the top of the barricade piling, shifting, and reinforcing things. What had begun as a row of parked cars and buses was now made unrecognizable as more ingredients were added. Tires, chunks of fences, doors, concrete, rebar, and bricks. It was bricks Gradenko passed now. One by one they found their way to the growing pile.

Others dashed to and fro, returning with yet more debris, furniture, scrap wood, cinder blocks, bicycles. The view down the road was blocked by the vast barricade. On the far side: the enemy. This side swarmed with life. The people of Moscow carried rifles and hung banners. Others painstakingly filled empty glass bottles with gasoline, stuffing rags in them and collecting them in sheltered points to be used in the direst emergency.

Direst emergency wasn't far off by the increasing sound of battle.

Gradenko knew that no amount of sentiment and good will could stop a tank. That had been proven in Warsaw, but—but not in Beijing. There, the people of the city—led by courageous college students—had started a chain reaction which had toppled the government. That it was a communist government didn't trouble him, the fact was that the People had won. It was a thought that kept him working.

One of the sentries atop the barricade shouted an alarm and fired off a few ill-aimed shots.

Like flipping a switch, the crowd of would-be revolutionaries scattered, but not in panic. The non-combatants melted back, taking with them what needed to be kept safe as others took up weapons—rifles and petrol bombs—and took places at the barricades. Together they joined their fire against the approaching army.

Gradenko was left momentarily flummoxed, blinking rapidly as he looked around.

"Comrade," a man in a dirty business suit called as he jogged over, head low as the battle grew only fiercer. Now the whine and pang of return fire echoed around them. "Strelnikov's men have crossed the river and reached the Kremlin," he said.

Gradenko didn't know him by name but recognized him as one of Ozerov's staff—one of the men who'd made a living pushing paper now called upon to direct battle.

"Where is General Mishkin?" Gradenko asked. "His mobile force must respond."

"We cannot find him," the staffer said without hesitation. "We have heard nothing on the radio. No one can reach him."

"And the mobile forces?"

The staffer shook his head, ducking as more gunfire cracked above the barricade.

Gradenko blinked rapidly as he took all this in. The city center was lost, what little they'd managed to scrape together of a professional army was all but annihilated by Strelnikov's steel fist. The people of Moscow were nothing but fodder to the enemy army.

"Then it is over."

He turned away from the staffer and found the eyes of the people were upon him. It was a haphazard mixture of government employees, broadcast studio personnel, and private citizens. They'd placed their faith in him, their lives as chips in his bet. It was a gamble he'd lost. Now they looked to him for salvation or comfort.

Gradenko was tired. He was tired of failure. Tired of the hopeless struggle against militancy and autocracy. He had nothing left to give.

"It is over," he said louder, struggling to be heard over the sounds of fighting. All he could do now was send them home.

"Comrade! Comrade Gradenko!" The TV studio manager threw open the door of the station, ducking at the chatter of nearby gunfire. "The radio!" he waved for Gradenko to join him.

The expression he wore was alien to Gradenko. It was hopeful. A smile. Something he couldn't remember the last time he'd seen expressed so earnestly. He followed the man into the station, joined by a growing mob.

The station manager turned the volume up on his radio as loud as it would go.

"—is the end of tyrants," a voice said, broadcasting on the civilian band. It was a voice Gradenko knew. Dmitriyev.

"Strelnikov be damned!" Dmitriyev said, "and all those who follow him! We have come for the People!"

Gradenko blinked away his shock and looked up at the others who erupted into frantic cheering. The celebration was cut short by a fresh exchange of rifle fire. The battle wasn't over yet, but now, with Dmitriyev and his army joined to their cause, it was turning.

37

The tanks of Dmitriyev's army were marked with white triangles, something Strelnikov hadn't recognized the importance of when he first saw them rolling down from the north, smashing through abandoned cars. It was only when they opened fire on his own tanks that he finally understood. They were the markings of the enemy, and Strelnikov had just given them the keys to his positions.

The loyalists—those loyal to Strelnikov—withdrew in chaos and panic. Accustomed to total fire superiority they had given themselves over to raw bloodlust, becoming strung out and over confident. Now the killers became the killed.

A shell burst a T-80 into a flame-spewing pyrotechnic display a block away. Strelnikov's infantry scrambled back from it, covering their heads as they ran. Sparks rained among them. Machine gun fire chopped them down in the open one by one.

"Back! Back!" Strelnikov shouted down into the BMPas the driver reversed, backing into a street lamp which bent and fell like an aluminum pine tree. The lamp smashed the pavement with a harsh sound, but Strelnikov kept his gaze fixed on Dmitriyev's armor, creeping down the street toward them. "Back!"

The BMP fired, the sound deafening Strelnikov. The shell burst on a pro-Assembly tank which slewed to a halt, boiling with black smoke.

The BMP commander deployed smoke, the smoke grenades caroming off the buildings flanking them.

Strelnikov—granted a momentary reprieve—ducked back into the BMP, pushing past a bewildered staff officer, and grabbed his radio. It only took him a moment to raise Sidorov.

"Draw your men back, south of the river and establish blocking positions," Strelnikov shouted. "We need fire support. Artillery."

"I cannot raise them," Sidorov replied, sounding abnormally calm. "I think Dmitiryev has taken our rear. He is on the radio now, saying that we have no choice but to surrender, that I am surrounded."

Strelnikov gawked at the radio mutely, unable to understand what he was hearing.

"Am I to surrender?" Sidorov asked.

"Fight!" Strelnikov exploded, spittle flying. All he'd tried to instill in his men was gone in an instant. "Fight, you damned fool!"

He didn't wait for a response. Somehow he doubted he would get anything intelligent out of Sidorov now. The frequencies for the airforce were dead, or at least they weren't responding to his messages now.

"Comrade, should we surrender?" a staff officer asked, terrified.

Strelnikov pinned him with a hatefilled glance. "Surrender," he said. "And I will kill you myself."

The staff officer's eyes flew to the carbine hanging around Strelnikov's neck and he swallowed.

Strelnikov returned to the hatch, emerging into the open air to survey what he could see with his eyes. If he could gather a company of men, good men, loyal men, the Old Guard–

His thoughts were interrupted by the flutter of helicopter rotors. A pair of Hind gunships banked around an apartment block and lined up with his BMP, taking a moment to identify him. He saw the flash of a missile launch.

Strelnikov heaved himself out of the hatch and leaped from the APC, landing hard, staggering, and stumbling a half dozen paces away before the BMP exploded behind him.

Pain, hot and razor sharp, slashed at his legs and his right arm. Strelnikov cried out, collapsing to the ground to roll onto his back.

The BMP was a rolling fireball, smoke pouring into the sky. A moment later, the two Hinds thudded through the smoke cloud, sending it whirling in all directions.

Strelnikov fought to his feet, or tried to, He cried out again and fell back onto his face. "Help!" he called.

All around him, soldiers fired wildly into the air, tracking the enemy helicopters before scattering in retreat.

"Help me!" Strelnikov demanded. He watched his men throw down their weapons and helmets and melt away, desperate to escape the noose of fire and steel that Dmitriyev had draped around their necks.

"Fight!" Strelnikov pulled himself up onto a park bench, his leg throbbing with pain. "Fight, you bastards!" He felt the carbine slung around his neck clatter against the bench. Seized with insane fury, he took it, reaching for the charging handle.

"Ahh!" He cried out as he lifted his right arm. A bolt of pain shot through him and he saw crimson dripping from his sleeve. Grinding his teeth, Strelnikov tried to load the weapon again but his arm wouldn't cooperate. He cried out again, first in pain, then frustration.

Now dizziness set in. Pain rose up from his legs, seeming to fill his body. He sat back on the bench, feeling rough wood splintered by shrapnel. His gun hung useless.

His men were surrendering in ones and twos. He saw soldiers raising their hands, dropping their weapons, and moving meekly toward Dmitriyev's men. No one would fight any longer. Whatever belief they had in the cause did not stand up to autocannon shells and anti-tank missiles. The Zagreb Guards had finally been destroyed

As the helicopters thundered away, the rumble of tanks made itself known. Strelnikov saw the enemy drawing nearer. The inexorable advance of armor shadowed by leapfrogging infantry. He laughed, dry and cold and lay his head back on the bench. "Then it's over," he said. "Finally."

***

Gradenko hadn't known Mishkin well enough to consider him a friend. They'd both—in theory—dedicated their lives to the same purpose, the service of the Soviet Union. In the end, their beliefs had overlapped enough to fight together, but they had never been friends.

Gradenko stared down at Mishkin's broken body, his face frozen in pain, eyes glazed and dead. He was not a friend, but he was a comrade.

Mishkin was one of dozens—the dead of the short-lived civil war laid out in grim ranks along the rubble-choked roads.

"This is him?" the staffer asked.

Gradenko nodded. "This is him." He couldn't help but think of his wife, of Dragomirov, of all the others lost to this madness. How many people had died for this insanity?

"Thank you," Gradenko nodded to the staffer and turned away. He walked slowly along, staring blankly at the death and destruction wrought on his beloved city. Had it been worth it? Maybe the men and women watching their new leader walk among them thought the same thing. They'd paid a price as steep as he had, sometimes steeper.

The throaty roar of a BTR caused everyone to look up, stop their work, tensing for battle. It would be some time before the army weren't seen as the enemy, Gradenko thought.

The white triangle on the BTR marked it as a friend, part of Dmitriyev's forces. It approached them carefully, weaving carefully the slalom course of barricades and debris.

Gradenko stopped, watching it approach. As it slowed to a halt he saw General Dmitriyev himself riding atop it. He clambered down once it came to a halt and offered a hand to Gradenko who shook automatically.

Dmitiryev's face was surprisingly devoid of joy for a victor. Maybe he too was thinking of the cost. "You have done it," Dmitriyev said.

"We all have," Gradenko corrected. "The lesson the tsars learned has been taught again. The tyrants are crushed."

"Are they?" Dmitriyev asked, eyeing Gradenko warily.

Gradenko nodded. "It is time for a change," he said. "Too long we have stagnated, too long we have relied on the bayonet to keep order. No more. No more."

"Order can only come from a bayonet," Dmitriyev said. "I only hope that it is the People who wield the bayonets."

Gradenko was a politician by trade, a diplomat, but now he felt that he had to be a philosopher. The Soviet government had been razed to the ground. Anyone who might oppose him was dead or hopelessly dishonored. There would be no better time to change things. He only had to decide how that would be done.

"We have captured him," Dmitriyev said. He did not have to explain who "he" was.

Gradenko gave him a curious look, squinting slightly. It wasn't welcome news.

"Wounded but alive," Dmitriyev said. "He wants to speak with you."

Gradenko felt... nothing. He felt only emptiness. He nodded. "I am sure that he does." He has more pressing matters than to spend time on a barbarian.

A silence lapsed, broken by the sounds of people clearing the streets.

"What do we do now?" Dmitriyev asked.

"We negotiate," Gradenko said. "We make peace. Before it is too late."

38

"Targets ahead," Janco said.

Adamcik couldn't recall the last time he'd slept. He hadn't been this exhausted since the initial push into West Germany at the war's start over a year ago. It had been a different world back then. He wondered if the world left after this war ended would be a better one than it was before.

He pressed his face to the padded scope and spotted the movement at once. It was a truck approaching along a country road in the pre-dawn gloom. It was a UAZ, Soviet made. A legitimate target, except this one flew a white flag from its radio aerial.

"Shoot them?" Janco asked, sounding as if he dreaded what Adamcik might say.

Adamcik thought of Ambroz. "No," he said. "No. There is no need for that." He relayed orders to the rest of his platoon arrayed in the cover of a line of trees and brush at the edge of the field, to hold fire. Instead he radioed Bear, asking a squad of infantry to confront the truck.

He watched a minute later as it happened, Czechoslovakians in woodland camouflage carrying American M-16s stopped the truck and a handful of men got out, hands raised. Poles.

Adamcik relaxed a little, feeling more justified in sparing them. He thought of what the Soviets had done to Poles who deserted, tried to surrender, or simply found themselves in the wrong place. For all the myriad of wrongs the Soviets had committed against his people, he doubted that the Polish would ever forgive or forget what they'd endured over a half century of brutal occupation. A century later he imagined they would still harbor a cold hate for the Soviets and Russians.

Bear checked the Poles for weapons, sent them back on foot, and moved the UAZ out of the road.

It was good timing on the part of the Poles. Had they made their desperate bid to escape just a few minutes later, it would have been too late.

Lacking the sophisticated night fighting gear of the rest of NATO, the Czechoslovakians still had to fight as they always had, relying primarily on daylight. The tanks and APCs of the Legion were arrayed in a broad semicircle around the city of Olawa, just south east of Wroclaw. It was their gateway to the Oder and—hopefully—what lay beyond.

"Tiger Company, this is Tiger Six," Vesely said. He broadcast on the company-wide network. "Begin the advance the moment the bombardment lifts."

Adamcik swallowed, his throat dry. He pulled his canteen off the bolt it hung on, took a sip, and put it back. He couldn't see Olawa, but he saw the smoke. Like so much of Poland, it was burning. This time he wasn't sure who was to blame for that, them or the enemy. Whatever the case, previous attacks had been beaten off with heavy casualties. The Germans had tried the day before and fallen back. Now it was the Legion's turn.

After a few tense minutes, the air overhead split with the freight train howl of incoming artillery. Each shell slammed, unseen, into positions ringing Olawa. The barrage was short, sharp, fierce. It lifted quickly.

"Driver forward," Adamcik said and the tank grumbled out of the hedgerow, joined by the others in the platoon, and the company.

The BMPs of Bear followed close behind, infantry ready to throw themselves into the jaws of death if their orders required. Adamcik wondered how many of them would come back intact.

"Tiger Six to all units, cease attack. Repeat, cease attack and withdraw to start positions," Vesely said, blurting the words over the radio.

Adamcik puzzled at it but relayed the command. A moment

later his tank reversed back into the hedges behind them.

"Six, this is One Six, what is the cause for delay?"

It took a few minutes to receive an answer. Adamcik imagined Vesely was confirming his own orders. When he did reply, it wasn't to him directly, it was to the entire company. "All units, this is Six. I have just been told that a ceasefire is now in effect. From now on, we are weapons hold. Fire only if fired on. I need confirmation you understand."

Adamcik felt only confused, but he gave his ascent. "Tiger One Six acknowledged." When he cleared the radio he tried to imagine what this could mean. Clearly NATO was not surrendering, but a ceasefire had to mean negotiations of some sort. Was the end at hand? Or was NATO about to sell out his people for peace? It would not be the first time.

"Adamcik?" Janco asked. "What is it?"

Adamcik shook his head slightly, not sure how to put it into words. The first part was easy. "There is a ceasefire." The second part was much harder. "I think," he said, scarcely believing it himself, "that the war is about to end."

39

From the moment Gradenko stepped off his jet at Vienna international airport it was as if he stepped into another world, an older world, a happier world. The world before the war.

Young men walked the streets.

Gradenko wouldn't have realized how odd that was until he saw it. He couldn't recall the last time he'd seen young men walking openly in Moscow. This terrible war had bled the Soviet Union dry. War's appetite was insatiable. Each class of inductees was smaller and less capable, older and younger. Soon there would be no one left. Which, of course, was precisely why he was here.

His driver, presumably an Austrian, did not speak as he drove the town car through the ancient streets of the city. The street, Museumstrasse, was closed to all non-official traffic. Metal barriers lined the road and it too was lined with the curious faces of onlookers, demonstrators, and press. They passed in a blur, kept at bay by a phalanx of Austrian policemen standing fingertip to fingertip.

The motorcade which surrounded Gradenko's car was ostentatiously large. Motorcycles flanked the car as it followed behind a column of police cars. A plainclothes officer sat silently beside the driver. His suit bulged from an ill-concealed ballistic vest and a submachine gun rested in the footwell between his legs. His eyes never stopped moving and the faint whisper of electronic voices carried from his earpiece.

The risk of violence directed against Gradenko, or anyone else participating in the conference, could not be discounted.

They passed the Vienna Palace of Justice on their left, its Neo-

Renaissance facade harkened back to a golden era of prosperity and enlightenment, a time when Vienna was the center of art, philosophy, and culture. This city once played home to Leon Trotsky, Joseph Stalin, and Adolph Hitler all in the same year. Now its relevance was long past, the Austrian empire had declined first into the Austro-Hungarian empire before collapsing completely, the Hapsburgs sliding into obscurity.

He had to wonder if the same fate awaited Moscow, Russia, and the Soviet Union. Maybe one day, but not today.

They turned left at the Volkstheater, then right at the Natural History Museum, each of these buildings no less impressive than the Palace of Justice.

The motorcade slowed as they approached the palace gates. The street was packed just beyond the police barricades. Cameras flashed and lenses caught in the morning light as they recorded Graenko's vehicle approaching the gate itself, a powerfully built, thick, stone construction whose entrance was marked with square columns. Across the top was an inscription in gold letters.

FRANCISCVS. I. IMPERATOR. AVSTRIAE. MDCCCXXIV

"Look on my works ye mighty," Gradenko muttered to himself, "and despair."

They halted at the gate and a veritable platoon of Austrian military and police surrounded the vehicle, sweeping it for bombs with dogs. His identity was quickly verified, though his beard seemed to confuse them slightly. No doubt he was a far cry from the man in their reference photo.

The car was waved inside and entered the Heldenplatz—hero's plaza. To his left, a bronze statue on a pedestal: a conquering hero mounted on horseback holding a banner proudly overhead. The statue was painted turquoise and white with verdigris and bird droppings respectively. To Grandeko's right, the bowl-like curve of the Hofburg Palace greeted him, tall, imposing, elegant, imperial.

From here he was ushered across a broad open expanse, flanked closely by Austrian security. As Gradenko walked he saw dark shapes edging along the tops of the palace. Snipers.

Inside, he was carried through the motion of formalities, shaking hands with various Austrian dignitaries. He did this all automatically and without enthusiasm. His attention stayed on the silent, grave-faced men hovering near the entrance to a conference room. The enemy. Westerners. The representatives of NATO assembled in their great numbers.

At his side, he had no one. Not even a token showing by the Warsaw Pact states. There would be no point, no reason to maintain such a facade, not now with every state but Poland in open rebellion.

After being introduced to his neutral Austrian hosts, he was introduced one by one to the Western delegates. There was no handshaking, only curt nods. Among their number he only recognized one, and was surprised to find that he did.

"Why do we do it, Andrei?" Andrew Carmichael asked. Carmichael was the British Foreign Secretary, Gradenko's opposite number when he had been head of the foreign ministry.

They were ideological enemies of course—Carmichael a capitalist and Gradenko a communist—but they understood each other, after years of opposing one another they understood each other well enough that Gradenko knew Carmichael was talking about war.

Gradenko thought for only a moment. "Because it is our nature."

"You think so?" Carmichael asked, more curious than challenging. He was sizing Gradenko up, measuring him before the real fight began. "What hope is there for us then?"

Gradenko looked back down the row of dignitaries, their eyes pinned on him, cold, unsympathetic. "Because," Gradenko said, looking back at Carmichael. "Peace is also our nature."

With that, the delegates sequestered themselves into the crowded, ostentatious conference hall and began the painful process of ending the war.

The started first as a trickle, tense, polite, and uncertain, but it soon became a deluge. Emotions boiled over and the bitter roots of war became exposed.

"Let's not fool ourselves," the American delegate said, glancing at the others for support. "You're losing." He looked pointedly at Gradenko. "I appreciate what you've said, that you desire peace, but you have to appreciate that we will have peace either way, through victory or negotiation makes no difference."

There was a time where Gradenko might have blustered at that. Instead he stared back, taking precious moments to collect his thoughts. "It will make all the difference to those who die," he said calmly.

Carmichael interjected quickly. "Mr. Gradenko, I think we all understand that. What my colleague is expressing is a sentiment we all hold to some degree or another. We want to know what it is you bring to the table. What do we gain by negotiation which we cannot achieve on the battlefield? While yes, these casualties are awful, we are more concerned with securing a lasting peace than we are with purely humanitarian aims. If preserving life were our only concern we could end the war ourselves by simply not fighting. What we fight for matters, you see?"

Gradenko absorbed all of this impassively. He had never expected this would be easy. There was a time, not so long ago, when the Soviet Union might have negotiated from a position of strength rather than coming, hat in hand, to beg for a truce, but that time was past. Besides, Gradenko doubted even then, even with motor rifle divisions pouring over the Rhine that the NATO member states would have sued for peace.

"You would make a desert and call it peace," Gradenko said. When he saw the horror and disgust on their faces he quickly explained. "Lasting peace is also what I desire. A truce for twenty years is a disservice to our children and our grandchildren. But you are mistaken in your belief that we can be beaten," he said. "Communism cannot be stomped out with bootheels. It is an idea which cannot be destroyed so easily. It is as much a part of the fabric of our society as capitalism is to yours. You believe in the freedom of choice. We believe in the inevitability of history. This conflict of ideology will not be resolved with bombs and bullets. The fact is plain that we are going to have to learn to live with each other, our ideologies in opposition, until one or the other proves superior and the second dies a natural death."

"As it did in China?" The West German delegate cut in bitterly.

They simply didn't understand. Gradenko shook his head. "You believe that if you persist, you will find victory. That you can march into Kiev, and Minsk, and Moscow and declare us to be liberated from our ideology." He stared at each member in turn. "And I tell you that if you continue on this path then you will start the war all over again. This is not yet a war of national survival and it does not have to become one."

"You are wrong," the German delegate pressed. "It is a war of survival, it has been a war of survival from the very beginning. For Sweden, Denmark, Turkey, France, and Germany. Our national survival is at stake. Why should the rules be different for you? For the Soviet Union?"

"Because we have nuclear weapons," Gradenko replied coolly.

The German delegate's eyes flashed anger but he bit off whatever he might have intended to say next.

"Do we really want this conference to degenerate into threats?" Carmichael said, trying to soothe the situation again. "Peace at the end of a gun—or beneath a bomb—is no peace."

"I make no threats," Gradenko said. "What I say is fact. The fact is that my people are willing to make peace because they have no stake in this war. This war does not concern the common man. Win or lose, it makes no difference. This will change if it becomes a fight for our survival."

Seeing contempt in the faces of his enemies he added, "nothing will galvanize our will to fight more than an attempt to liberate those who do not desire it."

"Aggression must be punished," France's delegate said, tone calm, words cutting. "For whatever blame the Americans bear for the attack on your naval bases, the fact is that it was Soviet arms which initially invaded Yugoslavia, Soviet arms which escalated this war to where it is now. Soviet ambition. Soviet prestige driving Soviet tanks."

Gradenko nodded. "I agree with you," he said.

This surprised the NATO delegates, rendering them silent.

"I agree that this war is a Soviet sin," Gradenko continued. "I agree that the West is not blameless, but I agree that it was our arrogance, our paranoia, our mistrust, hate, and greed which created this mess. I agree that we must pay the price for this." It was generally regarded as a poor negotiation tactic to admit fault, but Gradenko was unconcerned with that.

"It has all been a mistake," he continued. "Yugoslavia, Vladivostok, this war. Let us not make another. Think of your children. Think of tomorrow. We are willing to make concessions. But I cannot countenance our own destruction. Even if I were to agree, others would not. My power is tenuous, I will lose faith and then you will have no one else to negotiate with. Or someone worse."

Another Strelnikov.

The NATO delegates looked at one another, as if weighing his intentions, his ability to enforce whatever peace he was proposing.

"Gentlemen," Secretary Carmichael cleared his throat and rose to his feet. "I think we've been given something to consider here. Why don't we take a recess to report back to our respective governments and consider what Mr. Gradenko is suggesting. We can reconvene after lunch."

It wasn't a popular suggestion, but it went unopposed.

Gradenko sat silently at the conference table as the foreign delegates rose and left the room, singly or in small groups, whispering intently to one another. Eventually only Carmichael remained. He stood by one of the floor-to-ceiling windows overlooking a painstakingly manicured garden on the palace grounds. He glanced over and nodded to a staffer who pulled the wooden double doors softly closed. When he looked back at Gradenko, it was with confusion bordering on suspicion.

"What are you playing at, Andrei? What do you hope to achieve by threatening us?"

Even after everything, it seemed that East and West could not understand one another. Gradenko felt frustration but had to remind himself that his country had given the West no reason to trust them. After all, threats and protestations had been weaponized by the Soviet diplomatic corps for decades. That they should suddenly have a change of heart was improbable in the extreme.

Gradenko pushed back from the table and stood slowly. The muscles in his legs and back still ached from his time in Arkhangelsk. He wondered if they would ever stop. "I am not threatening anyone," he said. "I am only explaining the situation as it is. If this war continues it will destroy us both—the Soviet Union and the West."

"There's a saying in English," Carmichael said. "Perhaps you know it: when you hear hooves, think horses. Not Zebras." He smiled patiently. "So when I hear a Soviet say 'nuclear weapons' I assume that it's a threat."

"In this case," Gradenko said. "Imagine that I have black and white stripes." He sighed in disgust and shook his head. "This war has gone on too long. It has brought both our peoples to the brink of destruction, and for what? What will you gain from conquering us?"

"Peace," Carmichael said. "Peace for our children and grandchildren."

"I am not sure you can kill your way to peace," Gradenko said. "And even if you can, my people will not stand by and allow themselves to be killed." He looked away, out the window at the grass, sunlight, and flowers. "We are already defeated," he said. "You have proved beyond any doubt that the old Soviet system is too weak to survive into the 21st century. It is my desire to make a new system. A new model. A New Soviet Union."

"Should I take comfort in that?" Carmichael asked, tone unguarded.

Gradenko considered the question. "I would like to create a system which will benefit the people. A system where voices are heard within reason. A system which can live shoulder to shoulder with the West, seeking neither to conquer nor be conquered."

Carmichael was silent for a moment. "I mean no offense, but will your country survive such turmoil?

"I do not know," Gradenko said. "Maybe. Maybe not. But I see no choice but to try. If you press us, we will only harden our resolve. You will drive us further and further into madness. Do not seek to crush us with a fist. Offer us a hand of friendship. Be gracious victors. Accept the peace you have earned and allow it to last."

"We've tried that before," Carmichael said. "Thaws, detente, resets. It fails every time. Did you hear President Bayern's address to the American Congress?"

Gradenko shook his head.

"He said that it was delusion to think the human race could exist in peace, half free and half slave. What do you think, Andrei?"

"I think Mr. Bayern is correct," Gradenko said. "And I think that we are both in agreement about what must be done next. The slaves must be made free."

Carmichael gave him a tight smile. "Mr. Gradenko, I think we might be able to work with that." He gestured toward the door. "Lunch?"

***

"So, what are we talking?" America's representative said. "Real hard facts. What are you proposing?"

"Maintain the ceasefire," Gradenko said. "All Soviet forces will withdraw from all occupied territory in Sweden, Finland, and Turkey. The nations of East Europe will be permitted to hold free elections to determine their course." Gradenko had no illusions about how they would vote.

"Including Poland?" Germany's representative pressed.

Peace required good faith. "Including Poland," Gradenko said, knowing that particular concession would likely prove divisive back home. If Poland became Western-alligned, then it would put NATO right on their doorstep. "I can authorize withdrawals east as soon as we have signed an agreement here. The killing and destruction has already been ordered to stop."

"What about POWs?"

Gradenko thought of Johan and the others in Arkangelsk. "The Soviet Union and all her remaining allies will unilaterally release all prisoners of war through a neutral third party. I am sure Austria and Switzerland will provide the necessary apparatus."

Another show of shock from the Westerners. "If you hold true to that, we can sanction POW releases as well. Like for like."

Gradenko nodded. "Of course."

The delegates here looked wary, like men expecting an ambush. They were long used to Soviet obstinance, militancy, and belligerence. Gradenko's forthcoming behavior was unexpected.

"What of the other SSRs?" France's delegate asked. "The Baltic states, Ukraine, what of them?"

Gradenko thought about the bloody student protests in the Baltic, the quarreling Caucasian republics, the bitterly repressed muslim central Asian soviets. The Eastern Bloc weren't the only slaves held under the Soviet yoke. It might be that someday that they too would be free, but Gradenko was pragmatic enough to recognize that that was a bridge too far, certainly here and now.

"Any territory which is integrally Soviet is not up for discussion," he continued. "What happens within our borders is a domestic issue which is not up for discussion." He could not miss the thinly veiled disappointment in Carmichael's eyes. For all Gradenko's talk of change, he was still—at his core—a product of the Soviet Union.

Carmichael wasn't alone with this disappointment. The other NATO delegates weren't pleased with the idea, but they also had to yield to reality. As much as they might like to permanently dismantle the Soviet empire, that simply wasn't a demand they could enforce except down the barrel of a gun.

More Soviet concessions came. Reparations, financial and

economic assistance with reconstruction in war-torn areas, an international tribunal given authority to investigate and prosecute war criminals, and a staged disarmament. Gradenko agreed to all of it, willing to carry this weight if it meant peace. It was easier to bear this burden when he knew the alternative was destruction.

Over the following days and weeks, the treaty was revised, finalized, codified, and finally presented, a single master copy bearing the signatures of every NATO nation and representatives from the interim governments which now ruled in the Eastern Bloc.

Gradenko stared at the paper, keenly aware of the eyes of all the world on him. A year ago—before the war—being forced to sign such a treaty—such a surrender—would have broken him.

It was a delicate thing, a fragile thing, a bitter thing. Peace. The Soviets would lose most of their empire, they would bear the brunt of international condemnation, they would bear the cost of war indemnities and reparations. Truthfully, Gradenko didn't know if the soul of his nation could withstand this kind of brutal reckoning, but he knew they had a chance this way. A half-chance was more than no chance. And perhaps he could make a difference. Perhaps with everything he'd seen and felt and experienced, with everything he'd lost, perhaps he could make a change. Perhaps he could steer his nation back from the brink, away from slavery and death and towards something better.

The tip of his pen hovered above paper. Gradenko hesitated and finally spoke. "A nation—a people must atone for their sins. This is a start." He scrawled his name neatly and slowly—a scrap of paper to end the bloodshed. He drew the pen back, carefully capping it and tucking it into his pocket. "Gentlemen," he said, unwilling to consider the dark road ahead. He had to focus on the fact that there would *be* a road ahead. "Peace."

***

PEACE

"Peace hath her victories no less renowned than war."

JOHN MILTON, TO THE LORD GENERAL CROMWELL

40

Rayburn considered it a great irony that, as a corpsman, he hated hospitals. It didn't help that this particular hospital was Italian. It was not that he had anything against Italians or that their hospital was inferior in any way, it was that he did not speak Italian and their English wasn't the best when it existed at all.

He grimaced uncomfortably as his bandages were changed, enduring it until finally the nurse helped gently ease him over, lying half propped on his side in a crowded ward with other men wounded by shell splinters.

It wasn't just this room, the whole hospital was crowded, packed to the gills with the sick, injured, and dying. Even so, despite their grim surroundings, spirits were high among the men. They were high because they knew they wouldn't have to go back to war.

"Look at that, man. Crazy," Keyes said from the bed beside Rayburn's. His eyes were glued to a tiny color television mounted just above the doorframe of the room. It was tuned to the news and, although it was all in Italian, the images it showed were universal. Civilians celebrated in the streets, work crews dug out rubble, soldiers boarded ships and planes to return home, long Soviet columns withdrew over their borders. This was occasionally intercut with footage of the Vienna Peace Accords, the belligerent powers signing a treaty which amounted to a Soviet surrender. President Dewitt had called it "victory in all but name."

Rayburn wasn't thinking about victory though, he was thinking about the dead and wounded, about Sergeant

Washington, about Shelton, about the Hungarian children he'd seen cowering for Soviet artillery in the Budapest metro. A thousand threads of life, some severed, some frayed, others their fate uncertain.

"Should have kept going," another American said, his leg severed just above the ankle, the limb terminating in a thick nub of white gauze. "We had them on the run. Twenty years," he said. "Twenty years and we'll be doing this shit all over again. Mark my words."

"You think?" Keyes asked.

"Count on it," the soldier said.

"I think the peace will hold," Rayburn said. "I mean... it has to. Jesus, haven't we done enough dying?"

"Enough for my taste? Sure. For Ivan? Hell, Russians are bloodthirsty."

Rayburn didn't know how true that was. He had to hope that the Soviets had suffered enough to swear off war. "Doesn't matter," Rayburn said finally.

"Yeah? Why not?"

"I bet you in twenty years there won't even *be* a Soviet Union."

"Now there's a happy thought!" the soldier said, laughing. He had to speak up over the half dozen individual conversations that filled the ward. The wounded shouted back and forth to one another in a handful of languages like a microcosm of Babel.

"Lucky bastards," Keyes said glumly, eyes still on the television. He watched soldiers loading into commercial airlines, ready to fly back home. "When's it gonna be our turn?"

Rayburn snorted. "Not soon enough."

41

Major Pavel Fedorovich hadn't known a more miserable place than the Scottish countryside. The fact that he could only view it through tightly-woven wire mesh fences didn't help, but even so he despised it. Gray skies, cold wind, endless rolling moors, it was bleaker than the POW camp.

Fedorovich squinted miserably up at the overcast sky and longed for the distant days where he'd torn through the air in the cockpit of a Tupolev bomber at the helm of a regiment of planes. Now he slopped through the mud like a common private.

A light drizzle fell on the men of the camp as they assembled for morning roll call. This particular camp was for Soviet officers. A separate facility a few kilometers away housed the multitude of enlisted men who'd been scooped up by NATO. Every day their numbers swelled greater and greater.

"A bad morning, comrade?" Captain Babayev, his old co-pilot, asked.

Fedorovich grunted unhappily. "I have not had a good morning since we splashed down into the Norwegian Sea." He briefly recalled the gut-clenching terror of his bomber coming apart around them after a missile strike during an attack run. A final blaze of glory.

"It seems Colonel Nabiyev is no better," Babayev said, nodding toward the ranking officer in the camp.

Nabiyev had commanded a motor rifle regiment in Turkey before being run down by the British, his regiment all but destroyed, his command lost. He and Fedorovich had a lot in common that way. His dark eyebrows furrowed unhappily as he watched his brother officers assemble in the open.

Fedorovich eyed the folded slip of paper in Nabiyev's hand. "It seems the colonel has an announcement for us."

"Maybe we are to be sent home," Babyev suggested.

"We will see."

They parted ways, Babyev joining the assembled ranks. Fedorovich crossed in front of them, boots squelching in the black dirt to come stand beside Nabiyev. As the second highest ranking officer in the camp, he assumed the role of Nabiyev's executive officer.

"Morning," Nabiyev said.

Fedorovich nodded in greeting and looked over the men. They were an eclectic mix of all branches of the Soviet military. Air force pilots stood alongside army platoon commanders with a scattering of sailors among them. This last group had been plucked out of the icy waters of the Norwegian Sea just like Fedorovich had been. Among the longest serving prisoners here was a small collection of paratroopers—VDV who'd surrendered when the Americans and West Germans had retaken Rhein-Main and Rammstein. From there it was like a story of the war itself, lieutenants from the armored thrust to the Rhine and subsequent retreat, pilots from the fierce air war, sailors from the Soviet Navy's death ride, and now a growing collection of increasingly unqualified army officers.

A squad of British soldiers moved among the ranks of Soviet officers, counting them, verifying all were accounted for. When at last they were satisfied they stepped back, moving to the edge of the camp. Fedorovich glanced over to see the camp's commandant, a British officer, watching closely.

"Comrades," Nabiyev said finally. "I hope to dispel rumors with fact." He unfolded the paper, his sad eyes scanning the page. "The war has ended. This you know. I have been instructed to tell you that our government and the Communist Party of the Soviet Union have secured our release as part of a previously agreed prisoner exchange with the West." He lowered the paper. "We are going home."

Some of the men broke ranks to cheer or hug one another.

Others stood in mute shock, glowering silently at Nabiyev.

Fedorovich was in this latter group. Even as he watched Babayev cheering happily he couldn't help but feel nothing but bitter regret. The war was over, they'd lost. They were going home now but what had it all been for? Why had his men been sent down in flames over deadly arctic waters? What had it accomplished?

He looked at Nabiyev and the colonel looked back at him blankly. He seemed to read the major's thoughts. "Be glad," he said. "It is over."

"How can I be glad when it should never have happened?" Fedorovich countered.

"Because," Nabiyev said, crumpling the paper into a tight ball. "You have lived to regret it. Many did not." He dropped the paper into the mud and left, leaving Fedorovich staring after him, wondering what was going to happen now.

42

The dry, rolling countryside of the Turkish-Soviet border looked to Brigadier John Gates for all the world like the American Southwest. Not that had he seen the Southwest exactly, but he had seen plenty of Westerns. Blue-white skies, brown, dried grass, and a dotting of green shrubs and small, leafy trees formed a surprisingly scenic backdrop to an otherwise tense scene.

He stood in the shade of a twisted, branching tree sprouting from the top of a hill, and scanned the border through binoculars. To the north, only a few kilometers away, was the Armenian Soviet Socialist Republic, one of the constituent states of the Soviet Union. The border itself was an imaginary line traced by dense coils of razorwire and dotted with warning signs in Turkish and English.

A single road snaked along the valley between low hills winding its way up to a border post currently watched by a handful of Soviet armored vehicles. This was mirrored on the Turkish side by Turkish forces. A tense peace existed between the two sides, easier to enforce now that the Soviets had withdrawn from what little Turkish ground they still occupied the month before. The peace was shaky, but it was peace.

After a year of brutal fighting, the concept was as alien to Gates as he was sure it was to his men. Seeing enemy—no, not enemy. Soviet. Seeing *Soviet* vehicles parked in the open without being destroyed felt anathema to him. It was a good thing, of course. He was grateful for peace but—"Should have come bloody ages ago," he muttered, continuing to survey the enemy position.

"Sir?" Colonel Benson asked from beside him.

Gates shook his head. "Peace," he said. 'Took long enough."

"Yes, sir," Benson agreed.

A cool gust of wind from the north stirred the air, bringing with it the all too familiar sound of gunfire.

"The Armenians?" Benson asked.

Gates nodded, jaw set grimly. No sooner had peace been established than the Soviets began to fight one another. He had no way of knowing what it was he heard. Armenian separatists attacking Soviet soldiers? Clashes between Azerbaijani and Armenian militias? Soviet crackdowns on political dissidents? Time would tell.

"We ought to be helping them," Benson muttered darkly. "It's not right to sit and listen to them dying, is it?"

"No," Gates agreed. But they had orders and those orders were clear: under no circumstances cause trouble with the Soviets. If the Soviet Union was to die, it would die of natural causes. Finally he lowered his binoculars. "That's it then," he said, glancing at Benson. "Ivan has crawled back into his hole, we've blasted him out of the Free World, and liberated Eastern Europe for good measure. I expect we'll be sending the boys back home again before long. Maybe in time for Christmas."

"With the way the budget is I can't imagine we'll wait any longer than that," Benson agreed. "Seems like a dream."

"Yes," Gates said, the wind bringing the rattle of a machine gun again. "I wonder what things will look like when we wake up again."

43

Long lines of Canadian soldiers wearing American desert camo stood in the port at Izmir. Among them, Warrant Officer Michael Heathcliff watched his men—his platoon—waiting their turn to ascend a bouncing boarding ramp onto one of the dozen freighters tasked with carrying them all back home.

As he looked over his men, his gaze faltered, lingering on one of his soldiers. "Mandeville," he said, approaching and gesturing to the soldier's pack. "What the hell is that?"

Mandeville, who had been talking with Private Harper, froze, eyes wide. A sheepish grin spread across his face as he wracked his mind for a reasonable excuse.

Heathcliff opened Mandeville's pack and pulled the protruding object out. It was an AK-74, battered, scratched, but no worse for the wear. "Are you shitting me, Mandeville?" He wanted to be mad. Wanted to, but couldn't. A grin spread across his face.

"It's a trophy, sir," Mandeville protested.

"Trophy, my ass. No weapons. You can't keep this."

Harper laughed and Mandeville groaned, dismayed.

"You could've taken a helmet or a belt buckle—hell a knife. But a rifle?" Heathcliff passed the contraband weapon off to a patrolling MP he gestured over.

"Harper's got a Makarov," Mandeville reported, giving Harper a sharp look. Now it was his turn to blanch.

"I didn't see it," Heathcliff said. "And I'm going to pretend you didn't say anything. Now eyes front or you're going to miss the boat and we're not coming back for you."

Mandeville sighed and returned to line, shuffling forward

with the rest of the men of the battalion.

As Heathcliff watched, he could not help but think of the men of the platoon who'd come over to Europe to fight and would never again return home. Names and faces flitted at the edge of memory. Lost friends and comrades.

"Somehow we made it." Lieutenant Driscoll said, coming to join Heathcliff and watching the platoon file by. "Made it to the end."

Heathcliff was in no mood for such saccharine reminiscing. "Most of us, anyway."

Driscoll gave him a curious look, allowing a beat of silence to pass. "The ones that did make it made it because of you," he said. "At least in part."

"Thank you for saying so, sir, but you and I know that's bullshit," Heathcliff replied.

Driscoll raised an eyebrow. "It is?"

Heathcliff nodded. "Some of us just got lucky. We're going to have to live with that."

"Luck's part of it," Driscoll said as he and Heathcliff joined the line at the back of the platoon. "But not all of it. You did your share of hard work."

Heathcliff didn't want the praise, though he appreciated what Driscoll was trying to do. "We all did."

"Are you going to stay in?" Driscoll asked, walking up the gangway beside Heathcliff.

Heathcliff laughed. "Hell no. I've seen all I want to. Someone else can fight the next one."

Driscoll lagged with him. "I hope to God they don't have to."

Together they reached the metal deck of the ship, following directions towards the berthing areas and the waiting metal frame bunks.

"Driscoll," Heathcliff said haltingly. "When we get back home, we should stay in touch, go see a Wolves game, have some beers."

Driscoll grinned at him. "Yeah?"

Heathcliff allowed himself a smile back. "Yeah."

44

Jean had never been to Sofia before the war and she didn't imagine she'd ever come back here after it. It wasn't that she didn't enjoy the city—or Bulgaria for that matter—it was just that she wasn't the kind to stay in one place long.

She sat at a tiny, streetside table just outside a cafe turned bar. The night was full of celebration and revelry. Guns cracked in the air and drunks staggered through traffic to a symphony of car horns. Bulgaria's national elections had finished and the Communist Party had been destroyed in a landslide. That was reason to celebrate in her book.

Jean sipped her beer and glanced right at the small park which surrounded a neighboring cathedral—Saint Nedelya's. So far as cathedrals went, it was modest. Its cupola'd belltower rose only high enough to peek above the surrounding trees. The cathedral's bells chimed unceasingly as it was circled by a river of honking cars.

She thought about Dario, as she often did when things got quiet. She thought about others too, the people she'd met, the people she hadn't. She thought about Bulgaria and its people. They were free now to choose their own path. She hoped it was a bright one.

Pete asked her a question. It was too loud to hear him.

Grinning, Jean leaned over the table. "What?"

He leaned in closer, close enough to kiss. "I said 'what now?'"

She cocked her head. "What do you mean?"

"Yugoslavia's going to shit," he said. "Serbs, Bosnians, Croats all killing each other again."

"World War Three was just half-time for them," Jean said.

"What else is new?"

"So... are we going back?"

Jean laughed. She leaned back in her chair and downed the rest of her beer, eyeing Pete. "That what you want to do?"

He tried to keep a straight face but failed, it cracked into a broad grin. "I want to go where you go," he said finally.

Jean laughed again, helped in no small part by the alcohol sloshing in her brain. It wasn't just the booze though. She was a professional—mostly. Pete was her partner. Maybe he was more. There was a time she would have rejected the idea. She wasn't out here to make friends and find love, she was out here to get a story but... life was short. Life was just too damn short.

"So," Pete said, repeating the question. "What's next? Where do we go now?"

Jean considered the question, running a finger across the lip of her glass. She looked up as a truck cruised by, a pair of men firing Kalashnikovs up into the air. Police? Soldiers? Militia? Who the hell knew.

Jean grinned broader and leaned in again, beckoning Pete to do the same. When he did he was nearly nose to nose with her.

"I hear China's breaking up," she said. "Maybe we can do that next."

Pete laughed, loud and free.

45

Stockholm was little changed from how Sergeant Ingrid Karlsdotter remembered it. It was luckier than many other formerly Soviet-occupied cities that way. It had been seized without struggle and given up the same way, rendered untenable as NATO forces outmaneuvered their Soviet opponents.

All that had suffered were the people, and even they had been relatively lucky. There had been few executions and rapes and only light looting. All things considered, the Soviets here had been relatively disciplined. The same could not be said for everywhere in the country.

Still, life went on. The city swelled as people flocked home in droves, returning from rural cabins, other countries, and now returning from captivity.

Standing at the windows of the boarding gate, Karlsdotter gasped as she saw a Soviet Lufthansa flight taxiing toward them. "That must be them!" she exclaimed, gripping her mother's arm excitedly.

"I think it is," her mother replied.

Ingrid's father put his arm over his daughter's shoulders without a word. It was comforting, a strangely paternal gesture to someone who had very recently been leading infantry into combat.

Stockholm was nearly unchanged, but Karlsdotter felt like a wholly different person. She'd begun the war as a student—a reservist with a penchant for the outdoors and ended as... as a soldier, a fighter, a killer. But right now she wanted to be none of those things. She wanted to be someone fresh, someone brand new.

The airliner came to a halt, the boarding tube extended and clamped in place.

Police had to clear back the press of onlookers, friends, family, and reporters. A battery of cameras stood manned by a platoon of reporters, waiting to capture the first images of the aircraft's passengers.

Karlsdotter wormed her way through the crowd to the front, stopped only by a police officer.

"Ingrid!" Her mother exclaimed, surprised at her daughter's assertiveness.

Karlsdotter ignored her, gasping again as the doors came open and Sweden's prisoners of war came home.

The men walked, limped, or in some cases were wheeled out. They were skeletal, painfully thin, their clothes hanging loose. Some of them were clearly too sick to walk, or too badly injured. If it weren't for their smiles, it would be a grim procession.

People in the crowd called out to loved ones. Some wept. The police couldn't keep them back anymore and the news media filmed a dozen joyous reunions.

Karlsdotter kept scanning the crowd, checking the new arrivals, growing increasingly apprehensive. She knew he was on this flight, but she wasn't sure what condition he would be in. She was different now than she had been, would he be different also?

Then she saw him.

Johan stepped through the doorway, looking around at the crowd, bewildered and stunned.

"Johan!" Karlsdotter went to him, bowling through the crowd, dodging hugging couples until she reached him. His eyes lit up with joy a moment before she collided with him, wrapping him tight. She felt his shoulderblades, the knobs of his spine. He felt as light as a feather.

Johan put his arms around her and she broke down.

Karlsdotter had held herself together from the beginning to the end and every day in between. She'd fought and suffered, bled and killed. Now, with her arms around her boyfriend and his arms around her, she could hold it together no more. So she cried like a child, gripping him tight, her face pressed into his bony shoulder. "Johan," she said his name again, as if willing him to be real, willing him to be solid and permanent. "Johan."

He hugged her tight, hands running up and down her back until she'd gotten it all out, for now anyway.

When she pulled away she looked up into Johan's smiling face.

"Ingrid," he said finally, grinning at her. "Do you have a cigarette?"

46

Sabine Shuester was finally home. It was good fortune, she thought, that she even *had* a home to return to. For some, after long miserable months in crowded refugee camps in Belgium, France, and the United Kingdom, they'd had nothing to look forward to but more hardship—their houses and apartments flattened, burned, and ruined by war.

At least she had a home. Hildesheim was nearly untouched by fighting, but that wasn't the problem. It was her family which had been destroyed.

"*Mutti*, the house!" her daughter Sofi cried as they walked from the bus stop down the quiet suburban street. "I can't believe it!"

"Go," Sabine said, nudging her daughter on. "Run along."

Sofi ran, dashing down the sidewalk toward the house with joyful abandon.

Children, Sabine thought, had a remarkable ability to get used to anything. Sofi had quickly become used to their life in Belgium and had slowly gotten used to life without a father. She wondered how much of Herman her daughter would remember in another year, five years, ten years, twenty. Because that was the most painful part about losing someone you loved with all your heart. They were gone, but you remained.

Sofi reached the door a few paces before her mother and tried the knob. "It's unlocked!" she said, pushing it open.

Just how they had left it.

The people of Germany gradually filtered back to their homes, moving with typically German order and organization. There would be no haphazard scramble, no risk of squatters or looting. Everything was undertaken with precision. The town of Hildesheim's civilian population breathed life back into a place which had fallen into a deathless stillness under Soviet occupation.

The rush of memories was physically painful for Sabine. She put a hand to her chest as the familiar sights and smells of her home assaulted her at once. Their television was still here. It was a strange thing to note, but it meant that no looters had ransacked their house. What were the odds? After a year of dereliction apparently no one had been here.

The place was faintly musty, the air dense and still. Sabine busied herself opening windows, moving from room to room.

"*Mutti*, my room! Oh, I forgot about it!" Sofi said, digging through her things.

"I hope it's all there, *Maus*," Sabine said. She would give all of it away in a heartbeat—the TV, Sofi's toys, the house, all of it—all of it for her husband to be with her again.

The night they'd lost him in the chaos of the attack on the refugee column had been the worst night of her life. She'd known she should have gone back looking for Herman, but how could she with a child to care for? Sofi had needed her even more then than she did now. So she'd waited, waited, hoped and prayed for a miracle.

It had never come.

Others in the camp had experienced miracles as lost family resurfaced in another camp or arrived later. Herman had never come back.

Sabine sat on the couch and picked up the remote control. She blew a thin coating of dust off and pressed the power button. She was surprised when it snapped on, tuned to the news, just where they'd left it, as if they'd only been gone a day.

The news showed the chancellor in Frankfurt announcing Reunification. East and West to become one again. It was bittersweet. It meant that Germans would no longer be divided against their will, but it also meant West Germany would have to shoulder the burden of the ruined East in addition to their own troubles. No country, except perhaps the Poles, had suffered more acutely in the war than the Germans. It had been their homes which served as the battleground, their soldiers had been bled white in the opening days of the war. Now they had to rebuild. Again.

"The unification of our nation will also mean a unification of our armed forces," the chancellor continued. "Although there will be significant scalebacks, a general amnesty is being granted to all soldiers of the former East German army for activities undertaken under Soviet leadership."

Sabine wondered if it was an East German bullet which had killed her husband.

"*Mutti*, come see!" Sofi called.

Sabine turned off the TV and saw a dull reflection of herself. Herman was gone, but she had to go on, even if just for Sofi. She smiled faintly to herself as she stood up. "Coming, *Maus*."

47

Lieutenant Jan Adamcik's dress uniform was of an unfamiliar cut and style. It wasn't just that he was an officer now, it was that he was no longer a soldier of the People's Republic of Czechoslovakia. Soviet-style communism was dead now in his homeland, hopefully for good. The cut of the uniform was more similar to American dress uniform, bearing no communist iconography. It was a welcome change, but not one he would have to spend any real time getting used to.

His time as a soldier was finished. He stood along with the others of his regiment, back straight as a steel beam, arrayed in a neat grid. All of them faced a grandstand where a general stood. The man's face and name were unfamiliar to Adamcik, but he'd been the commander of the Czechoslovak Legion from its inception to its disbandment.

"I have been privileged," the general said, "to serve with such honorable and brave men. Each of you is a hero, each of you rose to the challenge of the enemy and did not flinch. You go home today as honored members of the greatest military unit of our nation's history." He saluted them.

Adamcik returned it. He did not feel like a hero. He did not feel brave or honorable. He felt like a bitter, empty man. A killer.

After some more ceremony with flags and musicians, the soldiers were released. The men cheered like a graduating class. A few even threw their caps into the air. Adamcik did not. He stepped from the ranks and joined a growing stream of soldiers moving toward the edge of the field which hosted this gathering.

Czechoslovakia's economy was floundering. It had had ups and downs under communism, but now with the war over, it was decidedly down. Hundreds of thousands unemployed, unhoused, others sick or wounded. The country did not need tanks and soldiers now, it needed doctors and laborers, men and women to build and heal, not destroy.

Where he fit into this new world, this new system, Adamcik wasn't sure. That was the curse of freedom wasn't it? He had no more orders, no more unbreakable boundaries. He was free to stay or leave, complain or not. He found himself drifting toward the still-ordered ranks of some of the lucky few who'd been retained in the army. These men wouldn't have to worry about finding a job or feeding their families for now. But even so, most of the men released wanted nothing more than to pick up their old lives, as broken or difficult as they might be. They didn't want to be soldiers any longer.

Among the ranks of the still enlisted, Adamcik saw Captain Vesely. As they locked eyes, Vesely raised his hand in salute, face tight, professional. A show of respect.

Adamcik froze and, to his surprise, felt something he hadn't known he had. Pride. After all, he'd done it, hadn't he? He'd made it. He returned the salute and Vesely grinned at him.

Adamcik turned away, joining the others filtering towards waiting friends and family.

"Adamcik! Adamcik!"

He looked up and saw Sergeant Coufal—now just Coufal, he supposed—leading Janco to him, both men grinning. "Adamcik, what did you go to school for?" Coufal asked.

"What?" Adamcik repeated, bewildered.

"School, do you remember that?" Janco added.

Adamcik stammered a moment, trying to recall ancient history. He had been someone before he had been a soldier. "Engineering. Mechanical engineering."

Janco snapped his fingers, turning to Coufal. "See? You see? I told you."

"So what?" Adamcik asked.

"My uncle," Coufal said. "He's a manager at the AZNP."

"The national automobile works?" Adamcik said, watching

Coufal bob his head eagerly. "And he tells me that there is discussion of an acquisition of the AZNP, a merger with a Western company. Maybe Volkswagen."

"So?"

Janco and Coufal laughed like Adamcik was the biggest fool on the planet. "So, this means big changes coming, big developments, new manufacturing lines. Lines which will need employees. I told him that I know a mechanical engineer."

Adamcik blinked in surprise. "Me?"

"Of course, you," Janco said, grinning. "And I told Coufal's uncle that I am close friends with a mechanical engineer and that he will need someone to drive him to work."

"So?" Coufal pressed. "Come with us, Adamcik. I promise you will never regret it."

For Adamcik, there was nothing else. But even if there was, maybe war didn't have to define him. Maybe he was more than a soldier and killer. "If he will hire me," he said finally.

Coufal clapped him on the back. "Yes! Excellent! We will call him. But first, we are free men. Let us drink like free men!"

To Adamcik, that sounded like his idea of heaven.

48

Major Ken Morris unfolded the small, weathered piece of paper and checked the hand-written address on it. The ink was faded, smudged slightly, but perfectly legible, the letters small and neat. He looked up at the house which bore the same numbers as the paper.

"This is so goddam dumb," he muttered to himself. His breath fogged in the chilly, autumn air. He'd always intended to come here, to Arvika, Sweden after the war, but intent and action did not always overlap. It had been nearly a year since he'd last even seen her. Surely she wouldn't be continuing to pine over a half-remembered American airman she'd known for what really amounted to a few short days.

And yet... how many romances started just like that?

"Fuck it," Morris said, folding the paper back into his pocket. He glanced back at the taxi idling at the curb. This would be an extremely awkward visit if Astrid's situation had changed since he'd last seen her. Well, at least he could go sightseeing. It wasn't as if he'd really been able to enjoy his last trip through Sweden.

Astrid's neighborhood was quiet, secluded. Taken on its own, it wouldn't have looked out of place in England somewhere. The homes were on the smaller side by American standards, but they were cozy, neat, orderly. Sharply pointed roofs marked most of the buildings, protection against excessive snow buildup in the winter, he imagined. Astrid's was smaller than most, assuming she even still lived here.

Mustering his courage, Morris moved up the short, paved walkway and came to the front door. He hesitated. This was his last chance to punch out before he was fully committed. Once that happened—

The door opened and an older man, probably in his sixties, stared curiously at him. "*Halla*?"

"Ah," Morris stammered. "*Halla*. English?"

The man looked annoyed and even more confused. He shook his head.

"Shit. I'm sorry, ah—*Jag...*" he struggled to recall what rudimentary Swedish he'd picked up before his trip here. "*Jag ladsen*." He couldn't keep it up. "I'm looking for a woman. *K*—" He closed his eyes, trying to recall the world. "*Kvinna*. Astrid. Astrid Alphand."

At this he blinked. "Astrid?"

"*Ja*," Morris was good with that word. "*Ja*. Astrid."

The man closed the door.

Morris blinked, staring at the door a moment. Well that was a bust.

The door opened again and Astrid was here, at first confused, then shocked, then overwhelmed with joy. "Ken!" She hugged him and in that moment Morris's whole trip, the airfare, the flight, the awkward negotiation with the taxi driver, it was all worth it. He would do it again in a heartbeat.

He hugged her back, breathing in her smell. It was new. She, like him, wore civilian clothes. Jeans and a t-shirt. Her hair was down, hanging between her shoulder blades. No more fatigues, no more helmet, rifle, camouflage, dirt, exhaustion, and sweat. This was Astrid, the real Astrid. And she was seeing him, the real him.

"Hey," Morris said as she finally broke the hug. "I hope you didn't get married." He glanced toward the house.

Astrid burst out laughing. "No! No. Ken, that is my father."

Morris laughed awkwardly. "Yeah, that was my second guess." Now that he had her, he didn't really know what to do next. He felt like the cat that caught the canary.

Astrid, to her credit, seemed to enjoy his discomfort immensely. "I did not think you would come," she said finally. "I was worried that maybe..."

Maybe he didn't survive.

"Yeah," Morris said. "I was worried about you too. Every day."

She blushed faintly which made Morris feel even more self-conscious. "But I am glad you did," she said finally.

"Yeah," Morris said again. "Oh! I have something for you." He half-turned, unzipping his duffel bag and reaching inside before hesitating. He gave her a furtive look. "You uh... you're still single right?"

She laughed. "What if I am not?"

"Then that would make this next part really awkward." Morris pulled out a thick wad of envelopes and letters, all bound together with a handful of rubber bands. "Uh... these are for you." He offered them.

Astrid looked at them, shocked. She said something in Swedish, following up with, "letters?"

"Yeah. I wrote to you but..."

She took the bundle carefully, looking it over. "So much."

Maybe this was weird. Morris kicked himself mentally. But then she smiled at him. All was well.

"I want you to read them," he said. "Maybe not right now, but... eventually. But first..." He grinned at her. "I think I owe you some coffee."

49

Dearborn, Michigan in winter was about as far from Fort Lauderdale as Lieutenant David "Rabbit" Barlow ever wanted to be. He was definitely a sunshine and warm water kind of guy. He felt like an alien visitor here with his tropical patterned shirt and khaki slacks. It didn't help that he was on a mission he felt woefully unqualified for.

Standing at the bar of a family chain restaurant, he stirred his drink, watching the ice slosh around, and grimaced. He really was a sucker to have offered to come all the way out here. He had no obligation to do it. Really what was the point? What could he do that would make any kind of a difference?

He turned around at the sound of the front door opening. He saw a woman with her husband talking to the hostess. The woman carried a baby basket, a neat bundle of white cloth within. That had to be them.

Rabbit raised his hand, waving slightly to get their attention.

The woman's husband caught his eye and pointed him out. After a brief conversation with the hostess they came in, going to the bar.

Rabbit glanced at the baby and wondered why the hell he'd waited at the bar and not at a table.

"David?" the woman asked.

"Yeah," Rabbit said, smiling. "Hi. You must be Eileen."

"Yes," Eileen said, flashing him a smile back. "This is my husband Craig."

"How's it going?" Craig and Rabbit shook hands.

"Thank you so much for coming out," Eileen said. "I know this was an inconvenience—"

"No," Rabbit lied. "Not at all. I was glad to do it." That part was true. Mostly. "I uh... I only hope I can..." he trailed off before finishing. "Bring you a little closure."

Eileen's smile tightened slightly, hurt lingering at the corners of her eyes.

"Let's grab a table," Rabbit said, guiding the family over to an empty table. He sat down across from Eileen, her husband sitting beside her, taking her hand in his, stroking the back comfortingly.

"I told you everything I could in my letters, but... I'm happy to talk about anything you want about your dad," he said.

"Can you tell us how he died?" Eileen asked.

It was both the obvious question and the one that he didn't want to address. He could tell her all the technical details of the operation, the kind of missile which had swatted Roy "Venom" Metcalf from the air, but what good would that do?

"Do you know what your dad did?" Rabbit asked.

"He was a pilot," Eileen answered.

"He flew a Prowler," Rabbit said. "It's an electronic warfare aircraft." He stopped himself, collecting the relevant details. "What that meant is he didn't shoot people, he provided support."

It meant nothing to Eileen, but she listened anyway.

"Your dad," Rabbit said, speaking slowly and clearly, "saved a lot of guys. He put himself in danger so that other people could live."

Hurt and loss flashed on Eileen's features. She was wondering why it had to be *her* dad who'd given his life. Rabbit was certain if, given the choice between Rabbit or her dad coming home, she would have sent Rabbit into the ocean in his place.

"I know that's not what you wanted," Rabbit said. "But that's the kind of guy Venom was."

"Venom?"

"Callsign," Rabbit said. "Everyone's got them." He hesitated, willing himself to relax. He was the last connection between Eileen and her father. It was the least he could do. "Want me to tell you about how he got it?"

Like that, the tension was broken and Rabbit told them all he could about Roy Metcalf as he knew him. It didn't feel like much, but to her it meant the world. They talked—or rather, they listened to Rabbit talk—for hours before he finally reached into his shirt pocket.

"Oh," Rabbit said. "Take this." He pulled a polaroid out and handed it over. "Your dad."

Venom wore his flight suit and posed by his aircraft along with his electronic warfare officers. Brothers in arms, they'd fought and ultimately died together. "George Bradshaw and Will Coleman," Rabbit identified them.

Eileen took the photograph gingerly and stared down at it for a few quiet moments. A tear ran down her cheek before she quickly wiped it away. "He never... he never talked about his job. Or much of anything. I... we mostly just fought." She tried to smile but it came out sad.

"He loved you," Rabbit said without thinking. It was true after all. "Venom wasn't good with people. He really loved you, but didn't know how to say it. Before we all went out..." he hesitated again, unsure if this would help or hurt.

Eileen clearly wanted the truth and looked at him expectantly.

"He wished he hadn't..." Rabbit tried to think of a diplomatic way to say it. "He wished you two were still close but he didn't know how to fix it. So..." he trailed off.

Eileen passed the photograph to her husband who likewise studied it. "Thank you," she said. "This has really meant a lot." Before she could say more, the bundle in the baby carrier stirred, mewing quietly. "Oh. Come here," Eileen cooed, picking her baby up, moving the swaddling aside to reveal a pink, puckered, chubby face.

Rabbit did not like children, especially babies but... "Hey," he smiled at the baby.

The baby stared back at him like he was an alien organism.

"This is Roy," Eileen said proudly. "Roy, this is Uncle David.

Rabbit smiled broader, wishing to God that Venom was here

to see this instead of him. "Nice to meet you, Roy."

50

There was no escape. The air reeked of burning plastic and charred flesh. The temperature spiked above boiling and into roasting. Flames licked at Don Vance's legs as he banged on the hatch of his tank, screaming.

He choked awake and struggled free of his entangled sheets.

"Don?" His girlfriend Molly woke up beside him.

Vance didn't reply straight away. His heart pounded in his chest and his whole body was sheened with sweat. He felt a familiar, tugging ache in his thigh, the remnant of splintered tank armor cast through his leg by a Soviet shell.

"I'm fine," Vance said, rubbing his chest. "Go back to sleep." He reached over and picked a glass up off the nightstand to take a sip. His hands shook fiercely.

The dream was almost always the same. It had been no different tonight. He wondered if it would ever stop.

Molly sat up too and laid a hand on his back. It was soft and cool. She rubbed small circles between his shoulder blades, not saying anything.

Vance took a cool drink and then another before setting the glass back down. He was home. He was safe. It was over. He looked at Molly and gave her a small smile. "Thanks."

She smiled back. "If you're up for good, I can make you some breakfast."

He considered it and glanced at the clock. It was just past three in the morning. Vance shook his head. "No," he said. "I want to try to get back to sleep."

Molly laid down and turned over.

Vance wrapped his arms around her and pulled her close. "I

love you, Molly."

"I love you too."

In a few minutes he was asleep. This time he did not dream.

EPILOGUE

August 1994

Two years after the first Soviet soldier crossed into NATO territory in anger. Two years of bloodshed, turmoil, suffering and chaos. Two years of hell on Earth. Now, two of the men who might be—at least in part—considered the architects of all this suffering stood face to face.

General Secretary Gradenko and Pyotr Strelnikov stood in the pre-dawn darkness at the edge of a runway, cloaked in shadow and fog. Gradenko wore a suit again, Strelnikov wore a uniform devoid of rank or decoration save for a single medal. The Order of Bogdan Khmelnitsky, Second Class. It had been his reward for the desperate, sanguine attack which had seized Zagreb in the Yugoslav War. It was the only medal Strelnikov had requested to be allowed. It was a request Gradenko had acquiesced to.

Strelnikov was leaving—seen off by no one, sent into a quiet exile far from home, far from his ability to fan tensions and stir trouble. The only others here were Gradenko's handful of bodyguards and a pair of stiff, statue-like army sentries. Though they shouldered weapons, the rifles were ceremonial, chrome-plated SKS, deactivated.

An aircraft taxied toward them out of the dark, props thundering as it revved up and down, moving closer.

"Your plane," Gradenko said.

Strelnikov looked over his shoulder at it, face blank and impassive. He watched as it parked, engines slowing to a low idle. Ground crew moved a stairwell into position and began to refuel the craft for its long journey.

Strelnikov's fate had not been an easy thing to decide. The

deputies of the assembly who'd suffered his cruel tyranny wanted him dead or crushed slowly in a gulag. Others, largely those in the military, respected Strelnikov too much to see him executed. Most of his most diehard supporters had been killed and captured in the fighting around Moscow. Most, but not all. Hardliners always waited in the wings, would-be Napoleons and Caesars.

Exile was the traditional punishment for those who the Soviet Union could not or would not kill. Strelnikov was unwelcome in the Western world, but fortunately for him there were plenty of tropical and subtropical communist nations willing to host him.

When Strelnikov turned back to regard Gradenko, his eyes were clouded with thinly-veiled anger. "I understand there have been more riots in Tbilisi. Demonstrations in Riga and Kiev."

Gradenko did not rise to the bait, he said nothing.

"A warning, Gradenko," Strelnikov said. "The Soviet people will tolerate many hardships. They will tolerate famine so long as it comes with empire. They will not survive a famine without an empire."

"That," Gradenko said, "is a hurdle we will have to overcome as one then." He spoke with confidence. He now held his post with some measure of support from the people, having won a contested election. It was still a one party system of course, anti-communist factions would not be allowed to vie for control of the nation, but he had soundly beaten Radomir to claim the post. Now, with Dmitriyev serving beside him as Premier, he had a mandate of the people, or something like one. Whether that would survive the ethnic and nationalist turmoil nipping at the frayed edges of the Soviet Union remained to be seen.

"They need a firm hand," Strelnikov said. "Someone to guide the team and ensure we are all pulling the same way." His scowl became a snarl. "That was all I ever did. My crime was to serve the Soviet Union to the best of my abilities." He laid a hand on his chest, over his heart. "Everything. *Everything* I have done, I have done out of love for my nation and its people. I am guilty only of believing in the promise of the Soviet Union."

An abortive defense, too little and too late. All Gradenko had to do was conjure the image of his wife's face, dead and bloody. No, Strelnikov was no hero, he was a monster waiting for another chance. He briefly reconsidered killing Strelnikov. It was not too late. The old ways were sometimes the best. No. To do so would create a martyr. He shook his head. "If that is true," Gradenko said finally, "then you will bear this for them. You will bear the burden of all you have done and all you failed to do for the people you claim to love."

Strelnikov bared his teeth. Were he armed he might have been tempted to try for Gradenko's life. A man who'd had everything and lost it all. With nothing left to lose he was perhaps more dangerous than he had ever been.

Gradenko eyed the aircraft, noting that the refueling lines were disconnected. "Your plane is ready. Farewell." He turned away and started back for the airport.

"Drop this charade!" Strelnikov barked.

Gradenko stopped, looking back at him.

"If you intend to kill me, to stage an accident, just do it and be done with it," Strelnikov said, glancing at the bodyguards. "Put a bullet through my heart and let me die a soldier's death."

Gradenko stared back pitilessly. Strelnikov truly was a barbarian. He had no business ever trying to run a nation. Finally he allowed himself a small, cold smile. "I do not wish you dead," Gradenko said at last. "I wish you to be forgotten." Then, he left Strelnikov—he hoped—for good.

***

The hangar bay of the USS *Norwegian Sea* echoed with Admiral Ernest Alderman's voice as he spoke to an assembled audience of hundreds. The audience was a mixture of sailors, dignitaries, and their families. Navy dress whites dotted the crowd like squares on a chessboard against darker suits and dresses.

President Jerry Bayern—*former* President Bayern—only half listened from his seat on the stage. Alderman discussed the vessel, the United States Navy, and the battle which lent her its name. Laid down as *Khe Sahn*, there was little debate when the name change was proposed after the conclusion of hostilities. While it was hardly a war-winning fight, many considered the Battle of the Norwegian Sea to be the turning point. That was the moment where NATO decisively defeated a Soviet force. Without the Soviet navy to cut off Norway and Sweden, the enemy had been locked into a prolonged attritional war, one they could ill-afford to fight. That front sucked in men and material and cost the Soviets irreplaceable war assets. Had they managed to cut Norway from the rest of Europe they might have crushed the Scandinavians and re-deployed vital divisions to other threatened fronts.

After some pre-amble, Alderman awarded sailors and airmen medals and recognition of their service in that brutal fight. This was followed by a moment of silence for those lost. Bayern looked over his shoulder at the projector screen hanging behind Alderman as it projected a series of names and faces. The human toll was difficult for Bayern to internalize and so he read the names of ships lost. He saw *Iowa* and *Raleigh* flick by, followed by a dozen others.

He looked away, struggling to maintain his neutral expression. After all, wasn't this all his responsibility? He took a glance to his left and right. He was surrounded by the other living presidents. Just to his right was Dewitt, cleancut and calm. To his left was an empty seat, ceremonially left open for President Simpson. On the other side of that was former president Slater. He leaned on a black walking cane, his wispy white hair combed neatly back, eyes on the presentation. Unlike Slater and Dewitt, Bayern wore his dress whites. He was still an active-duty naval officer after all. He hoped, eventually, that would be how he was remembered.

Alderman finally finished his part of the ceremony and Dewitt took his place, pausing to shake the admiral's hand. "Thank you," Dewitt said, calming the crowd as he glanced at the teleprompter just off stage. "It has been almost a year since the war ended. Two since it began. There are few among us who didn't suffer in that conflagration, or know someone who did. It was because of those noble, tragic sacrifices that millions of people can now claim the mantle of freedom. From Helsinki, Finland to Ankara, Turkey. Poland, Czechoslovakia, Hungary, Bulgaria, and Romania have been added to the roster of free nations."

Bayern noted that Dewitt conspicuously left Yugoslavia off that list. Maybe it was for the best given that continually unfolding tragedy.

"It was a blessing paid for in blood," Dewitt continued somberly. "A price we dearly hope and pray to God the father that our descendents never have to experience. Tools of that war—tools like this ship," Dewitt gestured about him, "linger on as reminders. It's my hope that this aircraft carrier will be the last built in a generation. I hope that she never has to launch a plane in anger, never has to experience the heartbreak of death and loss. I hope her hull is never marred by bullets or bombs." He paused. "I hope these things, but I know that..." he risked a faint smile. "Well, if wishes were horses then beggars would ride." His smile faded again as he found his place in the script. "The fires of war have gone out and we remain. Now all that is left to do is continue, to go forward." He looked out over the crowd. "We build a new tomorrow in the ashes of yesterday, and reach out—with open arms—to our new neighbors, our brothers and sisters in the human experiment that is democracy."

Bayern looked away, considering his role in all this. Dewitt would go down in history as the peace president. He would be the war president.

When the ceremony was over, the crowd began filing out of the hangar at the direction of ushers. President Dewitt made a beeline straight for Alderman, catching his elbow and talking animatedly with him. Alderman, Bayern thought, was on a short list for getting ships named after him, maybe the next Chief of Naval Operations.

Dewitt pointedly did *not* acknowledge Bayern. A wise move

politically. Bayern was persona non grata. There was still debate about just how much blame he bore for starting the war, but air strikes on Soviet territory certainly did nothing to ease tensions. Bayern's defendants held that the Soviets were simply waiting for their chance and if the US hadn't provided it, they would have made their own. His detractors... Bayern tried not to dwell on what they said about him.

"It's quite a ship!"

Bayern looked to his left in surprise, seeing Slater grinning at him. Slater, the man he and Simpson had replaced in the White House, was also something of a black sheep to his party. All his talk of peace with the Soviets had fallen on its face. His attempts at poverty reduction had backfired terribly, strickening the economy. Oh, he was respected, but he was respected in the same way a nutty grandfather was. No one took him seriously.

"I thought you might appreciate it, one Navy many to another," Slater continued. "You know, when they wanted to lay this down, I was against it. Wholly against it. We already had so many! Oh, but the Russians have their own now, they said," he continued. "Those ushankas or whatyoucallits." He took one hand from his cane to wave it around vaguely. "Well, how could I say no? Of course I fell in line."

"It's impressive," Bayern said. "Like Hoss said, I just hope we never have to use it."

Slater nodded knowingly. "Wars start at the drop of a hat but can't stop for—" he stopped, smiled. "Well, they don't stop quickly, do they?"

"No," Bayern said, frowning slightly.

"If it's any consolation to you," Bayern said, reaching out to put a hand on Bayern's knee. His crow's feet crinkled as Slater gave him a tight smile. "I would have done the same."

This surprised Bayern. Slater had a reputation for passivity, meekness. He was no warrior. "Why's that?" Bayern sensed Slater was just being nice.

"Well," Slater said, thumping his cane and looking away in thought. "I suppose we act with the intelligence we have. All signs pointed to a Soviet plot, didn't they?"

Bayern hesitated. "Yes, well... if we'd taken the time to think it through..."

Slater gave a half shrug. "Sometimes we don't do that. Sometimes we can't. It's very easy to criticize. I'm sure you have plenty of thoughts about how *I* ran things."

Bayern didn't answer that.

"But it's much harder to *do*," Slater continued. "It was maybe not the best call," he said with a sympathetic frown. "But we don't always get to make the right calls. Sometimes we make mistakes. I think, as far as mistakes go, you handled yours better than anyone else could have."

Bayern wasn't sure why, maybe something in Slater's disarming demeanor and casual tone, maybe because of their shared status as disgraced former presidents, but something about Slater made him feel at ease. He felt as though he was talking to a kindred spirit.

"I could have done something else.," Bayern said. He couldn't help but give voice to his critics' words. "I could have... done better. Done more."

Slater patted his knee. "Maybe. But you did your best. You did what you thought was right."

It was a hollow consolation, even if it was the truth. "Things could have turned out better," Bayern said finally, feeling strangely like a congregant seeking absolution.

Slater's smile widened. "Yes," he said. "But they could also have been worse." With a little effort and some help from Bayern he stood. "Come on, Mr. Bayern," he said, starting away. "I think there's still more for us to do. What did Hoss say? We've got to build a new tomorrow."

AFTERWORD

The success of this series came as a surprise to me. I've said it many times before, but I never intended Blue Masquerade to really find an audience. I wrote the book that I wanted to read thinking that I might happen to find some readers coincidentally. I continue to be blown away by the success and response of the series. I learned a lot and would do many things differently if given a second chance, but as with most things, we can only move forward.

I hope to continue to see you as I continue to write. Please keep reading for a taste of my next project and series. MAXIMUM BLACK. A retro-90s action-thriller.

Enjoy.

-TK

Also consider following me on Twitter to be kept aware of upcoming releases or feel free to drop me a line on email.

TKBlackwoodWrites@Gmail.com
https://twitter.com/TkBlackwood

MAXIMUM BLACK

November, 1991
Manhattan Exclusion Zone

8 years after the First-Strike War

The dead urban canyon echoed with the thunder of helicopter blades. A lone Blackhawk flew between the twisted, ruined towers of the city headed north, away from the epicenter of the blast. The sky overhead was as black as the bubbled asphalt racing by below. Onboard the Blackhawk, Sergeant Griff Mercer tracked the Delta Force helicopter's progress via the miniaturized screen fitted into his helmet-mounted eyepiece. The tiny computer display covered his left eye and flashed a digital map of the city in green monochrome, denoting the helicopter as a tiny triangle creeping along the ordered grid of New York's streets.

On his right side was Sergeant Sheila Dupree, his spotter, wearing the same gray and black urban camo combat fatigues he did. She kept her attention on the ruins outside, only glancing over when she sensed Mercer's attention on her.

Mercer flashed her a tense smile but was met only with a slight tightening of her lip. Like him, only her right eye was visible, sharp and bright in the dark. Her other eye was covered by the foldable eyepiece displaying the same map data. A moment later she covered her right eye too, folding down the long, black, night vision monocular mounted to the other side of her helmet. With her dark, short hair tucked away in her helmet there was nothing visibly human left about her save for her dignified nose, lips, and rounded chin.

Dupree was never one for levity, least of all on a mission like this. She was utterly unlike John Sparks in that way. Sparks sat to Mercer's left, grinning like a maniac and chewing mechanically on a piece of gum. He caught Mercer's eye, nodded, and then likewise flipped down his night vision device.

"Delta team, this is Control. I want a full systems check. This is our last chance to abort before we commit. All elements check in." Control's smooth, placid voice played out over Mercer's earpiece. As Sparks and his team sounded off one by one, Mercer checked his weapon—a McMillan TAC-338 bolt-action sniper rifle with an integrated bipod, suppressor, and detachable box magazine.

Mercer, as a professional marksman, knew the details and features of this weapon like someone knew the contours of their lover's body. His hands played over the black composite stock as he checked the action, magazine, and finally, the scope. He popped a plastic cover off each end and briefly sighted it at the yawning, window frames of a passing apartment building. An incomprehensible blur of gray raced by in his scope. Turning smoothly, Mercer aimed the rifle ahead of them, leaning partly out of the helicopter. He saw a shaky, greatly magnified view of New York's necrotic, carbonized streets. The scope worked.

"Control, Delta Nine, all clear," Mercer said, barely whispering, but pressing his throat mic into place to pick up the vibrations of his larynx. He flipped down his own night vision monocular and clicked it on. The dim, gray ruins of the city flashed up in flat shades of grainy green. Robbed of all depth perception it was hardly the best way to get around, but it would—in theory—give him a leg up on the bad guys.

A moment later Dupree followed suit. "Delta Ten, all clear." She re-secured her spotter scope and laid her carbine across her knees.

This dual assault on the senses—of a map in one eye and night vision in the other—took some getting used to, but Mercer managed it just fine. Consulting his helmet display map with his left eye, Mercer noted they weren't far from the landing point.

Weeks of planning, months of hunting, and days of drilling had all led to this final moment. They couldn't allow for any mistakes.

"Deltas, this is Danse, we're all go for Cardinal." Gordon Danse was something of an outlier to Mercer and the other Deltas. As an FBI director, Danse wasn't quite as 'tip of the spear' as they were, but this was his show, and by God, they were his monkeys. Unlike Control, there was a subtle tension to his voice, a load-bearing element. He was calm but only just. No doubt he was feeling the pressure of this operation—his operation—more than any of them.

This little excursion was the culmination of weeks of back-end intelligence gathering and old-fashioned police work, all honed to a knifepoint. Mercer tried not to dwell on the immense weight of the preliminaries which built to this climax. If he did, it might just crush him.

"We'll feed you any fresh intel as it comes up," Danse continued. "Relax, stick to the plan, and let's nail our guys."

The helicopter passed through an intersection and for just a moment Mercer saw straight through the city's dead heart. It was choked with shadows, a sea of broken glass glinting in the ash. Then they were past it, locked into the narrow canyon. The scale of the devastation here was mind boggling, even more so when added to the grand and horrible toll of the First-Strike War.

"Telemetry has the Fifth Wave helicopter en route, coming right on time," Danse said. "I've got word that our asset is onboard, codename Cockade. Try not to kill him."

Mercer closed his eyes, shutting out the dual assault of digital information. He pictured the man he knew as Cockade—one of the Quebecois separatists of the Fifth Wave. Small, dark hair, squinted eyes and a prominent nose. He knew the face—Mercer was good with faces—but whether or not he would recognize him through a low-light scope from five hundred yards away in a combat situation was another matter.

"More importantly," Danse continued, voice humming in Mercer's earpiece. "We've got confirmation that they have the warhead onboard. That's priority number one. Whatever happens, whatever the cost, we cannot let that weapon change hands. Period."

As if Mercer needed more reminder of that than the charred, warped, metal skeletons of the skyscrapers flashing by on either side of them.

"Priority number two is still Josiah Minnish."

Again, Mercer closed his eyes, recalling the man's face. Minnish, prophet-cum terrorist leader of the Crown of the Twelve Stars—the Christian accelerationists here to buy the nuke from the Fifth Wave. He'd studied the man so closely that he could recall his features in his dreams. Soft, kind eyes, crows feet, a faint smile, and strong jaw. He looked like an aged youth pastor. No wonder people trusted him with their lives.

"Dead or alive," Danse said. "Better alive, but I'll take what I can get. We nail Minnish, the Fifth Wavers, and recover that nuke and we're in good shape. Danse out."

"Three birds, one stone," Sparks said without activating his mic, shouting to Mercer over the stuttering rotors and whine of turbines. "Couldn't be easier."

"The fun never stops," Mercer agreed, trying to sound more calm than he felt. He wasn't afraid of dying, he never was, not in the heat of things. That fear would come later in the quiet hours, in the dead of night, when he lay alone in bed. No, it wasn't mortal fear that made his chest ache now, it was the fear of failure. That fear propelled him more than any other. Death and dismemberment came with the territory, but dishonor, now *that* was a personal shortcoming.

Mercer glanced again at Dupree, lifting his monocular. "You know what they say, Dupree," he said, raising his voice so she could hear him.

She mirrored him, lifting her own eyepiece. "Everyone dies."

Mercer smiled grimly. "But not us."

Again, she didn't smile, but he saw the corners of her eyes tighten. "Not today."

Their pre-mission ritual. Entire religions had risen over less.

Mercer considered it a bad habit, but a habit nonetheless, one he wasn't interested in kicking.

Control broke in over the radio again. "Thirty seconds. Going radio silent. Good luck Deltas."

Mercer restored his monocular and ground his teeth, looking down at the cracked streets and burnt out cars choking them. A swirling cloud of black dust stirred in their passing, the remnants of the city's residents, their possessions, and their homes.

The Blackhawk executed a stomach dropping turn, swinging wide across Sixth Avenue and circling the triangular Harold Square. At one time the square had trees in it, now it was blanketed with thick drifts of ash and soot like snowbanks. Open space was at a premium in New York so it made a suitable enough landing zone.

The Blackhawk dropped like a stone as Mercer and the other Deltas readied their weapons and gear, making last minute checks. The moment the tires met ash, they jumped free. Mercer's knees buckled slightly but he recovered instantly, sprinting away from the helicopter, rifle in hand.

Sparks and the others in the tactical team likewise fanned out. They took knees or went prone around what cover there was, mostly ruined cars.

Mercer slid in behind an overturned hot dog stand and glanced back over his shoulder. He watched the helicopter gun the throttle and climb into the overcast, ebon sky. It turned and flew back out the way it came in, weaving out of sight between New York's ruined towers.

As the sound of rotors died away, the Deltas became aware of the natural sounds of this place. Or rather, the lack of them. All they heard were the sounds of ruin: wind rushing through gaping window frames, the abrasive hiss of shifting ash, or the occasional squeak of rusted metal as something vibrated or flapped in the weak breeze. Though many of the buildings still stood—at least their metal bones—this place was as dead as its residents.

Mercer peered down the street, his gaze naturally traveling up the flanks of the buildings towering over it. The melted candle-stump of the Empire State Building gave him pause. He recognized it of course, what was left of it anyway. He'd seen pictures and knew they would be landing by it, but... He couldn't help but think of what it was before the First-Strike, before the war. It made him think of what this entire place had once been.

"We golden?" Sparks asked, glancing around at the other Delta operators. There were ten in total, his tactical squad and Mercer's sniper team.

Mercer flashed him a thumbs up and Sparks nodded. "Alright, let's move."

Soot and glass crunched underfoot, the shockwave of the blast had burst every window in the city nearly simultaneously. Mercer shuddered to imagine what it was like to be baked by stellar heat and flayed alive with hurricane winds of broken glass at the same time.

Skeletons littered the streets, lying exactly where they'd dropped. Without animals to predate them, they were undisturbed. Years of patient erosion had stripped the dead of all but the most rudimentary humanity. Nothing remained to showcase their suffering, to show they were once people like him.

Memento mori.

Further away from the blast, enough people had survived to flee to safety or at least die somewhere else. Closer to the blast zone they'd been vaporized, bones and all, but here these thin reminders remained.

Mercer tried not to look, but how could he not? What else was there to look at in this grim mausoleum but death?

The Deltas walked in two loose columns, one on either side of the street, heads always swiveling.

Mercer moved slowly, periodically training his rifle up on a looming building and peering through his scope. He saw only shadows and rust.

Sparks led the way, checking street signs each block, counting them down until—"Here." He pointed down a street. "West 38th," he said. "Your stop," He looked at Dupree and Mercer, gesturing like an usher directing them to their seats.

"Thanks for the escort," Mercer said, meeting Sparks' extended fistbump.

"I'd take you two on a walk in the dark anytime," Sparks replied with a grin, his teeth looking like military headstones in the night. "Good luck."

"You too," Dupree said before she and Mercer peeled away from the tactical team and moved down the more narrow side street.

After passing a couple buildings, Mercer looked back over his shoulder. The others were gone like they'd never even been there. He suppressed a shiver and followed behind Sheila

"I can't believe people used to live here," she said, her voice hushed. "It doesn't feel real anymore."

They deviated slightly, circling around an overturned taxi. A few patches of yellow paint remained, an odd remnant of color amid the desaturated skeletal frames of buildings, heaps of twisted steel beams, and jumbles of shattered concrete.

"When the war happened I couldn't believe it at first," Dupree said. "Now I can barely believe it wasn't always like this."

"Yeah," Mercer said, eyeing a dog's skeleton laid out on the sidewalk. It lay beside charred scraps of cloth pinned down by blackened bones, testament to the firestorm that raged here. "You can get used to anything." Surely there was more to be said, a more fitting eulogy for the millions resting here, but he couldn't think of it. Instead he saw the shredded tatters of an awning jutting out over the sidewalk ahead fluttering weakly like a ghostly death shroud. "I think that's the place."

"Archer Hotel," Dupree said, confirming it. "I'll take point." She moved ahead, shouldering her carbine, stepping through the empty frame of the revolving door and into the lobby beyond.

Mercer followed a few paces behind, the butt of his rifle snugged into the crook of his arm. He walked through the ruined lobby, stepping over scattered bones and broken glass. Death had come quickly for the poor souls here. Couches were blackened tangles of metal wire and springs, the front desk a charred altar, the guests and staff... Mercer's boot struck a femur bone which spun away with a dull clatter.

Dupree circled the check-in desk, checking corners and sweeping the area. She returned a moment later, lifting both eyepieces to regard Mercer nakedly. "All clear."

"How long do we have to wait?" Mercer asked, doing the same and moving into a corner to squat on his heels, back against the wall, his rifle across his knees.

Dupree slid up the sleeve of her fatigues, reading the radium dials of her watch in the dark. "Fifteen to thirty, depending on how long it took us to get here."

Mercer grunted softly and settled in to sit on the floor. He idly picked up a sliver of glass with a gloved hand and turned it over. It flashed as it caught the diffuse moonlight coming in through the blown out front entry. "This time for sure," Mercer said, partly to Dupree but partly to himself. "Minnish has a bullet with his name on it." He patted the receiver of his rifle.

Dupree sat beside him and brushed ash and dust off the legs of her pants. "Seems that way." She wanted the Crown of Twelve Stars leader as much as anyone else, but she did a much better job of hiding it. Sparks had always been fire, Dupree ice. Mercer thought he fell somewhere in the middle but was lucky to count both as his friends.

"Hell of a place for an exchange." Mercer looked around the grim tableau. "You think seeing this would give them second thoughts."

"It's neutral ground," Dupree said. "No border patrol, no prying eyes."

"I mean, how can you buy a nuke at ground zero?"

Dupree shrugged, eyes fixed on the moonlit entryway. "They're zealots," she said. "No cost too high, no price too great. Anything is permissible when you're fighting pure evil."

Mercer gave her a curious glance. "Sounds almost like you believe it."

"My parents," she said with a half shrug. "I grew up deep in the church. They took a lot of that doomsday stuff seriously. Made sure I read the Bible cover to cover. Tried to get my soul ready for Judgment Day."

Mercer smiled faintly. "I can see it. So how'd that go?"

She smiled back. "I joined the Army."

Minutes later the electronic click over Mercer's radio earpiece nearly made him jump out of his skin. He'd become too accustomed to the silence of this place.

"That's the go code," Dupree said, rising to her feet.

Mercer clicked his radio back twice in acknowledgement. "Lead the way."

2

They moved quickly and quietly, ghosting through the derelict hotel lobby and the back areas, laundry and kitchen. Ultimately they passed through a fire door hanging off its hinges. The rusted fixture had been caved in by the gigantic overpressure that ripped through this building.

"Up," Dupree said, gesturing with her carbine towards a partly buckled metal stairway.

It groaned and creaked loudly beneath them as they ascended one at a time and then crossed a rooftop towards a towering art deco apartment building. The steel skeletons of nearby towers frowned down on them in the gloom, sentinel-like.

The interior of the apartment was cavernous and dark. Only their night vision monoculars allowed them to navigate its guts and reach a stairwell.

"Up again," Dupree said, her voice a whisper.

"Up it is." Up they went, up, and up, and up until Mercer's knees and calves ached distantly. He should have been counting floors but he'd lost track. Lucky for him, Dupree never did.

She caught him by the back of his vest. "Here." She nudged the door open slowly, sweeping the hall with her weapon before moving in.

This entire floor had been gutted by the blast and the damage only got worse higher up the building. Individual apartments smeared together, walls blown in. Gaping holes connected everything in a charcoal labyrinth.

Dupree moved to the far wall, ducking into a crouch as she crossed the last couple yards.

Mercer tailed behind, glancing occasionally down to avoid stepping on loose debris and chunks of burnt drywall which crumbled into powder beneath his boots. When he had nearly reached the edge of the building, he lay down on his stomach and inched slowly forward. He paused only to listen to his heartbeat and the wind moaning through the ruins.

Finally Mercer brought himself into sight of the gray-black expanse beneath them, laid out like a game board. Bryant Park. Across from them, on the opposite end of the park was the New York Public Library. Its granite, neo-classical shell looked mostly untouched, but the former greenery of Bryant Park was scattered with evidence of human intervention. Rusted ambulances, tattered canvas tents, moldering stacks of MREs and burst water drums. All were the remains of an abortive attempt to bring salvation here, abandoned as quickly as it had been established.

Mercer was less interested in the scenery than he was in the people creeping around it. As Dupree laid beside him and set up her spotter scope, Mercer silently unfolded his bipod and pressed his cheek to the cool stock. Peering through his own scope he swept the park.

Men in army surplus and civilian gear stalked around the abandoned aid station. They were armed with a haphazard assortment of weapons, many of their faces were obscured by dust masks. Still, Mercer checked each one of them, hunting for Minnish.

"Any sign of him?" Dupree asked, likewise checking the gunmen with her scope.

"Nothing." Mercer whispered back. It was just as well. He

didn't know if he could resist the urge to pop Minnish early just to be sure he got him. "I count nine shooters."

"Ten," Dupree corrected. "There's one in the school bus."

Mercer pivoted his weapon, slow and smooth, and noted the hidden terrorist. "Ten," he said, eyeing the Kalashnikov the gunman carried. "Seems like a light crowd for a deal like this. Weren't we expecting more?"

"Twenty," Dupree said, still scanning. "The others might be distributed through—" her voice caught at the sound of an echoing thump deeper in the building. It was followed a moment later by heavy footsteps moving up the stairs.

Mercer and Dupree reacted instantly, withdrawing from the ledge as quickly as they could without drawing attention from the ground. They had just enough time to duck into cover by a waist-high interior wall before the stairwell door came open on their floor.

The Deltas traded looks in the dark, silently weighing their options. They knew this wasn't any of their people and no one else was alive in this city but Minnish's followers.

The steps meandered a bit, crunching through debris, before drawing gradually nearer.

Mercer's mind raced as he silently tried to decide what to do.

Dupree made a choice for both of them when she unbuckled the knife strapped at the small of her back. She drew it silently, the blade gleaming in the dark.

The moment the zealot stepped past them she lunged, plunging the knife into his back at the same time she clapped a hand over his mouth.

The gunman let out a startled grunt of pain, hands flying up to grab at Dupree's wrist.

Mercer kicked his fallen rifle away as Dupree drew her blade out and plunged it into his ribs twice in quick succession. Next she kicked the back of his knee, twisting and throwing him to his face. She let go of his mouth long enough to straddle his back.

He sucked in a wet breath before she pulled his head back by the hair and slit his throat, sawing her knife mercilessly back and forth. When she released her grip, his head dropped straight down, nose smashing into the floor. Dead.

Dupree looked up at Mercer, panting, eyes questioning. What now?

"They weren't supposed to have anyone out this far," Mercer said. "Maybe he wandered off."

Dupree looked unsold, her skepticism clear even in the dark. "Griff, that's not their MO. These guys are professionals. They wouldn't put someone way out here for no reason. Not unless they knew we were coming."

The thought froze Mercer's blood. If the missing Twelve Stars gunmen were in the surrounding buildings it would change the dynamic of the whole operation. He didn't have much time to dwell on it before the radio clipped to the dead man's belt squelched noise.

"Corinth, clear."

Mercer gawked at the walkie talkie as another voice came over it. Then another.

"Galatia, all clear."

"Ephesia, clear."

Bad guys checking in. Patrols. The guys doing overwatch for the deal, checking to make sure they were all in place.

"Shit," Mercer said. He unclipped the radio from the dead guy's belt, ready to check in on his behalf, when he realized he didn't have a clue what his callsign was. "Sheila—"

She hissed for quiet, brow furrowed, eyes darting side to side as she thought. Mercer could see her silently mouthing the names to herself.

"Phillipi, clear," the radio said followed by a pause. Silence. Their turn.

Mercer looked helplessly at Sheila, thumb hovering over the 'talk' button.

Dupree's eyes flashed with sudden recognition. "Collosians–uh." She screwed her eyes shut to think. "Colossae!"

Mercer half covered the mic with his thumb and then depressed the talk key. "Colossae, clear."

Another pause.

"Thessalonica, all clear here."

They both let out a held breath.

"We need to break radio silence," Dupree said, speaking slowly but deliberately. She wouldn't meet Mercer's eyes. "We have to rethink the operation."

They might be walking into a trap, but breaking radio silence might tip off their quarry. If they realized the Delta were here, then the Fifth Wavers would slip back to Canada with the nuke and Josiah Minish would get away.

Mercer chewed his cheek, looking first at the corpse and then towards the park, out of view. He shook his head. It would be better to walk into a trap than to walk away. "No. We proceed."

Dupree said nothing, only looked at him.

"They won't check in again for a while," Mercer continued. He was already feeling the time crunch. "And if they do, we just sound all clear again."

More silence from Dupree. The plan which had been so carefully laid out was in shreds. They were flying by the seat of their pants now. There was no telling how it would go.

"The Fifth Wavers are on their way," Mercer said, an edge of desperation in his voice. "This might be our only chance to get the nuke *and* Minnish."

"What about Sparks? We have to break radio silence to warn him."

Mercer wouldn't risk it. "Sparks can handle himself," he said, believing that was true beyond a doubt. "Besides, it's better this way. They won't expect us where their guy is supposed to be."

Finally, reluctantly, Dupree relented, her shoulders sagging slightly. "Fine. You're right." She wiped the blood from her blade onto the gunman's jacket and stood. "Let's get into position."

3

Within minutes of Mercer sighting his rifle again, they heard the growing thumping of helicopter blades.

"That's them," Dupree said as a civilian Bell UH-1 passed low over their crow's nest. Downwash from the rotors threw ash into eddying clouds that swirled around them before settling back in loose drifts.

Mercer exhaled slowly, adjusting his grip on the rifle, and sighted it on the helicopter as it came gently down in the center of the park.

A loose circle of Twelve Stars gunmen closed in, standing a casual distance away as they watched the Quebec separatists hop down and fan out.

The dead man's radio buzzed. "Standby. They're here."

The Fifth Wavers wore drab green fatigues and black berets—military surplus. Unlike the haphazard arms of the Twelve Stars, their kit was all French-made. Ten Quebecois formed a cordon around the helicopter, eyeing the religious zealots. Four more men climbed out, carrying a large silver case on their shoulders like pallbearers with a coffin. Though it was the size of a grown man, it clearly weighed much more and they struggled under the weight.

"That's the warhead," Dupree said. "And that's Cockade moving behind them. Next to their leader."

Mercer panned his crosshairs over the informant who glanced anxiously around. Next he surveyed the silver case bearing the nuke. "Do you see Minnish?"

"Not yet," Dupree said, watching through her scope.

Mercer ground his teeth side to side as he watched one of the Twelve Stars move forward. He was evidently their leader and had a cut-down pump shotgun hanging at his side. He kept his eyes locked on the Fifth Wave leader, Gustav Hervieux, his gaze unerring. The two men stopped a short distance away as the nuke was set down nearby. Negotiations started.

"He's got to be here or the Fifth Wave won't make the deal," Mercer said. His whispering vibrated the rifle enough to blur his sight picture. "Anything?"

"Nothing," Dupree said.

It didn't occur to Mercer that the Twelve Stars never intended to make a deal with the Fifth Wave until the Twelve Stars heavy lifted his shotgun and fired a blast of buckshot into Hervieux's chest. As he racked the slide, the other Twelve Stars opened fire on the Fifth Wave, the double cross in full swing.

The concealed gunmen on the upper floors of the surrounding buildings picked off the Quebecois in the open.

"Cockade is down!" Dupree blurted.

"Shit." The deal was bad. Minnish wasn't coming and Hervieux was dead. All that was left was to get that nuke. Mercer put his crosshairs onto a gunman in woodland BDUs and stroked the trigger, dropping him. He worked the bolt, gliding it smoothly back and flinging out the spent brass before sliding in the next round.

"Twenty yards left," Dupree said, directing him to his next target. "Guy with an M60."

Mercer sighted the machine gunner standing defiantly in the open, belting shells into the Fifth Wavers' helicopter. Mercer fired again, hitting his target dead in the heart.

The Fifth Wavers were caught in the open, but were far from helpless. Even as the pallbearers of the nuclear warhead were cut down, the other separatists fought back, going to ground and shooting wildly.

A group of Twelve Stars raced forward, heedless of gunfire whipping around them, and picked up the nuke. They withdrew hastily while their comrades kept the Fifth Wave pinned.

Mercer sighted and picked off the pallbearers as quickly as he could work the bolt.

"Leader, walkie talkie, ten yards right," Dupree said.

Mercer shifted, saw the heavy with the shotgun speaking into a radio, looking pointedly up at Mercer's position.

The dead man's radio buzzed with the leader's voice. "All units, we have heathens on the 15th floor. Converge on Colassae's position."

Mercer squeezed his finger and took the leader in the arm. Not a kill shot, but an incapacitating one. As he worked the bolt, he saw Sparks and the tactical team sweeping in from the left, clearing the field with precise bursts of fire.

"Displace," Dupree said, swiftly rising and stowing her spotter scope.

Mercer was just a moment behind her, crawling back as gunfire lashed at the concrete ledge. "Move!"

The stairwell door ahead of them flew open at the same time a burst of gunfire ripped through it. The zealot who stormed in unleashed a wordless cry of fury, firing indiscriminately.

Dupree dropped him with a three-round burst to the chest, stepping over his cooling body to put another bullet through his brain. "Up!" She leaned into the metal railing which spiraled up the center of the open stairwell and fired stuttering bursts down at more gunmen frantically climbing after them. They couldn't have the nuke, but they could have revenge.

Mercer took point, breathing hard as he took the stairs two at a time. He slung his rifle and drew his Colt M1911 in a fluid motion. The three tritium dots on his sights glowed dully against the pistol's silver finish. He breathed hard. In. Out. In. Adrenaline pumped through him, setting nerves alight and turning his muscles tight, like bundles of steel cables. Each corner he rounded might bring him face to face with—

Mercer fired before he realized he was pulling the trigger. One, two, three, four rounds into the jerking body of a zealot.

The terrorist staggered, firing his Uzi up into the ceiling as he collapsed, strings cut.

Five. Mercer painted his brains across the wall and continued up the stairs. Dupree was close behind, trading fire with the unknown number of Twelve Stars closing from below. Their angry voices echoed cacophonously in the concrete tube of the stairwell, sounding more like demons than men.

Mercer toggled on his radio earpiece. "Control, this is Delta Nine, requesting immediate evac! Negative contact with primary target, secondary target eliminated! How copy, over?"

"We read you, Nine," Control replied instantly. "Proceed to primary extraction, Sawhorse is en route."

"Copy!" Mercer had to shout over the banging gunfire coming from below. Concrete chips sprayed in his face as they ate away at the stairwell.

"Griff, this one!" Dupree shouted, jerking her head towards a door. He'd lost count again.

Mercer hardly heard the dry cough of a grenade launcher below them. He only became aware of it when the world exploded into noise and pain around him.

Mercer hit the ground, head spinning like a carousel. When he sat up he felt a dull sting in his right knee which erupted into searing pain as he moved. He hissed, clutching the wounded limb. His uniform was torn, perforated by metal splinters and slivers of concrete. His ears were ringing so fiercely that he wasn't aware he was nearly deaf until he saw Dupree tossing on the ground beside him, mouth open, screaming.

"Sheila!" Mercer shouted. He crawled to her, ignoring the pain in his leg. "She–" he brought his pistol up and fired the last two bullets in his magazine into a zealot who flopped back over the railing, nailing the back of his head on the next floor with a sick crack.

Tossing the empty pistol—no time to reload—Mercer came to Sheila. It wasn't good. Her face was a mask of blood, her fabric helmet cover shredded, testament to the burst of shrapnel which hit her. Her left side was a mess, uniform ripped, her blood running in rivulets. Her leg was worst of all, torn open, raw and bloody.

"I'm okay," she lied through clenched teeth. She had to repeat it before Mercer heard her. She looked up at him with one eye, her left eyelid was squeezed shut. Viscous blood oozed out.

"Jesus," Mercer whispered, feeling faint.

"Griff, I'm okay," Dupree said again, sounding faint. Her good eye drifted closed. She was going into shock.

Another burst of gunfire peppered the doorway, reminding Mercer that they had to move.

"Shut up," Mercer said, unslinging his rifle and tossing it aside. It would only slow them down. "Shut up." He reached around, slipping one arm under her shoulder and the other behind her knees to lift her in a princess carry. "This is going to hurt like a bitch."

He felt her screams as much as he heard them. Mercer tried to ignore her suffering, focusing just on the mission.

He tried, but he failed.

Turning, he hobbled with her in his arms, ducking through a gap in the exterior wall of the highrise and onto a broad ledge which held the remains of air conditioner units.

Dupree's left leg flopped sickeningly in his grip and more hot blood raced down his arms. She whimpered something into his chest, inaudible over the ringing in his ears.

"Just hold on!" Mercer snapped, feeling mounting panic.

Here in the open, all he could do was wait and pray for rescue.

He saw a flicker of shadows in the stairwell behind them, Minnish's crusaders come to finish him off.

Mercer turned away, shielding Sheila with his body for all the good it would do. He closed his eyes and his prayers were answered.

The Blackhawk swooped, dropping almost straight down towards them. The operator onboard peppered gunfire into the wall gap, pinning their pursuers back for now.

The helicopter was too big to land here, too big to do more than over a short distance above them. They threw down a rope ladder optimistically. It would be difficult to climb in ideal conditions, impossible with someone in his arms.

Mercer swallowed fear. If he left her here, she was dead. If he stayed, they were both dead. "Shit. Okay, hold onto me," he said, "tight as you can. Don't let go."

This time he heard Dupree's answer. "I can't... hurts too much," she said, shivering in pain.

"Don't you quit on me, Dupree!" Mercer shouted back, moving up to grab the ladder rungs. "Don't you quit! You're going to live, you hear me? We're not dying today!"

Dupree looked up at him with her remaining eye. Blood flowed from the other like tears, rolling down her cheek. She was speechless for an instant before she looped her arms around his neck. Grimacing, she grabbed a fistful of the back of his fatigues with all the strength she had.

Mercer took another steadying breath and then he climbed. He climbed somehow with Dupree clinging to him, crying out at each movement, straining to hold on, straining not to let go.

As he climbed, the helicopter lifted up and away, putting distance between itself and the building crawling with vengeful gunmen. Mercer looked down, which was a terrible mistake.

The necropolitic cityscape spun dizzyingly below. Dupree's legs dangled uselessly. Mercer's own right leg was streaked with blood, his knee throbbing. He tore his eyes away, fought down vertigo and pain, and forced himself to climb.

Finally, mercifully, he reached the lip of the helicopter's passenger compartment.

Friendly hands came down, grabbing at uniforms and limbs, pulling, lifting. Mercer struggled up, following Dupree into the Blackhawk to lie in the cold metal floor, gasping from exertion.

"Control," the helicopter crewman said as another operator ripped open a wad of bandages, wrapping them around Dupree's face. "We've got them. Two wounded, one critical!"

Mercer laid back, the back of his helmet thumping against the deck as he stared up at the ceiling.

One critical.

He closed his eyes, listening to Dupree's weak sounds of pain, the instructions of the helicopter crew as they fought to save her life. Mercer kept his eyes closed and just breathed.

-Available September 1-

ABOUT THE AUTHOR

T.k. Blackwood

T.K. Blackwood is a full time IT professional and part time writer who lives in North Carolina with his wife, child, and too many reptiles.

Printed in Dunstable, United Kingdom